IN THE DYING MINUTES

J.A. BAKER

First published in 2020 by Bloodhound Books.

www.bloodhoundbooks.com

Print ISBN 978-1-913419-79-0

ALSO BY J.A. BAKER

Undercurrent

The Cleansing

The Retreat

The Other Mother

Finding Eva

The Uninvited

The Woman at Number 19

The Girl I Used To Be

For family.
Always.

"Death twitches my ear;
'Live,' he says...
'I'm coming.'"
— Virgil

PART I

PROLOGUE

THE DIARY

He loves me, he loves me not.

Jacob, the love of my life, the only person I have ever truly adored, loves me not.

I am bereft, completely helpless, unable to function at the most basic of levels. All I want to do is lie in bed and think about our lives together, about the love that we shared and the unique bond we had. I want to ponder over all the good times we experienced, all the bad times even. How we melded together as one, complementing each other. Two bodies, two minds fused together for what I hoped would be forever. And now it's over.

We are over.

A cruel end to a beautiful beginning.

I've tried to speak to him, to tell him that us being apart is a big mistake but he refuses to listen. His mind is made up. If I could turn back the clock, do things differently, then I would. But I can't. What's done is done and cannot be undone. I made some mistakes and now I honestly don't think I can live without him. Jacob is all I have ever thought about. From the very first minute we met he has been on my mind – every day, every night, his beautiful face filling my thoughts, his gentle honeyed voice lulling me into a near hypnotic state.

I remember it so clearly – the first time we met. I was moving into my flat, my arms loaded up with boxes. I bumped into him as we passed on the path. He offered to help, his eyes, his voice making me weak with desire. I accepted and together we bustled our way inside, laughing simultaneously as we collided, becoming jammed in the doorway before falling into the living room in a heap. The attraction was instantaneous. It was love at first sight. Such a cliché, I know, but that's how it was. The way he looked at me made my heart flip. His conventional good looks and those eyes. Oh God, those eyes...

Two days later we were an item. It didn't take long. Why waste time with formalities when you both know it's meant to be. We spent every spare moment together, did everything together, loved passionately.

And now he's gone.

I'm lying here on my bed, crying again. I can't help it. I don't know what else I'm supposed to do. I'm nothing without him. Everything I did, everything I said, revolved around Jacob and now he's not here I have no idea what to do, how to live my life without him in it. He filled my every waking moment, my thoughts given over to him and how our relationship would develop in the future. Except it didn't. It came to an end and I have no idea how to react to that. I no longer know how to get through the day without him being here by my side. Everything is tinged with a dull impenetrable greyness that refuses to lift. I'm at a low ebb – rock bottom, actually – my life crushed. I've been sucked into a black hole, a great big void that is destroying me from the inside out.

I can't continue living like this. Something has to give. This isn't me. It's not who I am. I'm stronger than this, a fighter. Tough and resilient. Or I used to be. Now look at me. This is what he's reduced me to. This is what they have reduced me to.

When this sorry mess is over, I hope people will remember that I'm the victim here, that I did what I had to do to survive the bad times. My life has been ripped in two, the dry parchment of my exis-

tence crumpled to nothing in the palm of his hand. The pair of them watched my life disintegrate and turn to dust and stood by and watched, doing nothing to help.

I'm useless without him, a vacuous nobody. I have nothing to live for, nothing to lose.

So whatever happens next, should a dreadful calamity occur, know this – I was forced into it. They made me do it. None of what takes place from this point on is my fault.

1

PRESENT DAY

The train slices through the sprawling swathe of fertile green. Leah gazes out at it all; mile after mile of fields filled with crops, divided by lengths of crooked fencing and tangles of gnarled hedgerows. She keeps her eyes glued to it, her attention focused on the distant farmhouses, the impossibly straight lines of electricity pylons that stand tall and proud; huge silver entities that stretch over the spread of farmland and beyond. Her gaze doesn't stray, staying focused on the winding country lanes and the stream of cars that snake through them. She refuses to blink as she stares up at the azure sky, the wispy clouds and the white vapour trails that hang there like lengths of snowy candy floss – she sees it all, refusing to look away.

If she does that and keeps still, it may just be enough to stop the pain at the back of her head from developing into something more, something bigger than the current small nagging ache.

She keeps her eyes fixed on the smudge of green, staring intently at the starlings that scatter and scimitar above the rolling fields, their bodies a cloud of darkness as they take flight and flutter up to the heavens. Anything to stop her migraine from erupting. She counts trees and fields, studies grazing cattle, thinks about her journey, the reason for it. And stops, her flesh cold, her breathing suddenly laboured.

She rummages in the bag sitting beside her, her fingers trembling as she delves into its many side pockets. Why didn't she think to bring some headache tablets with her? Too many things to think about, too much to do, that was the problem. She closes her eyes and rests her head back on the seat, thinking about what her priorities actually were before getting here. Opening her eyes, she grits her teeth, refusing to give it head-space. Packing her meagre things and boarding this train – that was all she had to focus on and now she has done it she can relax. Nothing else matters. Nothing.

Her fingers continue groping about, landing on a bottle of water tucked away at the bottom. She pulls it out, unscrews the cap and glugs back the remainder of the liquid. It's warm but it soothes her throat and eases her headache. She shoves the empty plastic bottle back inside the bag, scrapes her hair back into a ponytail, tying it up with a band and pressing it in place with the palm of her hand. Her face is devoid of any make-up and if she were to look in the mirror right now, she feels sure the reflection staring back at her would be that of a stranger. This isn't her. Not the usual Leah. But then, something happened to the usual Leah a while back. Something that damaged her irreparably. She isn't the person people think she is. The person she used to be departed a long time ago. She no longer knows herself and – if she is being perfectly honest – now doubts she ever did.

A voice echoes over the PA system announcing the next stop – York. She feels a wave of tension begin to leave her, slipping out from under her skin, escaping out through her pores. Her fears, her many crippling anxieties get swallowed up by the surrounding noises and gentle pull of the train. The greater the separation from her starting point, the calmer she feels.

The headache that threatened to swamp her wanes as she massages the base of her skull, her fingers pressing and kneading at her flesh. The water has helped. That was a lucky find. Why wasn't she more organised? Why does she seem to spend her life in such a damn hurry? Always running, always escaping from the problems that trail in her wake. Dashing, struggling. In too much of a rush to leave her old life behind. Too eager to get away from Jacob, from Chloe, from their unreasonable behaviour. Too eager to escape from what took place.

She thinks of her destination, Aunt Mary's house in London, and allows herself a small smile. It's been such a long time since Leah has seen her that even the thought of Mary's face brings a lump to her throat. The world needs more Aunt Marys. A diminutive, elf-like creature, Mary is the epitome of kindness and compassion, always with a ready smile and a shoulder to cry on, always listening. Always caring. Mary is all she has left. They were always close, Mary like a second mother to her, speaking to Leah on the phone when she was a child, making sure she was happy and settled, letting her know that the guinea pigs were thriving, the only pets she ever loved and cared for.

Leah stares out of the window again. Aunt Mary will understand. She will realise why Leah had to leave Durham and head for London. Leah won't have to explain that Chloe's behaviour had become intolerable, as had Jacob's. It impinged on every aspect of her life until Leah had to pack up and go. She had to do it and now there is no looking back. She will spend time in London with her aunt, reflect on everything that has happened and then think about what her next move is going to be.

People fill the aisle as the train pulls into York station. The doors hiss. The crowds murmur and shuffle along, stopping to grab at bags and to pull on backpacks. Leah watches them step off the train, wheeling small suitcases, hurrying home to their loved ones. A sliver of envy creeps under her skin, pulsing and throbbing within her. She blinks back tears, tells herself to get a grip, to stop imagining how it must feel to be loved unconditionally, to have somebody who is always on your side and always by your side instead of having to suffer the excruciating loneliness that she has had to endure over the past few months.

More passengers board, their expressions unreadable, their shoulders hunched. She watches a couple of young women as they scan the carriage for their seats, checking their tickets and murmuring under their breath. They are both similar to her in age and have a pained look in their eyes as if they're carrying the weight of the world on their shoulders. Leah shakes her head in exasperation and looks away in disgust. She wonders what reasons they have for looking so dejected and miserable. She would like to challenge them, to compare her life with theirs, get them to understand what real misery feels like.

The boarding takes just minutes, the changeover seamless as new people step aboard and locate their seats, shuffling into them, placing bags at their feet and opening laptops and tablets, eyes glued to their screens as the movement starts once again and they continue their journey south.

Leah looks around at the eclectic mix of passengers – business people, shoppers, mothers with babies strapped close to them, even school children with their mussed-up hair and smart blazers. She bites at her lip nervously, pleased to have a seat with a table. It's a long journey when you're forced to stare at the back of a seat.

A low hum fills the coach, the sound of a moving train, of people talking, tapping at laptops and tablets, whispering into phones. Sitting opposite her is a man in his thirties. He's dressed in a black pinstripe suit, his attention focused solely on his computer screen. Standing up next to him, leaning over his shoulder, is a young woman wearing a beige cotton jacket. She has bright eyes, clear skin, her countenance one of eternal cheerfulness. She notices Leah watching her and nods, her mouth fixed into a wide grin. She reminds Leah of a sloth with her permanent smile, her dark eyes and short brown hair combed flat against her head.

Leah returns the gesture, nodding in return, wondering why she is still standing, her body rocking back and forth in rhythm with the movement of the train when there is clearly a seat available. She hopes this chirpy-looking female doesn't want to engage her in conversation. She isn't in the mood for chatting, for making inane talk about the weather and how diabolical and unpredictable British summers are. She has neither the energy nor the inclination for it.

'This is definitely seat 26B, isn't it?' the woman says, cautiously checking her ticket against the small sign on the wall adjacent to her head.

'It is,' Leah replies quietly, dipping her eyes away. She doesn't want to become embroiled in this. All she wants is to sit in silence, to enjoy some solitude away from her problems, from what she has left behind.

The woman remains still, her head turned, her eyes darting about the carriage before coming back to land on Leah. 'I'm really sorry to ask this, but I don't suppose we could swap seats? I'm not good with travelling backwards. It makes me nauseous.'

Leah doesn't answer, keeping her gaze diverted. She's tired and wants to be left alone to rake over her thoughts and plans. She definitely doesn't want this.

'Only, I did request a forward-facing seat when I booked my ticket but it looks like there weren't any left and I really do get quite bad motion sickness if I face the wrong way...'

Resisting the urge to tell her to go away, to find somebody else to pester, Leah nods and stands, figuring the alternative of a puce-faced vomiting woman sitting opposite her is far less appealing than switching seats.

'Thank you. I really do appreciate this,' the woman says, sliding her way into Leah's seat, settling herself in with more drama than is necessary. She gives Leah another smile and nods to the window. 'Rubbish weather, isn't it? At least it's warm though,' she says, indicating outside to the veil of drizzle that has started up, covering the landscape, colouring everything in a drab shade of grey.

'Yes,' Leah replies, doing her utmost to not bang her head against the Formica table in utter frustration at being held to conversational ransom with this person. It's all she can do to suppress a dramatic eye-roll and sigh out loud. Instead, she manages a tight smile, meeting the young woman's gaze and holding it for a little longer than is necessary. 'As you say, at least it's warm though.' She hopes this is enough. She hopes her attempts at responding in a polite, brusque manner will convey her need to be left alone. She isn't in the mood for talking. She isn't in the mood for anything except ruminating over what she has left behind and guessing at what lies ahead. She has given up her seat for this woman. What more can this stranger possibly want?

'I'm Rachel by the way,' she says, her travel sickness relegated to the back of her mind.

Leah nods and says nothing in return, thinking that Rachel's behaviour reminds her of a petulant child, suddenly chirpy and amiable once their demands are met.

'Awful that, isn't it?' the woman continues, eyeing up the newspaper she has laid down on the table between them. She places her hands either side of the page to hold it in place, taking ownership of it, her eyes sweeping over the words, studying the screaming headline with wide outraged eyes.

Leah reluctantly glances at it. She is inadvertently drawn to the picture. The walls of the train lean in drunkenly. The floor seems to fall away beneath her. She feels her breath catch in her throat, a pocket of trapped air pushing at her from the inside; sharp and angular as it struggles to free itself.

'Yes, awful,' she replies, her head full of noise, her blood like ice as she stares at the photograph beneath the headline. She swallows down vomit and feels its burn as it travels back down, settling in the pit of her belly like a raging furnace. Her eyes mist over. She blinks rapidly to clear her vision, disturbed by this unexpected image.

'Seems like there's nowhere that's untouched by these awful crimes.' Rachel's disembodied voice carries across the carriage, echoing in Leah's head. 'I mean this poor girl was in her bed when it happened. Imagine that, waking up to somebody standing over you with a weapon and then being beaten half to death while you're asleep and unable to defend yourself.'

Leah shakes her head, stars bursting behind her eyes, her movements laboured as she tries to focus, to concentrate on what this woman, this Rachel person is saying. 'Terrible,' she manages to croak, coughing to clear her throat. 'The whole thing is just beyond dreadful.'

'Didn't happen too far from here either,' she says, her voice carrying a small amount of glee and morbid curiosity as she stares down at the grainy photograph of a crime scene, at the yellow tape cordoning off a property and the attention-grabbing headline – WOMAN BLUDGEONED IN BLOODBATH ATTACK.

Unable to hide her disgust, Leah turns and stares out of the window, everything now an indistinct smudge. Her heart stampedes around her chest arrhythmically. She swallows, suddenly wishing this journey was over, wishing sloth girl would go and sit somewhere else. Somewhere far away from her. This is a conversation she does not want to be having. That headline is no more than sensationalistic tabloid nonsense designed to lure in voyeurs; bloodthirsty readers who will stop at nothing to pore over every bit of grisly detail they can find about murder and rape and any other heinous crime that will brighten their day.

Slumping down in her seat, Leah blinks away the film of fog that covers her eyes and stares outside, thinking how weak she is. If only she had the courage to get up and move to another seat, away from the newspaper, away from the glaring headline that is twisting her stomach into a tight ball.

She closes her eyes, squeezing them shut, feigning sleep. Her mind drifts away. In the background, she can hear people chatting, discussing the recent murder while others talk endlessly about work, using esoteric language about the minutiae of their jobs. The incessant drone of their voices swirls around the carriage accompanied by the rustle of newspapers and the gentle hum of the train which in itself is a strangely soothing sound that lulls her into a meditative state. For a few precious moments, she can clear her mind. Everything feels calm, the air soft with a welcome sense of equanimity. For a while, Leah forgets. She forgets about Chloe and Jacob. She forgets about the shreds of the life she is leaving behind. She forgets about the family who forgot about her.

And that's when it happens. A light rocking, her body swaying in time with the movement of the carriage, a rhythmic and recurring sensation, then an ear-splitting sound that cuts through the air like a bomb exploding. Next comes a deep thud that propels her forward, her body a tangle of uncoordinated limbs as she lands on a sharp object, her abdomen hitting the edge of the table with force. Leah whimpers, lets out a deep groan of resistance and collapses, her body crumpled. She is unable to think properly, to breathe properly. Everything is skewed, unfathomable.

More shaking and vibrating under her, around her, above her. A feeling that the walls are coming in, that the ground is disappearing under her feet. A terrible sensation that the earth is spinning wildly off its axis, taking her with it. She screams, is thrown forward again, clutches at thin air, finds nothing.

Then the grating and screeching of metal, the unbearable sound that causes her to shudder, making her skin crawl. And the shrieks, the soul crushing cries of terror. So much screaming, animalistic, feral. Terrified howling, cries of pain and dread, of confusion and fear.

Another sickening groan. Metal against metal. Another violent movement. This one tips her sideways, sends her spinning, the blood in her head swirling and gushing. She yells out, her voice low and desperate as she slides backwards then upside down, her body pressed hard against a solid surface, her hands jammed up against plastic or glass, something cold, something immovable and sharp. Too much chaos to think properly, to work out what is happening to her.

She can't breathe. Her lungs refuse to work, her throat constricts. Then the pain. So much of it. It pulses through her, wave after wave shrieking through her veins, biting at her limbs. Her eyes bulge, her chest heaves as a tiny pocket of air finds its way in. She tries to move but is held tight against something solid, something heavy and immobile. So hard to keep on breathing, to get enough air into her lungs. Oxygen. She needs more oxygen.

Moans and cries for help surround her, unearthly protestations; people begging, sobbing, howling. *What the fuck just happened?* She tries to move again, to look for the man with the laptop, for Rachel, the sloth woman. Where are they? Where is *she*? What the *fuck* is going on?

She tries to think straight, to fight through the thick veil of confusion. Not a dream. This is real. A crash. They've hit something at speed. Their train has crashed, come off its rails. Everything is broken and crushed, torn apart and burning. People are dying, possibly already dead.

Another sudden pain bursts inside her, an agonising ripping sensation that speeds through her diaphragm, cutting her in two. It's unbearable. Horrific. Worse than anything she has ever experienced. Her head pounds. A strangulated cry escapes from her throat. She's dying. Dear God. Oh dear sweet Jesus, she is dying. No other explanation for it.

Leah gasps and splutters, thick warm bile exploding out of her mouth, choking her. She coughs, gurgles, vomits, spits out the bitter fluid, trying to draw oxygen into her lungs, her chest wheezing with the effort of staying alive.

She waits, every second a minute, every minute an hour. Time stretches out before her, endless, infinite moments punctuated with pain. On and on and on... Everything is hopeless. She is choking, gagging. Praying.

An eternity. Too long. Everything is taking too damn long. Where are the doctors, the nurses, the firefighters? Anybody to get her out of here. Anybody. She just needs somebody to help her, to stop the searing pain that feels like knives are being repeatedly plunged into her stomach. Sharp blades, digging, gouging, slicing at her innards.

She's dying. She feels sure of it. Help. She needs help.

Please God, don't let me die. Not here. Not now.

Still nothing. No sounds. No more screaming.

Just emptiness. A horrible, lingering deathly silence.

It lasts for forever. All she can think of is how to breathe, how to keep her lungs working, to keep the oxygen flowing. In, out. In, out. She focuses what little energy she has on staying alive.

Seconds turn into minutes, minutes into an eternity.

She tries to count. Soon they will come. Somebody will help her. She gets to ten and keeps going. She continues to twenty and struggles to concentrate, to work out what comes next.

Agony. Not enough air... Thirty. Once she gets to thirty, somebody will arrive...

More time passes, an endless stretch of silence. She tries to ignore the pain, putting her efforts into staying awake, not slipping into unconsciousness, into a darkness that has no end.

Then at last, at long last, just when she has given up all hope, there are noises nearby. Sirens, voices, the crunch of heavy footsteps. Shouting, machines whirring, a high-pitched whine and the cumbersome creak and groan of metal moving, machinery tearing apart the carriage, metal fingers ripping their way through the carnage. *Somebody is here. Thank God, somebody is here.*

They've come to save her.

She tries to speak, to call out, to tell them that she's close by, that she can't breathe properly, that she needs air, but nothing comes except a stream of hot sticky liquid that fills her mouth, coating her teeth, settling in the recesses of her gums like warm oil.

A gurgling, gasping sound emanates from somewhere close by. She strains, listens and realises it's coming from her, her feeble attempt at shouting for help, impaired by her injuries.

Time is meaningless as she waits, the last pocket of air leaving her lungs until she feels she cannot hold out. Nothing left. No more oxygen. Just a growing darkness. A pinprick of light disappearing behind her eyes, getting smaller and smaller, her vision tunnelled.

Before the blackness descends, she hears something, a warped sound, distant – a voice, coming closer, getting louder until it's right next to her, a deep resonant tone; urgent, reassuring.

'Here! Over here. We've got someone.'

A figure leans close, a silhouette at first, then a face

surrounded by a halo of light, like an angel. A saviour. Her saviour.

She feels her hand being held, thick strong fingers caressing her wrist. Then a man's voice, strong, comforting. 'I've got a pulse. Quick! I need some assistance. She's still alive!'

2

'How are your nightmares?'

'Which ones?' Leah is restless. Will's talk of her nocturnal terrors makes her skin crawl. She has so many of them it's too difficult to set one apart from the other and place them in order of dread.

She shivers, her eyes drawn to the pieces of abstract art that line the walls of his office. She wishes Will had chosen something different to decorate his workplace, something softer, less harsh, with indistinguishable soft lines and pastel colours. Something that would soothe her rather than making her feel on edge. She stares at the largest picture and closes her eyes against the wave of revulsion that slides around inside her mind. Some would call it vibrant, exciting, innovative; artwork with a backstory. It isn't any of those things. It is a dark hulking monstrosity of a painting. The black ghoulish stripes that dance across the canvas combined with the vertical slashes of orange and red only serve to make her queasy and ill at ease. It's overpowering; sharp and striking, not something to be enjoyed, but something rather, to be intimidated by. She is sure that Will would tell her that she should be in awe of it, that she should admire its strength and fear its power. She feels none of those things. Staring at it fills her with misery, a feeling of inadequacy, of being trapped.

She opens her eyes, turns away and stares down at her hands.

'All of them. I take it you're still having dreams about the crash?' Will says lightly, as if they are talking about a grocery list or what to watch on TV and not the stream of disjointed visions that batter at her bruised and aching brain. It's she who suffers them. How could he ever begin to understand how it feels to wake with such terror and despondency hanging over you that you can't even remember who or where you are?

Leah nods, tears pricking at the back of her eyelids. She swallows, forcing them back. 'Most nights I dream that I'm dying, that nobody came to rescue me and I didn't make it out alive. My lack of memory doesn't help. I still can't recall what happened prior to me getting on the train or why I was even on it to begin with.'

'Retrograde amnesia.' Will says the words so casually, so lightly, as if it's a commonplace condition and not something that leaves her feeling as fragile as a leaf floating downstream, spinning and swirling, at the mercy of the elements. 'It's to be expected after an accident, and yours was pretty traumatic as accidents go. That, coupled with lack of sleep from the nightmares will leave you feeling fairly delicate and vulnerable.' He leans forward, his face coming into view out of the glare of the sunlight that is streaming in through the window behind him. 'Have you been taking your medication? The tablets to help you sleep?'

'They make me feel like a zombie. I can't seem to win. They help to dull everything but the more I sleep the worse the nightmares become,' Leah mutters. 'It's a vicious circle.' She is lying to him. She cannot recall being given any sleeping tablets but going along with what he says is easier than railing against him. Will is a force to be reckoned with, a rock in her unsteady world.

He leans back in his chair, idly running his fingers through his hair. 'And your painkillers? You're still on them?'

She feels inclined to grab them, arrange them on the desk for him to see, to prove how hard she is trying at getting better. Reaching into her handbag she is dismayed to find them not there. Her heart skips a beat, her skin grows hot. 'I must have left them at home. I'm pretty sure I take them regularly.' She isn't sure at all. She has no memory of any tablets but feels compelled to say the right things. The things that are expected of her.

Timed to perfection, the pain in her abdomen kicks in, sharp and raw as the day it happened. Will this ever end? She winces, takes a long breath, waits for the griping to dissipate, then gives him a thin tight grimace. 'I wish I'd never got on that stupid bloody train.'

Will smiles and exhales loudly, his nostrils flaring, his face appearing larger than ever as he places his hands on the desk. Leah can't help but notice how clean his fingernails are, how manicured and pale his hands are compared to his liver spotted face. She wants to ask him why his cheeks are so mottled and florid, why there are large marks on his skin when he isn't old enough to warrant having them. She guesses that he's in his late forties, early fifties at a push – yet his expression, his speckled flesh, is that of somebody much older. Somebody who has lived and seen things. Perhaps he has. Apart from speaking to him here in this place where all they do is talk incessantly about her health and her endless litany of ailments, both physical and mental, she doesn't know anything about him. He has a life, probably a family, a past she knows nothing about. She is an open book to him. Will is a stranger to her.

'You know, the mind is a funny thing, both terribly fragile and yet incredibly resilient at the same time. At some point everything will come back to you. It just takes time.'

'I'm still off work,' Leah mumbles as she picks at a piece of loose cotton on her shirt sleeve. She feels like a small child, a miscreant caught doing something terribly naughty. Work seems like a lifetime ago. She can't even remember when she is due to return. Everything is such a muddle, her logic in tatters.

'Well, there's no shame in that. You've been through a massive trauma. You just need to rest up, not be so hard on yourself and remember to keep breathing.' He chuckles at his own words, as if they're sharing a private joke.

Still picking at her sleeve, Leah remains still, waiting for his laughter to subside. She still has things she needs to tell him, odd occurrences, things she can't explain. Things that worry her beyond reason.

In the lull, she interjects, her voice low and raspy. 'I thought I saw my brother last week. I was on my way here and felt somebody watching me. When I turned, I could have sworn I saw him standing on the other side of the road staring at me. I let out a shriek, and then he disappeared.'

She waits for Will to respond, to come out with an explanation as to why she saw her dead brother in the middle of the street. Because she wants to hear it. She wants to be given a reason; some sort of medical terminology thrown her way to reassure her that she is not going completely mad. 'My brother is dead. He died some years back. How can you explain this latest incident?'

His manner is suddenly serious, an authoritative air to it. 'Now I know you might not want to hear this, or maybe you do, but obviously we both know it can't have been your brother. What I do know is that the brain is a complex thing and perfectly capable of misrepresenting things, allowing us to see what we want to see and hear what we want to hear.' Will coughs lightly and taps his fingers on the desk, a dull thrumming that pounds in her ears and fills the room. 'What about the rest of your family?'

Scalp prickling, Leah drops her gaze to the joints in the wooden floor, focusing on the ingrained dots of dirt lodged in between each one, hoping Will moves on from this subject. Thinking about her parents makes her skin itch. Her head buzzes at the very mention of them, at that memory of that awful, awful day. She shakes her head, her lips pursed. 'I don't see them, haven't done for many years now.' Her eyes bulge with unshed tears. She blinks them back. Ancient history. Time to look forward, to drag herself out of the rut she has found herself in of late.

'And you miss them?' Will has raised his volume, upped his tempo, forcing her to sit up straighter and delve into her past even though every nerve ending in her body is shrieking at her to step away from this conversation, urging her to say nothing and leave it be.

'Should I?' Ice fills her veins; her words are sharp, dagger-like, as they tumble out of her mouth.

'You've never told me why you're estranged from them. Do you want to elaborate, or should we leave that subject well alone?'

Leah thinks about what a clever man Will is, how astute and shrewd he is, cornering her like this, getting her to open up about the rift, making their future conversation about her parents seem like a fait accompli as if this moment was destined to be. He's a constant voice in her head, forcing her to confront her past, to think about those events and speak openly about them.

She shakes her head, shrugs listlessly, buying herself some time as a way of putting off saying what has always needed to be said. The lump in her throat is impossibly large, obstructing her windpipe. It's a wonder she can still breathe, let alone speak. She takes a deep breath, does her best to unburden herself. 'They no longer want anything to do with me. They lost one child and now refuse to communicate with their only remaining offspring. What sort of people would do something like that?' Leah doesn't mention Maria. There are only so many family matters she can bring herself to speak about.

Will's heavy breathing niggles at her as she waits for his response. She can feel his gaze boring into her, scrutinising her, wondering what is going on inside her head. He's the professional here. He should know exactly what she's thinking, be able to pre-empt her every word. And yet here he is, making her say things that she doesn't want to say, to utter words out loud that she doesn't want anybody to hear. He'll win. He always does. She has neither the energy nor the strength to fight him.

'And why is that?'

Another shrug then a sigh, affected and almost convulsive as an unexpected sob escapes from her throat. 'They blame me for my brother's death.'

The ticking of the clock on the wall booms in her ears. It sits there, a passive presence in the room, waiting for her to spill every secret, every sordid little detail. She waits, wondering who will speak next, her skin burning with the memory of it, her jaw rigid with resentment. Shaking her head, she blinks away unshed tears. 'I don't want to talk about it anymore. I'm tired.'

Leah glances around the room. Will's eyes are dark, the pictures on the wall monstrous, threatening. There is a bang. She jumps. Will remains seated, apparently oblivious to the noise. He is impervious to everything. Every noise, every distraction. He is in a permanent state of calmness, his manner always collected and unshakeable. Steady and solid in her wild and unpredictable little world.

'What was that?'

'What was what?' His expression remains blank, untouched by anything resembling emotion.

'That loud noise. The bang. Surely you heard it?' Leah says, her voice high, marginally hysterical. She coughs, clears her throat, tries to regain her composure even though her skin is burning and her nerve endings are on fire.

'Perhaps we should get back to talking about your nightmares.'

She can't take her eyes away from Will's face, from the liver spots that cover his skin, the large ugly blotches that appear to shimmer in the glare of the sun that is streaming in through the window, invisible waves that curl their way over her, heating up her pale cold flesh.

'Another time. As I said, I'm tired. It's exhausting going through this. Even thinking about it gives me a headache.' A memory springs into her mind, causing her to gasp. The train – something about having a headache, something about the journey, the reason for it. Why she was on it in the first place, why she was making that bloody awful journey, the one that has turned her life upside down. She tries to grasp it but it's too distant, too ethereal to pin down. It flits away, like all the other memories she is unable to hold on to, it grows smaller and smaller until it is out of reach altogether.

It's only as she stands up and is getting ready to leave that it dawns on her. She can't even remember getting to Will's office. Fear settles in her gut like bitumen, coating her insides, weighing her down. The exhaustion is overwhelming.

By the time she heads out of the main door of his office, she's so tired she can barely keep herself upright. She fights back tears once more. Is this what people who have suffered a trauma have to endure? Is this what she has become for the remainder of her life? She stumbles over to a bench outside and sits down, her leaden limbs glad of the rest. She closes her eyes, dips her head and shuts off to everything around her.

3

SUMMER 2005

A large crowd gathers at the foot of the cliffs, some of them local, most from elsewhere. They're here on holiday, magnetised by the beauty of the place. The sunshine has brought them out in droves, hordes of people walking on the pier, dotted around the promenade, spread out on the beach. So many of them milling around town and strolling over the sand like scurrying ants.

The town was full, the beach crammed with people when she fell over the edge, that tiny child, her small body spinning and tumbling, her screams captured by the wind and pushed out to sea. Yet nobody saw it happen. Not one single person saw her fall. They found her body afterwards, battered and broken at the foot of the cliffs, straw-coloured fluid seeping out of her ears, a thin line of blood oozing from her nose, her unseeing eyes pointed skyward towards the glare of the sun.

The noise, the pushing and shoving, the commotion as people try to get near the scene of the accident, is ugly. Despite the police arriving, despite them cordoning off the area and making an access space for the emergency services, people refuse to step back. They need to get closer, to claim the scene as their own. A crowd of voyeurs gather, their voices loud and brash against the backdrop of the incoming tide that rushes over the sand.

'I heard she slipped on the rocks, fell on the ledge and tumbled to the bottom like a bloody rag doll. Poor kid.'

'God, doesn't it make you feel lucky to have your own little ones here with you?'

'Bloody awful, isn't it? Gotta feel sorry for the parents. Poor sods.'

Chatter fills the air, eclectic emotions blanketing the crowd after the initial silence has broken. The ripple of shock turns to euphoria, everyone relieved it isn't their family, that this tragedy has impacted on somebody else. Every one of them is exempt from the grief, from the ensuing horror. All they have to do is be passive bystanders, to watch as the drama unfolds before them.

They twist their bodies to get a better view of the damaged child, to see her small head tilted in an unnatural position, to stare at her legs, splayed apart and jutting out at painful angles, to wince at the sight of her tiny mouth twisted into a half scream, the breath taken out of her, mid-cry.

Grayston-on-Sea, a small seaside town, known for its raspberry and lemon ice creams, its amusement arcades and long pier, isn't acquainted with death. It's a sedate place, synonymous with family holidays, golden sands, the shrieks of happy children as they paddle in the frothing waves; not the death of a tiny girl. Not this. Never this.

Questions fill the air, voices shrieking, desperate for answers, overlapping with one another. *Did she stumble over the edge? Are the cliffs unsteady?* There have been rock falls in the past, boulders and huge stones that have tumbled down from the top, landing on the sandy beach, scattering far and wide as they hit the floor. Is that what happened? Did the cliff give way under her?

Realisation dawns. People begin to disperse, stumbling back, their eyes cast upwards, a collective fear building and growing, ballooning in their gut at the idea of a rockfall raining down on them. They stumble and shift, a body of fearful people moving in unison to a place of safety.

The wail of sirens pierces the air. An ambulance expertly rolls down the ramp onto the soft sand with a thump and makes its way over to the watching throng. The bodies part to let it through, but people make sure they stay close by for fear of missing anything.

'*Where are her parents? Where did she come from?*'

'*Was she pushed?*'

The chatter continues, wild accusations thrown around with little or no evidence. Only the people above them, high up on the edge can answer those questions. They have their own version of events. And even those versions are disputed. Because their backs were turned when the child fell. They had been busy laying out picnic blankets, relieved to be high up, relieved to be away from the crowds below. They were like gods, up in the heavens, set apart from the people below. Their day had been peaceful. Calm and happy.

But not for long.

An argument had broken out between the teenagers, voices raised, a loud screech, a stumble or a push.

And then a protracted void where time stood still. A terrible moment that ripped their lives apart.

Nothing but the whistling of the wind, the rushing of the waves below them. And a small distant scream. Shouts and gasps had suddenly filtered up from the golden sands, up through the warm summer air, cutting through the calm ambience.

Then it came; the plaintive, wretched cries of anguish from the families on the cliff.

Blankets were discarded, food trampled underfoot as adults

ran and screamed and howled for help, voices raw, frantic, their bodies bent double with grief and horror as they leaned over the edge looking for the missing girl, for their child. Their baby.

But it was too late. It was all too late. She was gone, swallowed by gravity, her body broken, her soul departed. They shouted, howled, ran amok, asking how such a thing could ever happen. It wasn't real. It simply couldn't be. They only turned their backs for a couple of minutes. They are good people, caring, decent and attentive. Things like this only ever happen to others, neglectful people, parents who don't care. Not to them. It couldn't be real. It just couldn't.

The eldest of the teenagers had stood aghast. They were supposed to be looking out for the young child, keeping her safe. She was just a kid, an innocent being. And now she was dead.

They needed answers. Somebody was responsible.

Somebody had to shoulder the blame.

'It's your fault,' the young teenage girl had said, pointing to the taller boy. 'You were standing next to her when it happened. You were the closest.'

The young lad shook his head, the colour leaching from his face. His skin took on the texture of melting candle wax as he trembled and grew pale, his features slack with shock. He stumbled, fell backwards onto the grass, his limbs awkward and stiff with fear and revulsion.

The teenage girl turned to the two sets of parents; her voice cold, sharp as flint. 'I saw what happened out of the corner of my eye. He thought I wasn't watching him, but I was.'

A collective inhalation of breath could be heard, even above the howling wind and the screech of the seagulls that circled overhead. Everyone waited, eyes wide, ears attuned as she spoke with such authority and precision it shook them to their core.

'They were arguing, him and little Lucy. He said he didn't

want to be lumbered with looking after her. She cried and he told her to shut up and she wouldn't. So he pushed her.' The teenage girl remained calm, unruffled as she continued with her revelation, her features impassive. 'I saw it all. It was his fault,' she said flatly, not a tremor of fear in her voice, not a flicker of emotion in her face. 'He's the one who did it. Poor little Lucy. He killed her.'

4

PRESENT DAY

Leah is back there, in that road, at that place. Next to the house where it happened. Beads of perspiration bubble up on her forehead, prickling her scalp and trailing down her neck.

She can sense the dog close by, can hear its low growling, feel its heat. But worse than that, much much worse, it knows she is near, can detect her vulnerability and smell her fear. She visualises its twitching nose, sniffing her out. She tries to stem her growing disquiet to quell her terror and tell herself that everything is going to be fine, that this is just a dream. But is it? It feels so real, her senses attuned to every little movement, every beat of her heart. She has been here before, experienced this level of terror, felt the pain. She can't go through it again.

With a rumbling gut, she tentatively steps onto the road, away from the gate, doing her utmost to gain some distance. Everything is still the same and yet so very different.

It's the same old hedge, the same wrought-iron railings that she passed every day on her way home from school. The same ones she used to drag a stick across, back and forth, back and forth, over and over and over, the noise a jarring invasive clatter that echoed through the street. That's how it happened. The noise. It riled the dog. She knew that, was aware it would jump up and growl at her unwanted presence, at the rattling and grating of wood against metal. She knew no better, finding the noise pleasurable and the dog's reaction entertaining. That was all it was. No ulterior motive. No desire to be confrontational or oppositional. She was a child for God's sake. Just a kid.

That's not how her parents saw it. She was blamed, told to stop misbehaving and to stop being so keen to court controversy and danger at every available opportunity. Not in those words obviously – she was only ten years old at the time – but with the benefit of hindsight and experience, she can see that that was what was meant.

'Why do you insist on annoying that poor dog?' her mother had asked as they drove her to hospital, her father pushing through traffic and honking his horn as he manoeuvred around corners at top speed. 'The owner said he's asked you before to stop poking it with sticks. Honestly, Leah, why do you do these things? For a clever girl, sometimes you do the silliest of things.'

'Here's hoping this has taught you a lesson, eh?' her father had said as he swung the car into a space and yanked on the handbrake with such force, she felt sure it would rip up out of the floor of the car.

She had wanted to tell them that it wasn't her fault, that the gate had been left slightly ajar and that the dog had managed to escape. The owner should have kept it locked up and away from other people. But she couldn't say any of those things. The pain rendered her speechless; a screeching line of agony that raced up and down the soft underside of her arm. She hung on to it, pressing in place the towel her mother had given her to stem the flow of blood.

'Make sure you keep that in place,' she had been told as they slid in the back seat and fastened their seat belts, her mother eyeing the growing crimson bloom that was appearing through the thick towelling fabric. 'We don't want to stain the upholstery. Your dad's just cleaned the car.'

And that's how it was. That's what her parents' reaction was to her trauma. Perfunctory and judgemental. Unlike the time Ellis fell in a patch of boggy land when they were out walking. They had both been warned away by their father. He had seen the signs and told them both from under his brow that under no circumstances should they wander over that way. She had listened to every word, terrified by the prospect of sinking deep into the earth, swallowing clods of grass and mud, choking and gagging as the air was sucked out of her lungs and replaced by viscous, foul-tasting mud.

But Ellis didn't hear. He was locked in his own little world, immune to his father's warning and so stepped straight into that patch of marshland. His body slid under as swiftly as water down a drain. Leah had cried out, alerted her parents, screaming that he was gone, that Ellis was drowning. Her dad had thrown himself in after Ellis, clawing and gouging at the thick filthy fluid, his hands managing to grab at a clump of Ellis's hair. But pulling the lad out proved more difficult than he imagined. The surrounding land was slippery and the boggy earth sucked them both under.

Fortunately, two passers-by saw what was happening. They jumped in and formed a chain, helping to drag Ellis back out, laying him down under the haze of the watery afternoon sun. Leah remembers it all with such clarity; the ensuing furore, the howls of despair from their mother, how she swept Ellis up in her arms, holding his head close to her face and nestling her mouth against his grimy hair, ignoring the mud that clung to his scalp. She kissed his grey skin, wiped at his weeping eyes and wiped clean his hands with her own trembling fingers. No blame apportioned. No words of scorn at his lack of care.

It was apparent to Leah even then, that sometimes, no matter how hard she tried, no matter how hard she worked at doing the right thing, she would always be seen as less, never quite managing to get it right. Never quite managing to be as good as Ellis.

A low purring growl sends a buzz of terror through her. Heart hammering, she spins around, scanning the area, eyes sweeping over every hiding place, every dark corner. She lets out a protracted breath. She can see no salivating dog, no feral animal with bared fangs and drool hanging from the corners of its mouth, yet is unable to switch off, to step out of the shadows leaving herself unguarded and exposed. She's been here before. She knows what comes next and remembers this episode all too well.

The sound comes again, a deep resonating growl that sets her nerve endings on fire. Her feet twist and turn unsteadily as she attempts to walk away and save herself, but knowing also deep down, that it's too late. As if out of nowhere, the animal pounces, pinning her to the ground, the rough asphalt scraping against her back as she squirms about, trying to escape its clutches. It's not enough. She is no match for its bulk and strength. The animal lowers its head, strings of glutinous saliva stretching and shining, hanging loosely from its jaw as it dips its head lower and lower, sinking its razor-sharp teeth deep into her arm...

Leah stumbles up off the bench, her mind a fog, her vision hazy. Has she been sleeping? Outside, here in the open? She whirls around, an uncomfortable sensation settling in her stomach at the thought of being seen slumped, dozing, possibly even drooling, in public. She recalls that incident with the dog, her parents' reaction to their childhood accidents and the resentment that has never left her.

The pain in her abdomen is a sudden force within. She

squeezes her eyes closed, blinking back tears of self-pity. She is stuck on a hamster wheel, reliving the worst parts of her life, unable to escape.

She scans the nearby area, the empty landscape. Nobody here. The park is eerily devoid of people. No dog walkers, no pram-pushing parents. Nothing at all. A dull silence fills her ears, layers of nothingness building up in her head as she places a hand over the throbbing skin on her belly and walks towards Jacob's flat. She has no idea why she is doing this. She and Jacob broke up weeks and weeks ago, but she is feeling tired and scared and defenceless, susceptible to the horrors of the world and right now all she wants is a friendly face and a modicum of reassurance to keep her on track, to stop her life from unravelling completely. Speaking to Will often goes either way – she can leave him feeling buoyant and upbeat or she can leave his office feeling as if the weight of the world is pressing down on her. Today is one of those days. Putting one foot in front of the other feels like an ordeal. The weight of the world is hard to bear when your own problems are already pushing you deep into the ground.

The walk exhausts her. The pavement is soft under her feet, her legs like liquid as she heads out onto the main road and takes a right turn through the narrow Victorian street. The cobbles are slippery underfoot, the houses so close together they appear to lean in at a peculiar angle. Sinewy shadows dip and swoop at her, falling away into a thin line of greyness as she moves farther down the road and heads back out into an open space. She holds her breath, releasing it as she steps back out into the light.

Nobody sees her as she strides past. They're all locked into their own little worlds, eyes focused ahead, gaits angular and rigid. Lethargy eats at her but she has a steely determination to speak to Jacob. She'll suffer for it later, needing to lie still for however long it takes to let the pain ease, but to see Jacob and hear his voice, to see the twinkle in his deep blue eyes and know that it's reserved only for her at that moment, would make it all worthwhile. She has no idea if he'll be pleased to see her or whether this impromptu visit will set off a sharpness within him, forcing him to retreat into his lair. It's his speciality, being unpredictable and impulsive. For so long now, he has been unreachable. It's a gift of his. No matter how hard she tries to get past the barriers he has put up since their split, she always fails. She wonders if she ever really knew him at all.

It was a little over a year ago when they met. Leah rented a flat in the same street where he lived. She was working as an accountant and Jacob was – still is – a teacher at the local college. They clicked immediately after bumping into one another on the day she moved in. Their shared love of music and literature drew them together, as well as his quick wit and movie star looks that made her weak at the knees. They spent many, many memorable beautiful months together as a couple. Until things turned sour, that is.

Leah's stomach clenches. She tries to not think about it. A sudden feeling of gloom takes over as a memory pushes itself into her brain – Jacob standing over her, telling her to stop with the histrionics after one of their many arguments. The expression on his face as he glowered at her, his pleas for her to calm down still makes her guts swirl with dread. How on earth could she remain calm? What did he expect from her? She had seen him with another woman earlier in the day, ambling through the High Street like old friends, laughing, chatting, their body language telling her everything she needed to know. She didn't want or need to hear his excuses.

His ill-thought-out explanation that they were simply heading to the same shop to pick up a sandwich for lunch had insulted her intelligence and she had told him as much, roaring at him that he was a thoughtless shit.

He had shrugged and told her that it was the truth and there was nothing else he could say. It was his crooked smile that did it; that knowing look that he had in his dark eyes as he spoke. It had niggled at her, rippling under her skin, making her feel small and insignificant, as if their relationship meant nothing to him. As if she meant nothing to him. She had shouted and called him some terrible names, saying some unforgivable things about what a philandering bastard he was and how useless he was and that he couldn't be trusted.

He had taken a step towards her, his face dark with fury. She had shrieked and stumbled away, fearing he was going to do something to her. At that he moved closer to her again and they got in a scuffle. Somehow, her arms became entangled with his and she caught him with her fist. Leah shudders as she remembers the sensation of her knuckles connecting with his nose, the repulsive crunch of soft cartilage shifting and separating as she made contact. She recalls the sudden gush of blood from his nose, like a dam bursting; a river of crimson spurting from his face, running out of his nostrils and dripping through his fingers onto the floor of the landing outside his door.

There were tears as she screamed and tried to help him back inside, her arms wrapped around his shoulders, her voice soothing, apologetic, her hand guiding him back in, coaxing him, sitting him down while she cleaned him up, dabbing at his face with wet towels.

She had stayed for as long as it took to sort everything out, or at least until she was sure he had forgiven her, explaining through her bouts of sobbing that it was an accident and she hadn't meant for it to happen.

She eventually left for home, weak and weary, consumed with fear that his words meant nothing, that he was already planning on severing ties with her. She had to convince herself that they were just an average couple who had had an argument that had simply got out of hand. It happened to everyone at one point or another, didn't it? Couples fight and argue all the time. They were no different. She had texted him when she got home, making sure he was on the mend and not splayed out on the kitchen floor choking on a blood clot that was lodged in the back of his throat. He had assured her he was fine. Feeling relieved that he had forgiven her and not told her to stick her apology where the sun don't shine, she ran a bath, poured herself a glass of wine, comforted by the fact he was well enough to reply. Delighted that he still loved her.

The next day she awoke, the incident still in the forefront of her mind, giving her an aching sensation in the pit of her stomach, so she had called round after work and they had made love with such passion and fervour, she knew immediately that they had moved on.

Leah bites at her lip, digging her teeth into folds of loose flesh. She has a temper, she knows that, is acutely aware of it, and would even go so far as to say she lost control that day. But Jacob is far from innocent with his flirtatious behaviour and absolute refusal to rein it in when he is around other women. It wasn't all her fault. It was as if he enjoyed seeing her suffer, watching her reactions whenever he leaned in too close to a particularly attractive female to tell a joke or to regale his friends with one of his many anecdotes about working with teenagers and how they would send him notes asking for a date. Jacob thrives on female attention. He is a natural flirt. Leah wasn't solely to blame. She often tells herself this, consoling herself with this fact even though she knows her attitude was her downfall. The beginning of the end.

Turning onto Banbury Avenue, watching the flickering movements of birds circling overhead, listening to their effortless chirruping, she tries to visualise Jacob's surprised expression when she turns up on his doorstep. She thinks about his smile and wonders if it is now reserved for somebody else. She hopes not. What they had was different, a special connection that can't be easily broken. She feels sure that Jacob knows this and that their current separation is no more than a hiatus, a brief respite from the norm.

She spots it as soon as she rounds the corner – Chloe's car. Her stomach plummets. She grips on to a nearby wall for balance. The houses ahead begin to spin, the lavender velvet sky turning a murky shade of grey as she attempts to regain her composure, stiffening her shoulders in preparation. Chloe, the person who stalked Jacob for so many months, the one who sent him love notes making her and Jacob so nervous that they considered calling the police, is here at his flat. Leah's skin shrivels. Surely Jacob hasn't relented and allowed that woman into his life knowing how unpredictable she is? That would be absurd, terrifying even. Leah's dark moods and quick temper are nothing compared to Chloe's manipulative devious ways. He knows that. Jacob bloody well knows it. So what the hell is he thinking?

Her heart crawls up her throat as she nears his house, passing the flat that she was forced to give up after losing her job a few months ago. Another thing to drag her down and make her feel utterly miserable. General cutbacks and losing a major account meant she was first to be given the push as soon as redundancies were announced. Within weeks, she managed to procure another position at a nearby firm of accountants, but the hours were longer and the salary lower. Paying her rent and other bills would have been impossible.

After many fruitless viewings of flats, many of which were practically uninhabitable, she found one on the other side of town. It meant sharing with two other people. She was also farther away from Jacob, at least two miles, but she had a roof over her head. And that was the main thing. After losing her previous position, she was relieved that she had a job at all. Had she and Jacob still been together, she could have talked about moving in with him, taking their relationship to the next level, but they had already parted ways and even though she was working on repairing what they had, there was no way she could have asked him if he wanted her as a lodger in his home.

She is her own person, unaccustomed to looking to others for support. Having parents who no longer want anything to do with her has given her an independent streak that she simply cannot shake no matter how low an ebb she is at. And by God, she has been at some low points in the past few months, but she is still here, giving life a go, getting by as best she can. That's one thing she can say with true conviction, that she has always been a trier. Even now, despite everything losing its shine, despite losing her boyfriend and being in constant pain, she is doing her damnedest to remain positive. It's not easy. There are days when she wants to rage and shout, to raise her fists to the sky and scream that everything is so fucking unfair. But she doesn't. She just gets on with it. Day after day after day.

She squints against a shimmer of light radiating from the line of cars parked at the side of the road. Shielding her eyes with her cupped hand, she stares at Chloe's immaculately polished Mini Cooper with its perfect cream paintwork and impossibly clean badges and chrome handles. An incongruous sight, parked in between other less salubrious vehicles that have seen better days, it is crying out to be noticed. An invitation for damage.

Hands slung deep in her pockets, Leah wraps her fingers around her keys, running the soft skin of her fingertips over the serrated edge of the Yale key to her flat, thinking how sharp it is, marvelling at the damage it could do to an unprotected length of shiny new metal. She can almost hear the deep grating growl it would make as she traces a long gratifying line across the bodywork of the pristine vehicle. She shivers and stops, closes her eyes and sighs, and leaves go of the key, knowing it would be a childish thing to do. Churlish and crass. For all she knows, Chloe could be visiting somebody close by. She may not even be in there with Jacob. She could be at any number of places. Leah stares up once more at the window, resentment and bitterness building in her chest. She isn't at any number of places though, is she? She is in there, with him. It's too much of a coincidence. This street isn't anywhere near the town centre. She has no other reason to park here. She's here for Jacob. Chloe is here for Leah's boyfriend.

Ex-boyfriend.

She swallows and runs her fingers through her hair. Ex-boyfriend for now. But that's not going to last. Things are about to change. She can feel it in her bones, sense it deep in her gut. There is a good chance they'll get back together. And soon. Never say never.

Chloe won't stop her and Jacob picking up where they left off. She is nothing. A fly in the ointment is all she is. No more, no less. Chloe strolled into their lives so rapidly and casually that she can be just as easily dismissed again.

Leah turns away from the flat, stands for a second then spins back around, her eyes drawn to the upper bay window. She thinks of them up there, in his home, the place where she and Jacob spent so much time together. The place where they made love with such hunger and desire, the thought of it still makes her weak and wanting. The place she is going to keep a close eye on until he sees sense and lets her back into his life. She waits for a little while longer, her mind full of ways she can approach him, ways she hopes will make him see her point of view. Because whether he realises it or not, it is obvious to her that they cannot live without each other. It's just that he doesn't know it yet.

But he will. Soon enough he will wake up to what Chloe is doing. His eyes will be opened. He will become aware of how he is being led by somebody who will never have the capacity to care about him the way Leah does. Soon he will realise that she is no more than a transient part of his life, a shallow lover he will live to regret. And then he will cast her aside with the realisation that he and Leah were never meant to be apart.

5

PRESENT DAY

It's dark, the sun hanging lazily in a bruised russet sky. Leah has no memory of losing the light or getting home. She lets herself in, careful not to disturb her flatmates. They have demanding jobs, busy lives and are always asking for peace and quiet, complaining that she is clumsy and noisy if she so much as *dares* to close a door too loudly. It doesn't bother her too much, their moans and complaints. It's a decent flat and given that they are always studying or working, it's not so bad. The serious feeling around the place helps to clear her head and restore some balance in her muddled chaotic life. When the many thoughts and memories she has going on in her brain collide, leaving her feeling woozy and out of sorts, a quiet house is exactly what she needs. She has no idea if either of them is in their rooms but takes care anyway, keen to avoid an unnecessary skirmish. Her life is difficult enough. She definitely doesn't need any more conflict.

Unable to eat, she sits by the window thinking about Chloe's car outside Jacob's flat; she thinks about the jolt it gave her. A sharp reminder of her predicament closely followed by a wave of anger so strong it almost swallowed her whole. She suppresses a yawn and closes her eyes, her head resting against the glass, savouring the chill as it spreads over her skin, alleviating the burning hatred that is still flickering deep within her belly. She should be the one who is up there with him. Leah and Jacob, not Chloe and Jacob. Never Chloe. Never her. How could he? He's got it all wrong. Everything is skewed, her life out of kilter and heading in the wrong direction.

She stays there, leaning against the cool of the glass for longer than intended, the cold sensation lulling her into a welcome state of detachment, the pain in her abdomen shrinking as her skin develops an icy sheen, becoming anaesthetised and comfortably numb.

A sudden noise from the hallway drags her out of her reverie, forcing her to her feet. She stands, walks to the door and stops, seeing it as soon as she steps into the hallway – the small white envelope on the coconut matting, pale and discordant against the dark brush of the rug. She paces closer, aware that it has been hand delivered, aware that it's a strange time for anybody to be posting notes, thinking immediately that something is awry. Blood rushes to her head, making her dizzy as she bends down and snatches it up. A tremble runs through her arms, down to her hands, reaching her fingertips as she holds the letter aloft, staring at the name written on the front.

Her name.

The handwriting isn't familiar. It isn't Jacob's slightly left leaning cursive script that she admires and has tried to emulate. This writing is small. Neat and precise, written in heavy black ink as if to draw the eye and make an impact.

Gripping the envelope tightly, she heads into her room to open it. She doesn't want to read it in a communal area where Grainne or Innes could appear. She wants privacy. Sitting down on her unmade bed, she looks around, the letter clutched tightly in her slightly damp palm. It's a disgrace in here. She needs to start looking after her own private space, to tidy it up, get some order back into her muddled untidy little life. She is only thankful that Grainne, who owns the house, doesn't do spot checks. Grainne is a special needs teacher at a local school and likes everything to be orderly. She is also a trained counsellor and a huge believer in feng shui. Leah thinks that feng shui is a load of old bollocks but refrains from airing that particular opinion in the presence of the person who has allowed her to rent a room in her house when many other places were unsuitable or she was declined occupancy for reasons unknown.

The other flatmate, Innes, is a lecturer at the university and dresses like somebody who hasn't changed his clothes in months. He wears corduroy slacks and tweed jackets and smells of mildew. Leah suspects his room is as bad as hers. If Grainne ever decided to check up on them, she hopes there would be lenience shown. This is a big house and Leah doubts Grainne could afford to keep it running on just her salary alone. Both she and Innes are quiet, keeping themselves to themselves. They will undoubtedly be considered half decent tenants in a city full of students who have very little money, along with a number of undesirables who are desperate for cheap rooms and easy-going landlords. Neither she nor Innes bring people back here. They are both employed and aside from their untidiness and Leah's purported clumsiness, they cause Grainne no problems.

Her eyes sweep over the detritus stacked in all four corners of the room, surveying the mess that is hers and hers alone. It's not healthy living like this. She should do something about it. It was only a few weeks back when she was unable to put her hands on some documents she required for work. Also buried amongst the piles of papers are duplicates of the letters she sent to Jacob after their split and her angst-ridden diary entries. If she hasn't the energy to take care of those, then what has she become?

She swallows and rubs at her eyes, promising herself she will set to and tidy it all once she has read this letter. The letter that for some inexplicable reason she is delaying opening. It arrived at a peculiar time, or at least she thinks it did. Keeping track of time is another ability that seems to elude her now. She cannot seem to pin it down and work out whether it is morning, noon or night.

Leah casts her eyes downwards at the envelope clutched between her damp fingers. Her stomach growls, her skin grows cold. For all she knows, it could contain something unpleasant. What she does know is that this isn't an ordinary occurrence, receiving a hand-delivered letter after sunset; it's unusual and she isn't a fan of surprises, agreeable or otherwise.

Her fingers tremble, vibrations pulsing under her skin as she rips at the fold, slipping her nail inside to slice it apart. Inside is a small piece of paper neatly creased in half. A swarm of angry wasps take hold in her head, the room tipping and tilting as she opens it and reads the words written there.

Leah,

I write this in the hope you understand what it is we're trying to say. Please don't make us call the police because we will do it if this stalking behaviour doesn't cease. We are asking you to stop following Jacob and me around. We saw you earlier standing outside the window staring up at us. It is unnerving and unnecessary. Jacob has made it clear for many months now that he wants nothing to do with you. We hoped you moving away would solve the problem but that hasn't worked. If anything, you seem more determined to watch us. Your behaviour is obsessive bordering on dangerous and we really think you need to get some help.

Don't be angry when you read this. That sort of reaction won't help. We're trying to be patient with you but you have to do your bit as well. We realise you're lonely and initially wanted some company but following people around and refusing to leave them alone isn't the way to go about making friends.

Have you thought about seeing a doctor? Perhaps you should bear this in mind. And please don't think we're bluffing when we talk about calling the police because our safety is important to us. Having somebody standing outside watching us for hours on end is unsettling and actually rather frightening.

Please think about what we're asking. Stop stalking us or you will end up with a police officer knocking on your door.

Chloe

A rage burns inside her as she scans the letter, reading and digesting each word, skimming over every line again and again. A switch has been flicked somewhere deep in her gut, churning everything up, starting a furnace that is spreading through her veins.

How dare she? How fucking *dare she*?

Leah perches on the edge of the bed, gripping at the pain that slices over her abdomen. It rips through her sternum, pulsing up her neck and filling her mouth with bile until she feels unable to breathe properly. She switches from cold to hot. Sweat stands out on her forehead, tiny iridescent beads of frustration and hatred. She wipes them away with the back of her hand, looks up to the ceiling, her eyes dry, her temper building. She has never been the crying type. What good does it do? It won't change anything and it won't make this awful letter disappear. The unthinkable has happened. Chloe has done it. She has succeeded in her attempts to snare Jacob permanently and has now wormed her way into his affections. She is well and truly ensconced in his life and by the sounds of it, his heart. Leah shivers at the thought, an unwanted sob lodging at the back of her throat like a jagged rock.

A picture of the two of them blooms in her thoughts. She banishes it to the back of her mind. Too sickening to contemplate; Chloe and Jacob wrapped in one another's arms, lying next to each other in his bed, possibly even planning a secure future together, a permanent one. It's all so unfair. Jacob was hers until Chloe came along and now she has Jacob and Leah has nothing. She cannot allow this. She won't allow it.

It has to be stopped.

She picks up the porcelain shell ornament she has had since she was a teenager and hurls it at the nearest wall, watching mesmerised as it shatters into a thousand tiny pieces. Hopefully, Grainne will be out and Innes, even if he is in, will undoubtedly have his head immersed in some book or other, too deep in his thoughts to hear the smash. The sound as it hits the wall makes Leah's chest swell with excitement. Her pulse quickens and her heart thumps around her ribcage. Then she sees the mess and thinks about how long it will take to clear it all up. As if this room isn't enough of a dump as it is. Why does everything have a downside to it? Why the hell is everything so fucking difficult? She can't even manage to be angry properly.

Leah wonders how it all came to this. How did she let the love of her life slip away into another woman's arms? Careless doesn't even cover it. Perhaps Jacob was right all along and she was too controlling, too possessive. But then how was she supposed to react to his endless flirtations and wandering eye? He made it so difficult for her to remain calm, seeming to bring out the worst in her every single day. She did try to approach things differently, play the waiting game, hoping his latest fancy was a passing phase and that he would return to her, mired in regret and begging for forgiveness, but it became so much more difficult once Chloe came on the scene. She changed things. She changed Jacob.

They had been together for a few months when Chloe came dancing into their lives. Apparently, she was a colleague, a peer, which was a change from Jacob's usual trick of flirting relentlessly with students who had developed a mad crush on their young good-looking teacher. This was a step up for him. And an unwelcome one at that.

That particular evening, Leah had planned on the two of them spending time together but Jacob had informed her that he was going to see friends and colleagues. Leah knew immediately what that meant. She had listened to him talking about Chloe, seen the way he looked at her if they happened to bump into her when they were out in town. And they bumped into her a lot.

That was when it dawned on her. Chloe was following them, trailing after them, making sure she was seen as she stood at the bar, draping herself over it, nodding and smiling at the barman, fluttering her long dark eyelashes and laughing loudly at his jokes. It was sickening to watch, knowing what her ulterior motive was. Jacob. He was her target. That was all she wanted. And by stealth, she finally managed it. She snared him. Chloe stole Jacob from under her nose and now they are an item; a tag team sending her notes warning her off. Accusing her of being a stalker for God's sake. Such a ridiculous notion.

Her stomach tightens as she recalls that evening. The evening Leah lost Jacob for good. She had followed him into town, ducking behind road signs and hedges, dipping into doorways every time he glanced around or crossed the road. That was what he had reduced her to – a jealous snooping partner who followed her boyfriend around town to keep tabs on him. It was Jacob's fault, lying to her, forcing her into a corner where she had no option other than to do such things. None of it was her fault. If only he had remained faithful and not lied to her.

If only he hadn't gone out to that restaurant with Chloe. But he did.

That evening was the worst of times. A low point.

She had watched as they ate together while she stood outside in the rain, water dripping over her face, clinging to her eyelashes like drops of dew, falling on her face and running down her neck, saturating her clothes and soaking her skin. A terrible memory and such an awful cliché. Such complete sadness that no matter how hard she tries, cannot be erased.

At one point, Jacob had leaned over the table and kissed Chloe before filling both of their glasses with red wine and raising a toast. And all the while, Leah had stood there, soaking, freezing, despondent and completely powerless. That was when she made a promise to herself to get him back, to keep Chloe away from her boyfriend. Jacob she could forgive, Chloe she could not. He was a chatty charming guy with oodles of charisma and the swarthy looks that sent most women into a swoon. There was no denying that Chloe was a glamorous woman with her own appeal and charisma, but the fact she had stepped in and taken somebody else's partner made her tinged with something dark, something brooding; an aura of wickedness that Jacob was blind to. She was a siren luring him to the rocks and he had fallen for it, casting Leah aside like an old sock.

The letter flutters in her hand, the slight tremble in her body now a violent shudder as she struggles to contain her anger and misery. Even thinking about it after all these months brings it back to her so clearly. It's as if it happened only yesterday, the memory punishingly lucid in her mind, never leaving her, reminding her of how unhappy she is, how desperate she is. How lonely she is.

She sits, close to tears, aware that she will do anything to get him back.

Anything at all.

Solitude is a cold and unforgiving place. An eerily silent and despairing place. She doesn't like it and doesn't want to be here. What she does want is her life back to how it was. The life she had with Jacob. Her perfect life, the one she admittedly took for granted before Chloe came along and ruined it.

Dropping to her knees, she gingerly gathers up the fragments of the porcelain shell, placing the small shards in her cupped hand one by one. A stinging sensation whips over her skin. Leah looks down to see a pool of crimson gathering in her palm. She lets out a small cry, blinks, and looks again to see nothing. All she can see is the pile of sharp fragments heaped up in her palm like a tiny mound of rubble. No blood. No cuts to her skin. Nothing.

She breathes heavily and stands up, small pieces of the shattered ornament crunching underfoot, sending a small ripple of revulsion though her. It reminds her of the time when as a child she stood on a snail, the tiny crack of its shell causing her to stop and shriek until her father assured her it was an accident. He didn't really understand why she was upset. It wasn't the thought of killing the snail that repulsed her; it was the actual feel of the crunch and pop of its shell as she stood on it that made her skin crawl. It was only later when she was tucked up in bed that she thought of that snail and how it had ceased to exist because of her. The very idea of wielding such power sent a thrill of excitement through her, flames tingling in her veins and diffusing inside her. That was the first time she had experienced supremacy. It fired up her senses, made her feel alive. No longer was she a small inconsequential child. She was somebody who could control who lived and who died. It was a pivotal moment and the memory of that raw surge of power has never left her.

Leah shuts her eyes, her palm still stuffed with the broken pieces, sharp serrated edges cutting into her soft unprotected flesh as she closes her hand over them and presses down. She wonders how she was able to experience that feeling of control as a child but as an adult, finds herself incapable of exerting any influence over the important things, like winning Jacob back. Perhaps she's just not trying hard enough. Perhaps she needs to be more attentive to what is required and find a way around this thing instead of making a fool of herself by standing outside his house like an unwanted guest.

She lets out a yelp as a piece of the porcelain cuts into her skin. The pain is a release, freeing her of the pent-up anger and frustration that eats at her. This time there is blood. Real blood. She feels it as it covers her palm, its warm stickiness a reminder that she is still alive, that she is still here and able to do something about the shit that is thrown her way.

Opening her hand and unfurling her fingers, she lets go of the shards, watching as they drop to the floor, spreading far and wide, smeared with her sticky scarlet blood, a metaphor for her life.

That is who she is now. This is her life – she is broken and bleeding like an exposed vein.

But not for much longer. Not if she has her way. She has plans to get Jacob back. Whether Chloe likes it or not, she and Jacob are destined to be together, so that woman had better be prepared because Leah is not about to give up without a fight.

Stripping off her clothes, she stands in the shower, watching as a thin ruby river trails its way down her legs, feathery swirls of pink circling around her feet and down the drain. The water is soothing, silky and calming against her skin. She stands, enjoying the sensation, relishing the smells, inhaling the light floral scent that billows out into the steamy air. The smell of summer. For a short while, she forgets.

Her eyes are heavy as she turns off the tap, steps out and dries herself.

Tomorrow is another day. For now, she will sleep. She will conserve her strength, be the stronger person and not allow herself to be dented by their threats.

Empty threats, that's all they are. Empty threats that they wouldn't make if they really knew her. If they knew what lengths she is prepared to go to, to get Jacob back.

6

SUMMER 2005

The funeral is just the beginning, signifying the horrors that lie ahead. Sitting at the back, refusing to be close to his family, the teenage lad keeps his head low, his eyes fixed on his lap. All around him mourners hold handkerchiefs to their faces, their eyes swollen from the tears they have shed, their faces pallid and wan.

His jaw is clamped firmly together. It wasn't his fault. None of this is his fault. Not that his pleas and repeated requests to be believed actually mean anything. After that day on the cliff, after that awful fucking day when little Lucy's body lay battered and broken at the foot of the craggy cliff face and fear and raw terror reigned supreme, his life has gone into free fall, his emotions spiralling downwards faster than a hammer drill gouging through wet mud. And the worst part is that nobody seems to notice or care. They are all too wrapped up in their own personal grief, a huge mantle of misery pressing down on them all, obliterating everything else. Obliterating reason and compassion and logic.

'Of course we believe you,' his father has said time and time again, whenever he protests his innocence, when he tells them that he didn't fight with Lucy or push her, either deliberately or by mistake, but his father's eyes tell a different story. The damage is already done. His sister's words have bored a hole in everybody's thoughts, forcing them to question his credibility, his integrity and sanity. Is he capable of such an act?

He has had a few incidents at school – nothing major, just a lack of interest in schoolwork and an unwillingness to engage with lessons – but is now thought of as a nuisance by certain teachers. He is labelled and neatly categorised and now everybody doubts him. The die is cast. But getting into scrapes at school and being less than eager to engage with English lessons is in a different league to pushing small children to their deaths. He is innocent. There is no question about it. But his sister's words have sowed the seed of doubt in everybody's minds and now the damage is done.

He hadn't even wanted to go with them that day. He was fifteen years old – too old for picnics at the seaside with family and friends. Too old to be stuck on a clifftop with his sister and mum and dad and their friends and young daughter who was both cute and annoying at the same time. She was six for God's sake. All six-year-olds possess those traits. And yes, he had complained that she was getting on his nerves but that didn't mean he wanted to kill her. Everybody was getting on his frigging nerves that particular afternoon. His mother, his father, his sister, Johnny and Petra – his parents' friends – and little Lucy. Having been told that he wasn't allowed to stay home alone as some sort of warped punishment for not doing his homework, he had been dragged along, sulking and full of hell like a petulant child. He can't even remember what happened as Lucy fell. All day long, he had been busy checking his phone, hoping for a return text from Lauren Bixby that never came – another reason to feel completely fucking miserable.

All he remembered was a scuffle, then a scream – that

scream – then he and his sister crashing into each other in a confused, hysterical frenzy. And next the utter terror, that gut-sinking feeling as the enormity of what had just happened dawned on him. His mind slowed down, struggled to process it all. His skin had turned cold while his blood ran hot through his veins.

And then his sister's wild and unsubstantiated accusation. Those words. Those fucking stupid senseless words that cut him in half, reaching in to his very core; cold hands grasping at his heart, ripping it out of his chest, holding it aloft for all the world to see, his dying pulsing heart that since that day has felt completely out of sync, never quite beating in time and feeling as if it is slowly rotting inside his body.

He hasn't spoken to his sister since her mad unwarranted accusation. He can't bring himself to. He can barely look at her or be in the same room as her. She knows it wasn't him, has always known it. She was just pissed off with him. That is her default emotion; permanently pissed off with a whacking great chip on her shoulder. He is older by two years. They may be close in age but as far as any sort of bond goes, they are poles apart. It's as if they aren't really related at all. But that's how she has been for most of her life; aloof, dispassionate. Different.

Lucy's aunt stalks past him down the aisle, an uncharacteristic swagger to her walk, her eyes dark and condemnatory. He wonders if that look is meant for him, a way of trying to punish him. That's how it's been since the accident, second guessing everything, presuming every negative word is aimed at him, every black look, every single hissed accusation about Lucy's unexplained death, all intended to frame him and make him appear guilty.

Johnny and Petra spoke to the police after the accident, as did his parents. He has no idea what was said. His parents assured him it was just a formality and that nothing would come of it. The police also spoke to him and his sister who, much to his surprise, said nothing about her earlier accusations. She obviously thought better of it, knowing her account wouldn't stand up under close scrutiny. But mud sticks. Johnny and Petra haven't said anything to him directly but their looks and body language tell him everything he needs to know.

'I saved your arse,' his sister said after their police interviews. 'I didn't tell them what you did. I kept quiet but that doesn't matter because everybody already knows anyway.'

He had felt his innards writhe and twist at her words. He has no idea why she told everyone he pushed little Lucy, no idea at all. What irks and baffles him the most is why she is the way she is. She has had a good life, the best. They have decent caring parents – hardworking and compassionate. They have been given unconditional love. He and his sister may have grown up together but when it comes down to it, he doesn't really know her at all. She is a stranger to him. She is a stranger to all of them.

The eulogy delivered by Alice, Lucy's aunt, is without doubt one of the most moving heart-rending speeches he has ever heard. Despite trying to stop them, his tears flow freely every time that little girl's name is spoken, the lump in his throat boulder sized, his eyes sore and gritty.

He leaves the church feeling wrung out, thinking that if this is how he feels for little Lucy, then how desperate must Johnny and Petra feel? How hurt and despondent must they be? He has no idea how they are still able to function, to attend their own daughter's funeral, sitting close by the coffin that contains her tiny battered and broken body.

Afterwards, he makes his own way home, refusing to get into the car with the rest of his family. His mother cries, his father pleads, his sister smirks and turns away. How can he possibly sit close to them when his dignity is in shreds, his reputation in tatters. The journey to the church had been bad enough, the atmosphere thick with resentment and mistrust. He isn't prepared to put himself through it again.

His parents still don't quite believe him, he knows it for sure. It's evident in the way they sneak glances at him, watching him when they think he isn't aware, their minds ticking over, wondering if, wondering how, but most of all, wondering why. His sister is good at it, you see, this lying caper. Better than him. She can be eloquent when required; charming and persuasive. Everything he isn't. He stumbles over words and flushes scarlet when faced with problems. And he can't see a way out of it. He can't see a way of getting them to believe that he really is innocent, that all he is guilty of is being less able to lie than his sister, less able to engage with people and get them on his side.

They may have said those words, that they think him blameless but that element of doubt will always remain. He will always be that kid, that lad who was accused of pushing a little girl off a cliff. Whether he did or not is irrelevant. It's out there now, words whirling about. And there is nothing he can do about it. His life will never be the same again.

Everything is ruined. Everything has turned to shit.

7

PRESENT DAY

Everything is wrong. Messed up and wrong. Leah looks around. She has no idea how she has ended up outside Chloe's flat. She has no memory of getting to this place, just a vague recollection of the ground moving under her feet, objects floating in her peripheral vision. The world sailing past as she made her way somewhere, which is apparently here.

She is fully dressed which is odd as she is certain she had recently showered and was in her nightclothes. A vision flits into her mind, a vivid recollection of pain and anxiety. She remembers her hand and the smashed ornament. She stares down at her palm looking for blood or stitches or anything that will convince her that the memory is real, that that event really did take place. A line of thin scars cover her hand, small pink streaks of a past injury. Leah blinks, swallows down her misgivings and tries to put it down to fatigue. She is confused and tired, that's all it is. Her body clock is skewed, her mind still processing everything that's happened since the accident. She thinks about Will's words – *the brain is a complex thing and perfectly capable of misrepresenting things, allowing us to see what we want to see and hear what we want to hear.*

Above the rooftops, birds congregate atop the mass of wires strung across the street, an elongated huddle of small black bodies sitting silently, their feathers sleek, their songs muted. She doesn't even know what time it is. Her wrist is bare of a watch and the entire street is deserted. The sun is a hazy ball of orange, slung low in the sky. Sunrise or sunset? Leah runs her fingers through her hair, separating the strands with her fingers, pulling it back off her face to clear her vision. Her mind is blank. She has nothing to go on, no clues. What time is it and how the hell did she get here? At what point did her life get to be so bad that everything feels as if it is falling apart?

As fast as she tries to clear her mind, more thoughts and memories muscle their way in; random unpleasant occurrences from way back. Like finding out by chance that she wasn't who she thought she was. That particular memory stabs at her making her flinch; an icicle ramming into her flesh, reminding her of how she never really belonged. Everything that had happened, everything that she had felt for so many years, all those deep-rooted emotions that she had been unable to explain, suddenly began to make sense after her discovery. It all slotted into place. She was an imposter, an interloper. A stranger in her own home, in her own family. She wasn't their first choice. She was an afterthought. Still is.

Leah shakes the thought away. She has more than enough to deal with at the minute without allowing rogue unwanted memories to push her closer to the edge. She has other pressing issues to deal with; important matters that cannot wait.

A distant echo of footsteps sends a frisson of electricity through her; an uneasy tingling that races through her veins. She has no idea why, no clue as to what is going to happen next. All she knows is that she is on edge, her nerves jumping and pulsing, her heart thrashing about under her sweater. A distant figure marches up the street towards her, a small silhouette, grey and characterless with no definable features. Leah squints, attempting to work out who it is. They look angry, or if not angry then at least prepared for conflict. She stiffens her spine in anticipation, her body braced for whatever may occur next. The figure picks up speed, closing the distance between them until eventually she can see him, is able get a good look at his features and stance. He seems brusque and business-like, unaware of her presence. Unaware that she is staring straight at him.

She relaxes, loosens her muscles and lets out a small chortle of relief. There was no need to be fearful. It's nothing and nobody to be concerned about. Just a middle-aged man, dressed in a suit, clutching a briefcase, on his way to or from work. A tic takes hold in her jaw. Something about him is familiar to her, some feature or expression, possibly his gait. There is something about him that dances on the periphery of her mind but refuses to fully reveal itself. Turning away from him, she tells herself it's not important, that she has to stop focusing on the minutiae. Instead she should think about sharpening her thoughts and getting her brain to function properly, to focus instead on her movements and stop herself from wandering aimlessly with no direction or purpose.

The suit wearing man passes by her, barely giving her a second glance, his eyes fixated on a point in the distance, his attention absorbed in things other than her presence. He's just a normal man going about his daily business; and yet the idea that she knows him still bothers her. The familiarity she initially felt is still there, nagging at her.

A quick flare of heat pushes under her skin as she turns and stares once again at the stranger's retreating shadow. She knows then, the memory a jabbing blade in her consciousness as she realises who it is. Him. It's him. And yet it can't be. It's too much of a coincidence. Why would he be here? And yet, why not? As chance encounters go, it is an odd one, improbable but not impossible. She brushes the thought away, refusing to consider such an idea. It's a ridiculous notion. She's confused and worn out, that's all it is. Her mind is doing its damnedest to trip her up, make her question her sanity and she is tired of it. She is better than this. At least she used to be before that awful crash impacted her life, turning everything upside down.

Blinking, she stares at him, trying to organise her thoughts, to slot them into some sort of coherent order.

There is no denying who he is. It's him, the guy from the train. The one who was sitting opposite her when the crash happened. Her blood runs like sand as she observes his stance, his confidence and swagger, as if that horrific accident didn't affect him one iota when it has ripped her world in two. And why here? Why would she see him here on the street in the middle of Durham City? The chances of such an encounter must be almost zero, yet here they are, passing strangers with a deep and lasting connection, the two of them linked by an event that has left her traumatised and struggling to know her own mind while he strides away, seemingly untouched by it all.

Tears prick at her eyes. She blinks and takes a deep breath, oxygen bursting out of her lungs in ragged chunks. She tries but is unable to obliterate thoughts of that day and yet this man is breezing along the street as if it didn't happen. How has he managed to escape the anguish and the atrocious levels of pain she experiences every minute of every day? Here he is, happily strolling down the street while she barely knows her own mind and seems to stumble from one disaster to another with no idea of how to live a normal life anymore. How is any of it fair or just?

She clamps her jaw together, bites at her lip until the metallic taste of blood floods her mouth then she looks up the street for the familiar stranger, but he has already disappeared. There is a cold emptiness around her. It's as if he was never there at all. Perhaps he wasn't. Perhaps he was a figment of her imagination and she really is going mad.

Leah sighs. In the property opposite is the woman who has ruined her life. That's what she needs to focus on here. Not some random stranger from a fated journey that went nowhere. A fated journey that it would appear, has no end, following her wherever she goes, leaving a trail of stricken memories in her wake.

As disconcerting as that may be, the woman who snatched Leah's boyfriend away from her, acting in the most insidious way possible, is close by, almost within touching distance. She shouldn't let old memories draw her attention away from that fact. Everything Chloe did, every single move she has ever made has led Leah to this point. Chloe started off as an irritant, an unwanted bystander in their lives, but her presence grew and grew, spiralling out of control until she eventually became a permanent fixture, always there, always close by. Wherever Jacob was, Chloe was there too. And no matter how many times Leah tried to keep her at arm's-length, she would appear with her saccharine smile and that innocent air, giving Jacob long lingering looks of adoration plastered all over her face, the glowing varnish she wore to snare her man.

Chloe always had the upper hand in every situation they found themselves in, playing at being the victim, the poor down-trodden innocent girl who happened to be in the wrong place at the wrong time. And she was good at it too. It was yet another ploy to gain Jacob's attention, to turn his head and lure him away. Like the time she turned up at his birthday party uninvited, dressed inappropriately in a short skirt and low-cut top, carrying a gift for him that was neither needed nor wanted, much like her presence there that night. Leah had tried to intervene as Chloe approached him, her tits on show for all the world to see, and was thwarted by Jacob whose eyes were out on stalks as Chloe sashayed towards him. Enraged and feeling more than a little humiliated, Leah had suggested they eject Chloe from the room.

And that's when all hell broke loose.

Jacob had rounded on Leah, telling her not to be so ridiculous and that Chloe had as much a right to be there as anybody else. His eyes blazed as he stared at her, his voice was filled with anger. Leah knew then that Chloe had ceased to be just a colleague to Jacob and that their relationship was about to progress to the next level.

Startled by Jacob's visceral reaction, by the sheer ferocity of it, by his need to protect a colleague and put her needs above those of his girlfriend, Leah had taken her drink and thrown it over him, silencing the room in seconds. Not content with spoiling the party by turning up dressed like a complete tart, Chloe then sidled up next to Jacob, took his arm and began dabbing him dry with a handkerchief that she miraculously had to hand. The whole scenario was so contrived, so sickeningly affected and overly dramatic that Leah had been unable to contain her anger and had attempted to push Chloe away. What began as a happy evening at a local pub to celebrate Jacob's thirtieth birthday, ended in catastrophe with Chloe falling backwards and being surrounded by a group of people who insisted she receive hospital treatment for a purported wound that Leah doubted even existed.

Leah spent the remainder of the evening sitting alone in her flat, drinking vodka and sobbing hysterically. That was the evening that sealed her fate and ended her relationship with Jacob for good. Perhaps she overreacted, perhaps she shouldn't have pushed Chloe. Perhaps Jacob did the wrong thing by inviting her in the first place, but what was done was done. There was no changing the past, just a chance to shape the future. She still has an opportunity to get Jacob back and for them to go back to how things were before that dreadful woman came along and ruined everything.

Staring over at Chloe's flat, Leah knows what she must do next. She has to confront Chloe, warn her off and remind her of who she is dealing with. Leah may be unable to pinpoint what day it is or keep tabs on her memories and thoughts but she is no pushover. While the rest of her life is falling apart, this thing, this meeting she will have with Chloe is clear in her mind. She knows exactly what she has to do, what she will say to send her running. And when it's over, she and Jacob will be back together. Everything will be back to how it was. It will be perfect.

Back to how things should always have been.

All around her the empty road slowly comes to life; street lights turn off in an eerie sequence, people appear at windows as blinds are opened, the birds overhead disappear in a dark swoop as a car engine kicks into life. It is morning. The world is waking up.

Unwilling to be seen, Leah turns and walks back towards her flat, her mind sifting through the details of what she must do next, sorting through the details and intricacies, smiling at the thought of it. It keeps her going, puts fire in her veins, stokes a furnace in her soul. This is what she needs – a plan, a purpose, a way to get her life back.

A way to get Jacob back by her side. Right back where he belongs.

8

The fabric of the chair scratches at the back of Leah's legs. It reminds her of cinema visits as a child; the coarse material that resulted in her being reprimanded for squirming and fidgeting while the rest of the family sat quietly watching the film. It reminds Leah of her brother, completely inactive, a bag of popcorn in his hand, eyes fixed on the screen while she, bored, would bend and twist, spilling her food, splashing her drink until eventually her father would escort her outside, his hand holding her firmly in place in case she decided to run off. Memories like that remind her that she has always been trouble, never quite fitting in. Always different from the rest.

Will watches her as she tries to get comfortable, his gaze eventually resting upon her fingers. She places them on the desk; they are splayed, bare of any jewellery. Seeing his contemplative look, she removes her hands, places them on her lap, thinks about how unadorned and naked her fingers feel without any diamonds or glittering stones. No gold, no silver. Unlike lots of women her age whose fingers are heavy with engagement rings and weddings bands, hers are unembellished. She traces the skin around the third finger of her left hand, touching it lightly, a painful reminder of how lonely she is, how anxious she is to get Jacob back into her life.

'How are you?' Will says softly, as if he too, can sense her loss, her need to be reunited with the only man she has ever loved.

Leah doesn't know how to respond. She left Chloe's street feeling buoyant but has no memory of getting home. How can she begin to tell him about the plans she has for the future when she can't even recall the present? 'The same. I'm just the same.' She keeps her eyes averted from his, refusing to be scrutinised, refusing to look at the ghastly painting over his shoulder, the one that reminds her of what it must be like to be cast deep into the bowels of hell.

'And how is that?' Will asks, his penetrative stare making her feel uncomfortable. She shifts around in her seat, her hands hot, her fingers itching to scratch at her scarred arms over and over or to pull at her own hair until it snaps and comes away at the root.

'I think we both know how it is. My life is a mess. I live in a flat with two other people who neither know nor care whether I live or die. My boyfriend is with another woman who stalked him and stole him right from under my nose. My parents want nothing to do with me and I keep seeing people in the street who are connected to me in some way yet they don't seem to see me or recognise me, including my dead brother. How's that for starters?'

Will nods, his body language one of neutrality. Just this once, she would like him to say something to make everything better rather than giving off an aura of detachment and complete impartiality. Just for once, she would like somebody to be on her side.

'I've suffered,' she says, a tremble evident in her tone. 'A lot. I've been through more than most.'

A look of resignation crosses his face, or perhaps it's a look of compassion. Leah can't quite work out what he's thinking. She wishes these sessions were easier. It feels like a one-way street, her voice filling the airwaves with her cries of pity and self-loathing. All she wants is her life back to how it was. She wants her mind to be clear and to get her thoughts in order. Progress seems impossible and she finds herself wondering if these sessions are really worth the effort.

'You have suffered a great deal,' Will replies, catching her unawares. 'And I'm here to help you out of it, to stop your pain and make everything better. We'll sort this out, I promise.'

His words take her by surprise, unaccustomed as she is to receiving help and hearing kind words. A lump swells in her throat, tears burn at her eyes. The pain in her abdomen increases. She places her hand over it, pressing down to alleviate the dull ache that is ever present.

'I'd like to talk about my parents,' she says as she bites down on her lip. That wasn't planned. She has no idea why she even suggested such a thing. The words seemed to spring out of nowhere and she now wishes she could take them back.

'I'm listening,' Will says as he leans forward, his pupils dark with curiosity.

Something inside her stirs, a feeling of unrest that refuses to go away. She hates these memories, hates talking about them, hates every bloody thing about them. Yet here they are, fresh in her mind, about to unfurl, ready to show themselves to both her and Will, a man who knows nothing about what went on.

She closes her eyes, reluctant to look at him anymore, to be subjected to his silent scrutiny as she reveals her innermost thoughts and waits for him to assess them, to dig and probe and analyse and pass judgement. She counts to ten, thinks about what she is going say before opening her eyes again and glancing his way. Will appears closer than she remembers. She lets out a juddering breath and digs her fingers into the edge of the chair, clutching at it for support. The walls feel as if they are crushing her. She can almost feel the heat of Will's body and hear his low breathing as she starts to speak, the words pouring out in a rapid unstoppable stream.

'When I was thirteen years old, I found out that I was adopted. Nobody had told me. I always knew I was different, and not in a good way. I didn't fit. I was a square peg in a round hole. I didn't think like they did.' Leah stops to take a breath before continuing. Her throat is dry, a slow pounding builds in her temple. She uses her fingertips to massage at the thin skin there. 'Mum and Dad are quiet reflective people, much like my brother, although he had his moments. He was two years older than me and had started to get into some trouble at school. Nothing major really but we were very different and didn't get on all that well. I suppose most siblings don't. Especially teenagers. They're built to argue, aren't they? I guess it's part of their DNA. They're hardwired to fall out with each other, aren't they? Or maybe it's all those hormones racing around their system. Anyway, I was looking for something in the old wooden bureau one day and came across my adoption certificate.'

She looks at Will, observing his features, searching for solace from him, some succour to reassure her that not all of what happened was her fault. He is sitting, not looking disinterested but neither does he look interested either. Once again, he has assumed a passive stance, absorbing her words, allowing her to unburden herself while he sits and watches.

'I presented it to my parents who tried to bluff their way out of it, saying they were going to tell me when I was older, that they thought I was too young to understand. But that's not the truth at all.'

'So, what is the truth?' he says, an edge to his voice, as if he knows what's coming next.

'The truth?' Leah says more forcefully now. 'The truth is that they were never going to tell me because everybody knew I was different and showing me the certificate would have just confirmed it. It would have affirmed everybody's belief that I was an outsider, not a proper member of the Browne family.' Hot tears bite at her eyelids. She blinks them away, wipes a shaky hand across her brow.

'And did it make you angry?' Will's voice is quieter now, calmer.

'Yes of course it made me angry. Fucking furious, actually. I felt like a complete fraud.' She looks away, fresh fury uncoiling within her chest. The memory of it is still raw, the feeling of not belonging a gaping wound. 'So I did things, made life difficult for them by way of punishment.'

A silence takes hold as she gives Will time to process her words, to let them really sink in. If she expected further probing or questions to get her to open up completely, she couldn't have been more wrong. Instead, he takes the conversation off on a tangent, steering her away from the wreckage that has been her entire life.

'And how did that make you feel? Making things harder for them, I mean. Did you feel vindicated? Did it make you feel better about yourself?'

A sting takes hold in her face, an army of red ants crawling over her flesh, biting and burning leaving a trail of fire in their wake. Does she feel vindicated? Was all her hatred and bile actually worth it?

Sickness wells up in her gut making her nauseous and dizzy. And why is Will even asking her such questions? She feels certain it's to provoke guilt, to get her to dig deep within her psyche and reveal her deepest most private thoughts, to lay bare her soul for him to see. She won't allow that. Absolutely not. She will protect her soft underbelly, cover herself up and live to fight another day. Will is supposed to be here to help her, not to expose her vulnerabilities and weaknesses. She does a damn fine job of doing that herself and doesn't need a helping hand to make her feel even worse about her shitty life.

'Well,' she says proudly, 'it didn't make me feel worse, if that's what you mean.'

Will smiles, his mouth moving but the sentiment not quite reaching his eyes. Leah digs her nails into her palms, into her old scars, thinking how quickly the wind changes, how rapidly the direction of a conversation can change trajectory, leaving a person feeling wounded and out of their depth.

'Okay, so what about your split from them as an adult? Are you ready to talk about that yet?'

A dart of annoyance spears through her. Even thinking about that part of her life irritates her, makes her itchy with rage and fear and guilt. It's not somewhere she chooses to visit if she can help it. But this is different; talking about that point in her life is expected when she's within these four walls. This is a safe place even though she doesn't feel particularly secure when she's here. If she's being honest, being here puts her on edge. Will's searching questions; the choice of artwork; his proximity; even the way her scar seems more painful when she visits all make her feel a thousand times worse. Coming here is a necessary evil, somewhere she visits to purge herself, to be absolved of her sins.

She ruminates over the final argument she had with her parents and decides that that particular story is for another day. It's all too complex, too difficult to condense into a half hour's conversation. She has given him the beginning, the concealment of her adoption and that's enough for now. That's when it all started. Or at least, that's what she tells herself but, in all honesty, finding out she was adopted was simply a point in which she could stick a pin and say, *it all started here.* She knows

– and they know – that her story began long before that. Her parents spent their lives trying to mould her, to get her to fit into their neat little family unit, to wedge her into their values, to squash her into their perfect little life and yet the more they tried, the greater the distance grew between them. She was their wildcard, their erratic, unpredictable child. The one who never really belonged.

'I'd rather tell you about my lapses in memory. I stagger from one hour to the next, one day to the next, unable to keep track of time, unsure of how I get from one place to another. How do you explain that? And please don't tell me my brain is a complex thing because I already know that. I just wish it weren't. I wish it would just function as it's supposed to, but I guess it's all down to the effects of the crash, isn't it?'

Will picks up a pen, twirls it around in his fingers like a small baton then drops it onto the desk with a sharp click. The noise jolts her, causes her to sit up straight in her seat. She notices it then – the smell of burning. She stares at Will, who appears to not notice the pungent odour that is slowly filling the room. It grows stronger, becoming more and more powerful as it snakes itself around the room.

'What is that?' Leah says, eyes wide, incredulous that he hasn't noticed. The stench is intense, filling her nostrils, setting off a growing panic in her head.

'What is what?'

And then she sees it, the sudden burst of flames behind him accompanied by a thick plume of black smoke that billows out from the wall. Will remains seated, composed, unruffled. Utterly unaware.

Leah lets out a stifled gasp, brings her hand to her mouth, blinks, looks again. And it's gone.

She stares at the bare wall and presses the heel of her hands into her eyes, rubbing at them savagely before looking again, her jaw slack with shock. Everything is back to normal. No smell, no smoke. Absolutely nothing at all.

She suppresses a sob, swallowing it down with a loud gulp. She is going mad for sure, losing her fucking mind. There's no other explanation for it.

'Everything is going to be fine,' Will says, completely unfazed by her sudden reaction. Everything is silent, the room back to how it was before. 'I'm here to help you. Try not to worry about things you can't change. Just take it easy and soon you'll feel a lot better.'

'It's difficult,' she says quietly, a buzzing filling her head. 'I can't seem to keep track of anything. I'm seeing things that aren't there and my memory is shot. I don't even know what day it is, for God's sake.'

Will places his large pale hands on the desk. Leah's eyes are drawn to them again, to the paleness of his long fingers, almost white like chalk and in direct contrast to his liver spotted face. She looks away as he nods at her and smiles. 'How is your pain?'

'Still there,' she murmurs, the memory of the crash sharp in her mind. It's always there, blinding her with its lucidity. She's still on the train, in that carriage, stuck under the wreckage, unable to get out. Unable to breathe. She can feel herself being thrown sideways, backwards, forwards, her body in agony, her mind desperately trying to comprehend the awfulness of it all. She can feel the heaviness, that crushing deadweight as it presses down on her, cutting into her soft flesh. She can hear the glass shattering, can feel it slicing through her skin, scoring her bones. The terrible screaming fills the space around her, the groan of metal pulses in her ears, the screeching of brakes causing her to shudder as the train stops, derails and tips over. Then nothing. An empty silence. Just a sinister unending fear.

And now she is back in the room.

Lowering her head, she fights back tears. She can't keep

going through this. It will be the undoing of her. She needs to snap out of it and work out why she was there, what it was that caused her to leave Durham and catch a train to London. She desperately needs to find that elusive chunk of time before the crash so she can determine what compelled her to head south. She hasn't been to London since she was a child and can't for the life of her remember making any plans to go there. She wouldn't leave Jacob. Since meeting him she hasn't ever left Durham. Why would she? He's all she has, and all she will ever need. Nothing and nobody else matters.

'I have to go now, Will.' She is spent. No words left in her. She has given all she can give for today.

He nods, making no attempt to stop her, instead leaning back in his chair, a look of understanding on his face. She doesn't say anything else as she closes her eyes, takes a deep breath and thinks about going home.

9

AUTUMN 2005

He has to leave. As far as he can tell, there's no other option open to him, no other way out of the living hell that has become his life. Everything has stopped – his hobbies, his love of photography, seeing his friends, trying to get back on track with his schoolwork – they have all taken a back seat since that day. He has spent the past few months putting up with so many snide comments and the hints to his family and friends that he is guilty and he has had enough. Deranged, fucked up, some sort of childish vendetta, call it what you will, his sister has made no bones about the fact that he is the one responsible. She may have remained silent about it to the police but she has bleated incessantly to anybody else who will listen about how he was there when little Lucy fell to her death. She always chooses her words carefully, edging around the issue, giving listeners long lingering looks, leaving painful interminable silences as she recalls the events of that terrible day before stepping back and letting them put two and two together so they can come up with five.

So many times he has thought back to what happened, trying to work out what actually took place on that clifftop. The closest he has ever come to an answer that makes any sense is that Lucy was too close to the edge and slipped. Both he and his sister were there with her when it happened but everything is such a blur in his mind. One minute they were playing and the next he and his sister were arguing. Tempers were frayed, emotions running high. Lucy was there with them as they fought. And then she wasn't.

He has tried and tried to remember the turn of events but nothing makes sense. He has a recollection of his sister pretending to drag little Lucy closer to the edge but then she was standing next to him. Perhaps she ran back to the edge again to look over? He simply can't remember. There was so much toing and froing. It was windy and noisy and he was angry and upset. Lucy was just a kid with no real sense of danger, no idea of what a fall from that sort of height could do to her tiny, frail body. Maybe she just slipped.

The one thing he is sure of is that he didn't push her. He wouldn't. He couldn't. He doesn't have it in him to do such a thing. He is a young lad, interested in girls and cameras and fast cars and trains. He isn't a killer. What disturbs him the most is that people even consider it a possibility, that they have so little faith in him, so little belief in him as a decent, caring person that they actually consider his sister's words. That hurts. Despite the coroner's findings of misadventure, that nobody was to blame, neighbours and friends still shun him, deciding to believe a teenage child over figures of authority. So much for a sense of community and for practising forgiveness and tolerance. They couldn't wait to get their teeth into a bit of idle gossip, twisting and turning it until the story went that although nobody saw it happen, he did probably push her, that he had had an argument with his sister and snapped, taking his temper out on somebody smaller and younger than him who couldn't fight back.

His parents will be upset at him leaving, that much he does

know, but everything is closing in on him and he can't take it any longer. The teachers at school are pretty neutral about the whole thing but word about his possible involvement soon spread in class and the taunts and bullying have become unbearable.

His only chance to escape it all is to disappear.

He leaves early one autumn morning as a thin line of light is just beginning to reveal itself on the distant horizon, a streak of hazy sunlight slowly rising and growing as the earth wakes up to the day ahead. A copse of trees is silhouetted against the backdrop of a burning amber sky. That's where he will go – somewhere with cover and water where he can be alone and not have to see those knowing glances or endure the whispers that echo and boom in his head every time he walks into a room.

Nobody will miss him. Perhaps his parents will feel his absence keenly but they'll soon get over it. They still have another child to pour all their love into. And God knows she needs it. She needs as much nurture and love as they can give to melt her frozen heart.

Shrugging his backpack over his shoulders, he closes the door with a quiet click, posting his key through the letterbox before stepping out into the empty street and setting off hastily, never once looking back.

The weather grows wilder throughout the day – gale-force winds blowing in, driving rain battering against his skin, plummeting temperatures that nip at his exposed flesh – they all hinder his progress, stopping him from getting as far as he had hoped, but none of it stops him completely. He continues regardless, body bent double against the howling wind and stinging rain. A bit of adverse weather is nothing compared to what he's had to put up with at home and at school over the past few months. If one positive thing has come out of this whole shitty debacle it's the fact that he has grown to know himself more than he did before. He doesn't necessarily feel any stronger for it but he does feel older, as if he's matured ten years in ten weeks.

He thinks of the look on the faces of his parents as they read the letter he has left for them propped up on the kitchen table. If they get it, that is. His father is usually the first one up but it's the weekend and on the odd occasion, his sister sometimes gets up before him. There's no telling what she will do with his heartfelt plea if she gets to it first. Anything is possible. His heart crashes around his chest at the thought of her throwing it away, at the thought of her wicked smirk as she tears it up and stuffs it in the bottom of the bin, his words disposed of, his parents never knowing why he left. He still loves them. He just can't take any more of living in that house, living the rest of his life with that great big weight of doubt hanging over his head.

Did he kill Lucy?

It's an unbearable burden to carry. All that hatred directed at him. If that day at the beach has taught him one thing, it's that people enjoy directing malice at others. They love it, thriving on the drama and the upset, living for spreading lies. It puts a spring in their step. Their inclination for lying and wrecking other people's lives gets them out of bed on a morning, giving them something to look forward to. All those loose tongues, the many clacking mouths that never seem to stop. And yet after all the untruths and gossip and downright lies, he doesn't hate them. Far from it.

He pities them.

They are the ones who have to go through the rest of their lives knowing what they've done, knowing they have ruined his life. It sounds dramatic but he can't see beyond this point in his miserable existence. No matter how hard he tries, he just can't see a way around it, which is why he has chosen to leave. He has some money, not a lot, enough to see him through for a few weeks but it's all he needs. His plans don't stretch too far. He's living day to day and that suits him just fine.

Battling against the blustery wind and barrage of rain, he edges his way over the road that runs parallel to the river. Soon he'll be at the foot of the hills. Once up there, hidden amongst the trees and bushes, he can find shelter, light a fire, eat some of the food he has brought with him. He needs to keep his strength up. Falling at the first hurdle and succumbing to the elements isn't part of his plan.

In the distance, the church bells ring out loud and clear. 8am. Even with a lie-in, his father will be up by now. He tries to picture his dad's face as he reads the letter, taking his time as he digests the words written there, realising that their son can no longer stand living with people who mistrust and doubt him. He will read those words and feel a pang of sorrow and regret but will also know that they'll be better off without him around casting a shadow over their lives. His dad isn't the emotional type. Any reaction he has will be muted. Maybe he'll think it's a childish hysterical response and shrug it off or maybe he will march upstairs, shake his mother awake and go looking for him. He can't see that happening but then he never expected his life to take the trajectory that it has. Anything is possible.

He shivers, steps up his pace, aware that pretty soon search parties will be out looking for him. He needs to hurry up. Newspaper headlines will scream out about the lad who was recently accused of killing a young girl and that although nobody can prove anything, doubts still remain. His disappearance will cement the idea in everybody's heads that he did it. *The guilt weighed too heavily*, they will say. *He has fled to escape justice.* His skin prickles at the thought of it. Let them think whatever they want to think. He no longer has to look into their faces, to see the mistrust and malice there or to listen to their idle gossip, to the lies peddled about him: that he was always a disaffected troublemaker, that he has committed the ultimate crime and that everybody will be better off without him. Perhaps they'll even hunt him down, an army of vigilantes with their metaphorical pitchforks meting out their own form of justice.

The fact of the matter is, he is just an ordinary lad, a teenager who enjoys football, fancies girls in his class and isn't too struck on being holed up in a classroom all day long and being made to learn about the life cycle of insects and rotational farming methods. He isn't bad, he isn't evil and he most certainly isn't a killer.

It takes him half an hour to make his way deep into the woods, the traffic no more than a distant hiss as he climbs up the side of the steep bank. It's damp, the ground underfoot soft and spongy, but it's manageable. His boots grip the soil as he pushes his way up under the shelter of the trees. He tips his head up, closes his eyes and smiles, letting out a satisfied sigh. It's perfect, just as he'd hoped it would be. Nobody knows where he is. Nobody can get to him. He's completely alone.

Sitting cross-legged, he opens his backpack, takes out an apple and bites into it, miniscule sweet pulpy flecks bursting out and running down his chin. He looks around at the piles of twigs, the low-lying shrubbery and carpet of rotting leaves. This is his new home. For now. He isn't so naïve as to think he can camp out here permanently, but for now it's just what he needs. He is shut away in his own little enclave of anonymity, away from the gossip mongers, the haters, the white noise that has been his life for the last few months. He only wishes he had done it before now. He could have saved himself a whole lot of misery. A sudden gust of wind whirls above him. Leaves quiver, a metallic susurration that pierces his dark musings, gives him pause for thought. He has always enjoyed experiencing different kinds of weather, keen to expose himself to all that the natural world has to offer. He's never been one for sitting indoors playing computer games the way many of his pals do, preferring instead the rugged outdoors and its many challenges, preferring to sit on the loam, feel the beat of the earth beneath his skin and marvel at its resilience, its capacity for change, season after season, year after year, decade after decade, often taking pictures for posterity, recording life as it happens.

Tears flow as he sits, clearing his thoughts, enjoying the moment. The pent-up emotion he has kept at bay for so long now eventually breaks down and spills out of him. It's not misery that is driving this outburst; it's relief. He's away from it all. For how long, he doesn't know, but for now he is alone, and it feels good. He closes his eyes and attempts to put it behind him – the clacking tongues, the knowing looks, the accusation that started it all in the first place.

He doesn't want to think about her; the sister he would sooner forget. The sister, who it seems, hates him with every fibre of her being. There's no good reason for her actions. It's just how she is. It's who she is. Hatred comes effortlessly to her, a smooth fluid emotion that oozes out of her. He doesn't hate her back. He's not entirely sure how to hate. He has seen hate in action and would rather leave it alone, let it contaminate those who lack basic compassion and take pleasure in seeing other people suffering. All he wants is to be left alone.

This is all her doing, however. His current anguish, his sullied name and reputation, it's all down to her. It is entirely her fault. His own sister. She did this to him. She owns this.

And although he doesn't hate her, there is one thing he does know for sure: he can't ever forgive her. People talk about forgiveness like it's an easy thing to do, a throwaway word that means nothing to those who have never been wronged. In reality, forgiveness is one of the most difficult things to dole out. So although he may not hate her, he feels an element of bitterness towards her. Perhaps it's because, although they are not particularly close, he hoped for some sort of sibling bond, something that would keep them connected to one another. But she broke any chains that linked them together after she said those words. And he doesn't think they can ever be repaired.

10

PRESENT DAY

Once again, Leah is standing outside Chloe's flat with no recollection of how she got here. Her nerves are jangling, her flesh burning with the dread she feels at her lack of control. Her seething anxieties are growing and multiplying by the day, a nest of vipers coiling themselves around her internal organs, slowly crushing her. She takes a deep breath and presses her nails into her palms until a soothing wave of pain scratches against her skin. She can't continue like this, unable to keep track of her movements, moving through each day like a fallen leaf on the wind, directionless, following the breeze with no idea of where she is going, or why.

Leah looks over towards the window, her eyes heavy with exhaustion. Why is she so damn tired all the time? Fatigue follows her around, trailing in her shadow, dragging her lower and lower until she feels so close to the ground she can barely stay upright. She can't remember the last time she felt energetic or positive or anything remotely resembling happiness. Everything is such an effort. Even breathing feels like a chore.

The lights are on in Chloe's flat. She's in there, doing mundane things. Leah stares at the small square of light, wondering if she's alone or if Jacob is in there with her. Jealousy and resentment build in her chest, ballooning and expanding until she feels as if she is about to explode. The thought of the two of them in there together, locked in an embrace or worse still, in bed making mad passionate love, makes her feel physically sick. She is dizzy with envy and rage. A rock sits at the base of her belly. She sways on her tiptoes, balls her hands into tight fists, locks her jaw together and stands watching, waiting for a flicker of a movement, a darting shadow, anything to let her know who is in there and what they are up to. Not knowing is the worst thing. It's so insulting to be ignored by someone you used to be so close to. There was a time she knew all of Jacob's movements, was able to track him and account for his whereabouts. But not anymore. Not since Chloe came along.

Only when her teeth begin to ache does she release everything, unfurling her fingers, unclamping her jaw before looking away, disappointment rippling through her at the lack of movement inside the place. Surely somebody must be in there? Why would the lights be on if nobody is home? What the *fuck* is she up to in that flat?

A crow caws in the distance, a car passes by, footsteps echo down a nearby alleyway. Still she waits and watches, feeling the pulsing of her skin, the beating of her own heart. She counts to twenty, takes a deep breath. Wishes she were somewhere else. Except she isn't. She's here, and she has to know. She has to see them, to speak about her relationship with Jacob. She has been put in an impossible situation. Her life is an uphill struggle. Surely they can see that? She isn't asking a lot. All Leah wants to do is talk to Chloe, to reason with her, let her know how desperate she is feeling. If only they would listen. If only Chloe or Jacob would act like reasonable human beings and hear her side of the story.

And then it happens. She appears. She is there – Chloe's

outline at the window, staring out into the street, a solitary figure. And she is alone. Leah waits, her body tensed, ready for Jacob to appear, for his arms to wrap themselves around Chloe's slim shoulders, for their eyes to meet, their loving gaze, easy manner and relaxed body language displaying to the world just how much they adore each other, how much in love they are. Except they're not. They can't be. It's too soon for either of them to have developed such deep feelings for one another. Too soon after Leah for Jacob to transfer his affections elsewhere. It's all too much. It's all far too soon.

Vomit rises in Leah's throat, burning her gullet, a reflux of hot bile that almost tumbles into her mouth. She swallows and rubs at her eyes. It should be her who is up there with him. They should be staring into one another's eyes, his hands trailing down her back, his fingers slowly slipping under her blouse and unfastening the hooks on her bra. Her skin tingles at the thought of it. She imagines his scent, heady and musky with overtones of magnolia, thinks about the texture of his naked flesh as he strips off in front of her and pushes her backwards onto the bed. Her body pulses, waves of pleasure rippling through her as she stands, staring at the woman who stole her life right from under her nose.

A sheet of ice suddenly cuts her in two, settling deep in her gut at the thought of it. She feels as if cold water has been poured over her, the warm sensuous feelings now replaced by revulsion and hatred. Taking a clump of her own hair, Leah pulls at it, tugging and twisting, closing her eyes and sighing, enjoying the line of pain that screeches over her scalp. She would like Chloe to feel that pain, to know the agony of loss, the unbearable loneliness and fear that stabs at you when your life is ripped apart and trampled upon, ground into dust by those who think nothing of you, by people you thought loved you when all the while they had other plans. Plans for another life that didn't involve you.

She leaves go of her hair, tossing a few beige strands to the floor where they sit strewn around her feet, dead pieces of her, just lying there on the ground. She knows what she has to do next. She's just prevaricating. She has to challenge Chloe and tell her what she thinks of her presence in Jacob's life. That's why she's here. Her mind may not be completely focused but there is a part of her brain that is acting on its own, her subconscious thoughts directing her, showing her what needs to be done. That's how she has ended up here. Hiding away and licking her wounds hasn't worked. It's time to tell Chloe that she needs to leave Jacob alone or face the consequences.

With a thumping heart, she marches up the path to Chloe's flat, her knuckles ready to rap on the big oak door. Her attention is focused on this point in time, this one act of revenge and retribution. There's no way out of it now. Forget Chloe's letters threatening her with police action, forget the risky situation she may be about to put herself in, this is something she has to do, an itch that has to be scratched.

She raises her hand, a breath suspended deep in the hollow of her diaphragm as she steels herself for the inevitable backlash, and is stopped by a noise behind her. She spins around, sees nothing, hears nothing else, and returns her attention to the door, to confronting the woman who has ruthlessly stampeded across her dreams with such recklessness and arrogance it takes her breath away. Today is the day when she will tell her to leave. Today is the day she will hopefully remove Chloe from Jacob's life forever. She has no right being with him. She's an imposter, an unwanted toxic presence, contaminating everything and everybody she comes into contact with and it's about time somebody told her as much. This meeting is long overdue.

The noise comes again, then a movement, a sudden breeze

that passes over her prickling flesh. She shivers, steps away from the door and catches sight of somebody walking down the street. It's a male figure, a shadowy entity. His hands are slung deep in his pockets, his shoulders slumped, his head dipped. His gait is unsteady and wobbly as he heads in her direction.

Leah stands and watches him, something about his presence unnerving her, stopping her dead in her tracks. A sickness wells up inside her. She waits, hoping he deviates, takes another route, yet somehow knowing that he won't. It isn't him again, the guy from the train. Different size, different posture. She places a hand to her breastbone, trying to still her thumping heart. It bounces around her chest, fluttering and dancing under her ribcage as she watches him approach. She feels horribly sick. Stars burst behind her eyes. This is wrong. So very wrong.

There's a sound; low, unexpected. A whisper. She hears it again; her name being called. Her pulse races, she swallows, holding on to the door frame for balance, doing her utmost to stay calm. This is ridiculous. She's mistaken, has misheard it. It wasn't her name being called at all. It's just the breeze warping a distant conversation, twisting the words. Not everything is about her. She's nervous, her muscles coiled tight, her senses heightened, her imagination in overdrive. Apart from Chloe, nobody knows her in this part of town. She is a stranger, an outsider. A nobody. So why does she feel so fucking nervous, as if her world is about to shatter into a million pieces?

And then it comes again, her name travelling up the street on the breeze. The voice is as real as she is, as familiar to her as her own skin. A voice from the past, one she recognises and knows all too well. A voice she never ever thought she would hear again. Her legs buckle as she turns to see him, her brother, Ellis. But it can't be. This is all part of the trauma she has suffered. This is her brain playing tricks on her, putting her through yet more shit.

It's not real. It can't be. Ellis is dead and has been for many years now. It's an illusion, a hallucination. This is all a mirage cooked up by her deluded damaged brain to stop her from knocking on Chloe's door. It's a small part of her that's frightened, that's all it is. A small part of her that is worried about what will happen once this Pandora's box is opened. And yet the terror she is feeling is real.

Ellis turns briefly and watches her, his eyes dark and disapproving, a brooding expression on his face. She attempts to speak, to say something, anything, but the words refuse to come. Her mind has frozen, her mouth remains stubbornly closed, glued together with fear and dread. She tries again, this time managing to prise her lips apart and say his name.

'Ellis?' Her voice is a murmur, barely audible, drowned out by the thrashing of her own heart as blood pushes through her veins, roaring in her ears.

The ground moves and sways beneath her feet, the air around her thins. He doesn't answer, turning instead, away from her. She closes her eyes, prays to be somewhere else, anywhere but here, then opens them again to see nothing. Nobody is close by; nobody is in the distance. The street is empty. He's gone, that is, if he was ever there to begin with. Leah lets out a ragged breath. What a fucking awful deluded state she is in. What a stupid sorry mess she has got herself into.

Delving into her pockets, she grasps a tissue, a handful of coins, a wad of old receipts. Anything to convince herself that she is real – that this situation is real, that it's not one big nightmare. She leaves go of them and taps at her head, rubbing her fingers over the tiny bald strip of skin where she pulls at her hair with grasping desperate fingers. She circles her finger over the smooth, slightly ragged patch of skin. The sensation of touching the flesh where there should be hair, helps to soothe her and slow the racing pulse that is rattling away in her neck.

Another noise behind her makes her blood fizz. She whips around, her balance faltering, her vision blurred and misty. She is greeted by Chloe's stern face, her piercing eyes. Her obvious palpable anger.

'What do you want, Leah?'

She has been caught unawares, on the back foot, and once again struggles to find the right words, standing speechless, a useless lumbering being as she tries to calm herself down, to slow her pulse and keep herself upright on liquid legs.

'I meant what I said, Leah,' Chloe says curtly. 'If you don't stop this, we'll have to call the police. Enough is enough.'

A rage builds in Leah's chest, her initial fear subsiding, replaced by anger as it balloons deep within her. How dare she? How dare this woman speak to her like this – with such condescension and arrogance? Jacob was hers until Chloe came along. The pair of them were ticking along nicely until this conceited bitch strolled into their lives and tore them asunder. Chloe is a selfish cow but she is, however, right about one thing – enough is enough.

A storm rages in Leah's head, a roller coaster of emotions rising and falling. She tries to speak, to tell Chloe why she's here but all that comes out is a low moan and a steady flow of tears. They stream down her face, small unexpected rivulets of misery that she can't seem to stop. She wipes them away with the back of her hand, angry at herself for being so weak, for being so fucking pathetic. Sniffing and spluttering like a child, she grapples in her pocket for a tissue.

'Look,' Chloe says more softly now, an air of exasperation in her tone. 'I really think you need help. I can give you the number of a friend of mine who can talk to you about what is going on in your life.' She briefly moves away from the door, her head craned to one side as she peers over her shoulder back into the dark hallway behind her. She leans inside and reappears holding something. It's a small card bearing a logo.

Leah doesn't respond, staring instead at the small rectangular business card with dismay. She shakes her head and bites at the inside of her mouth roughly, hoping to draw blood, to feel the sharp tug of pain that will remind her that this isn't an illusion, a figment of her imagination. This isn't how she planned it. In her mind she was going to confront Chloe, be strong, be in control, to tell her to leave Jacob alone and then go on her merry way. And now look at her, a weak insipid creature who can barely string two words together. This isn't how it's supposed to be. She had plans, big plans. Chloe was going to be terrified. She was going to listen to what Leah had to say, then she was going to apologise and promise to leave Jacob alone, but like everything in Leah's life, it has turned out all wrong. She should be used to it by now but if anything, it gets harder to accept, each rejection, each failure chipping away at her self-esteem like a sculptor shaping their latest creation, chiselling away until only the very core is left. Leah wonders what is at her core, whether she is a work of art or whether a demon lives inside her, furled up, waiting for the day when it will be unleashed into the open.

She takes a breath, composes herself, tries to not think about how she looks compared to the manicured creature standing in front of her. Drawing on reserves of strength she didn't know she possessed, Leah looks directly into Chloe's face, clamps her teeth together and smiles.

'No,' she finally manages to croak, as Chloe holds out the card for her to take. 'I don't need your help. I don't need anything from you except Jacob. You broke up my relationship with him. You've ruined my life and I will never ever forgive you.'

A sigh, an eye-roll then a loud guffaw. Chloe's laugh is shrill, loaded with venom. She shakes her head pitifully and glares at Leah from under her long lashes, almost spitting out the words as she speaks. 'Okay, I've had enough of this charade. No more being nice. If this is how you want to play it, then so be it.' Leaning forwards, Chloe lowers her voice to a hiss. 'Get the fuck off my doorstep, you useless deluded piece of crap. I've just about had enough of you and your lies. I've tried to warn you off, I've tried to be nice to you but it hasn't worked so now I'm going to tell it like it is. If you don't shift your arse, I'm going to call the police and report you for harassment.' She steps back into the shadows, smiling, arms folded over her chest triumphantly.

It's all Leah can do to stop herself from stepping forward and launching herself at this woman, jabbing her in the chest and reminding her that she and Jacob were an item long before Chloe came on the scene, that she knew the feel of his skin and the contours of his body long before Chloe did, that she knew the sweet aroma of his warm breath, his voice as he murmured her name over and over while they were making love in his bed.

Leah remains in place, her feet locked together, her eyes boring into Chloe's. She is determined not to be browbeaten by this woman. She knows her own mind and she also knows that Jacob still harbours feelings for her. He's not so cold as to be able to switch them off so easily and so rapidly after meeting Chloe. What she and Jacob had was something special. Something permanent. Chloe is a blip, a pimple on the horizon. Soon she will be gone.

'I know people, tough people,' Chloe whispers as she bends down to stare into Leah's wan face. 'So, if a visit by the police doesn't scare you off, then maybe a visit from some of my hard-knock friends will.' She leans even closer to Leah, eyes dark, narrowed in anger. 'Can I make a suggestion? That you fuck off right now, or I'll call them and send a picture of you so they know exactly who it is they're looking for.' Out of nowhere, she produces a mobile phone, holds it in front of Leah's face and begins snapping, taking a series of photos, one after another after another.

It's a spur of the moment thing, a reaction provoked by Chloe taking the pictures without her consent. She didn't mean to do it. It just happened. Leah's arm raises and connects with the mobile, knocking it to the floor where it spins around, the screen splintering into a hundred fine cracks.

A second passes, perhaps two, a stunned silence hanging between them until Chloe steps forward and grabs Leah's arm, her fingers digging deep into the flesh, nails pressing on bone. 'You'll be getting a bill for that. Now do me a favour and piss off before I really lose my temper, okay?'

Leah steps back, stunned at the ferocity of the reaction. She didn't know Chloe had it in her. She watches her bend down and scoop up the mobile, turning it over and over in her hands as she inspects the damage, her eyes glittering with untethered fury. Leah knows it then, that this is the moment when things will change. They've crossed a line. *She* has crossed a line. The damaged phone is just the beginning. She has no idea how she knows this but a tight sour sensation slithering just beneath the surface of her skin tells her that something unpleasant is about to take place. The tang of retribution is heavy in the air. Perhaps not now, not here in the next few minutes, but soon.

Leah moves forward, perhaps to placate her nemesis; she doesn't quite know why she has closed the gap between them but before she can stop herself, Leah has touched Chloe's shoulder.

Chloe recoils as if burnt.

'What the hell do you think you're doing?' Chloe's eyes are on fire, a rage burning deep within them, a flickering of hatred focused directly at Leah who shivers, trying to stem her own feelings. It doesn't work.

Without thinking, she brings up her hand and slaps Chloe across the face, the sting on her palm causing her to take a step back. She stares at her reddening flesh then up at the flare of pink of Chloe's cheek. It was a hard hit, a lot of negativity and hatred behind that strike. She shouldn't have done it. It's too late for regrets and second thoughts now though. It's all too late.

Chloe stumbles back, her head shaking from side to side, her shoulders dipped, her whole body looking as if it's about to combust.

Fire bursts through Leah's veins, an unexpected feeling of authority coursing through her as she observes how weak Chloe suddenly looks, how pitiful and characterless. No more the confident, controlling woman who just a few seconds ago, was ordering Leah about, telling her what to do. Threatening her. She is now a reprimanded child, submissive, passive, her eyes glassy with tears, her mouth hanging open.

Leah hadn't meant to hit her; she didn't plan to come here and mete out any form of physical violence, but Chloe threatened her, leaned into her face, her features contorted with fury. Leah had to protect herself, to let Chloe know that she's not to be messed with. She and Jacob have already done enough damage to her, crushing her confidence and stripping away her dignity bit by painful bit. It's about time the tables were turned.

Leah would like to say she is sorry for hitting Chloe, but she's not. It actually feels rather good. It has empowered her, elevated her flagging confidence and self-respect.

Turning away, Leah takes three long strides to the end of the path before looking back over her shoulder to a now weeping Chloe who is clinging to the side of her face, her long pale fingers covering the patch of reddened skin.

'Don't think this is the end, Chloe, because it's not. I'm just warming up. Let this be a warning to you. And I don't want any police involvement. It's only my word against yours anyway, isn't it?' She spreads her hands apart and looks around at the empty street, a long avenue devoid of life. Parked cars, no people. Just a long line of beech trees that stand proudly, stoic and solid with their gnarled arthritic limbs and smooth grey bodies. 'There are no witnesses, nobody to say any of this actually happened. So if I were you, I'd step away from your threats and I'd step away from Jacob because no matter how hard you try to convince yourself that he's yours, I can assure you, he isn't. He and I are meant to be together and I won't stop my visits until everything is back to how it was before you turned up in our lives and ruined what we had.'

Without waiting for a reply, Leah turns, the click of her heels echoing down the street as she slams the gate behind her and makes her way back home.

11

Leah is standing outside her parents' house, staring in the window, her fingers pressed against the glass, her fingertips hot against the cool surface. Her heart swells. Her throat is tight with anxiety as she watches her mum and dad, intrigued as they go about their lives inside their home, unaware of her presence.

The house is as she remembers it. It's been years since she has visited and she is surprisingly satisfied to see that everything has remained the same. The overstuffed chair in the corner still needs to be re-upholstered, its pale lilac fabric as threadbare and ragged as she remembers. The coffee table in the centre of the room is still home to a wad of magazines and badly folded newspapers, and her father's reading glasses are still perched on the arm of the old brown leather sofa. The ancient squat wooden clock is still sitting on the stone mantelpiece, its gilt face peppered with dirt, its hands struggling to keep time through lack of maintenance. Leah takes a deep breath and swallows down the lump that has risen in her throat. It's as if she has never stepped away from the place where she grew up; it is a moment in time, frozen and preserved to tear at her emotions and fill her with grief for the childhood she misses, for the family who shut her out. Leah blinks, swallows, tries to stem the sadness and crippling anxiety that bites at her, reminding her of who she is.

And what she did.

A lone tear escapes and rolls down her cheek. She wipes it away, angry at the loss she feels, angry at herself for allowing her emotions to get the better of her. She's usually tougher than this, but then the accident has weakened her, left her feeling vulnerable and fragile. It's as if her outer layers of skin are slowly falling away one by one until only her centre is left, naked and unprotected against the world, defenceless against its many blows.

Leah moves away from the glass, unsure why or how she even got here. In a strange way, she is now becoming accustomed to these unexpected ventures, finding herself in places that she knows well, with no memory of getting there. It's as if she has stumbled upon them in some sort of somnambulistic stupor, her subconscious leading her to places that are deeply embedded in her memory and pivotal to her existence. There's a reason why she is here, there has to be. She just doesn't know what it is yet.

She watches her parents, observing how they carry on behind the glass as if she isn't even there. Her father moves over to her mother who is slumped in a chair in the corner, her head lowered, her eyes shielded by her cupped hands. Her body language screams wretchedness and misery. On her lap is a small green box. Leah shivers. She knows what that box is, what it contains. It sat for so many months on her mother's dressing table before it was moved, before they took it to the top of the cliff at Grayston-on-Sea and scattered her brother's ashes into the four winds.

She had argued that it was a bad call, that it was the last

place he should be laid to rest. That town, that clifftop held nothing but bad memories for everyone, but her parents had been insistent, arguing that Ellis had been fond of little Lucy, that there was nowhere else he could go. Her mother couldn't stand the thought of him being buried in the ground, his remains rotting into the earth.

Leah suspected there was another motive, that her parents feared vandalism once word got around about where he was buried, that his final resting place would be desecrated by locals with no shame. Even death didn't stop their hatred and warped views of what was right and what was wrong. Her parents denied it, of course. They claimed that they wanted him to be free, to go wherever the weather dictated and to be at one with nature. Her father had said that Ellis had loved the outdoors, that they were doing what he would have wanted.

Nothing she said at the time could persuade them otherwise but Leah knew the truth, that her tiny mousy mother simply couldn't bear the thought of her dead son being visited by gangs of thugs who believed that what they were doing was right as they knocked over the flowers on his grave and graffitied his headstone. They would say that they were doing it for little Lucy, that they were simply evening things up, restoring the balance and giving him exactly what he deserved when in truth they were just thugs looking for trouble.

'And where do you suggest he should go, Leah?' her father had shouted when she reiterated her belief that the location was all wrong. She hadn't replied and ended up lowering her head away from his piercing gaze. That steely stare was another reminder of who she really was, his subliminal message telling her that she was an outsider, an addition to the family after Maria's premature death.

That's why they had adopted her. She was no more than a substitute, a damaged toddler adopted from the care system in a desperate bid to replace their previous child. Leah's own parents had been too interested in drugs and alcohol to take an interest in their own daughter and so social services had stepped in and removed her.

Her new parents were an older grieving couple with a daughter who had died just a few weeks after being born prematurely and a young son they had had later in life. They had tried for another baby and unable to have any more after Ellis they looked at adopting. They had initially fostered Leah and then took her into their family. She was too young to recall any of it but had felt overwhelmed with anger at not being told the full story, at not being allowed to know about her real parents. Who were they? Where had they lived? After discovering her true origins, she became angry. She had always been given to bouts of rage but the savage wrath that burned inside her after that day of discovery was like no other. She became rebellious, her temper ready to boil over at the slightest provocation. That was why she did what she did, to get back at them all for forgetting about her, for pushing her away and pretending they were all one big happy family when they were anything but.

She removes her hands from the glass, looks down at them, at the tremble in her fingers, at the whiteness of her own skin. She can't think about this anymore. It's all in the past and too late to undo the damage and the hurt. What's done is done.

Inside the house there is a movement. Her head snaps up. She watches her mother stand, clutching the box close to her chest, her father's arm draped over her shoulders. They look smaller somehow, as if sorrow has squashed them, pushed them closer to the ground, gravity and grief forcing them deep into the loam. How has she only just noticed this? Their misery, their ageing faces, lined with worry and angst, how did she not see it earlier? They turn and leave the room, grief for their son etched into their features. Another death. Another child to mourn.

Before she can stop it, tears begin to fall. She has to stop this. For years she refused to give in to regret, priding herself on being a hard-nosed individual who has survived many setbacks. But things have changed. She has developed a softness in her centre, the very essence of her altering, relaxing and becoming more pliable, and more susceptible to hurt and remorse.

The room is empty now. She waits, sees nothing else happening within and turns to leave. She will never understand why they scattered Ellis where they did. They could have buried him with Maria, *should* have buried him there alongside their other daughter. She thinks that perhaps they did what they did to get back at her, to make certain that that day at Grayston-on-Sea would always be there, like a huge stumbling block in their lives, a hurdle they would never get over.

More tears spill out, obscuring her vision. She blinks, looks again at the house and sees that it has changed. A bubble of air sticks in her chest. She lets out a hiccupping sigh, her fingers fumbling through her hair to find that smooth patch of skin on her scalp, the place that gives her such comfort, helping her to realise that pain can indeed help alleviate stress.

Rubbing at the flesh with her cool fingertips, Leah can see that she isn't standing outside her parents' house after all. It's not her childhood home. She is here, outside her own flat looking in the bay window of her room. Memories, that's all it was. Dark, painful memories that flood her mind on a regular basis of late, crowding her in, making her think she is going mad.

She steps inside the grey shadowy hallway and closes the door behind her, the dull click reverberating around the empty space. Grainne and Innes must be at work, which is where she should be once the effects of the crash have worn off, once this shroud of loneliness and the pitiless bouts of excruciating pain leave her. If they ever do, that is.

A stack of mail is piled up on the old console table farther down the hallway. Leah sorts through the envelopes, retrieving her own letters and examining them with a critical eye. Most of it is junk mail from people selling her insurance and offering services for repairs and maintenance to a house she doesn't own. One though, stands out from the others – a brown envelope with her name and address printed on it. There is no stamp and it's been franked. A sliver of anxiety slips under her skin. Just another thing to worry about, that's all this letter is going to be. Just something else to knock her off balance and drag her down into the gutter. As if she doesn't have enough going on. As if losing her boyfriend and being in constant pain isn't enough.

A noise to her right causes her to stiffen. She had presumed the house was empty, everybody at work. A door groans, a floorboard creaks. There is the shuffle of feet and suddenly Grainne is standing next to her, an expression of concern on her face as she watches Leah with a preciseness that alarms her. Grainne's face is sharper than usual, angular and unaccommodating. Her grey eyes sweep over the wad of envelopes clasped in Leah's hand.

'Can I have a word, Leah? It's about your rent.'

Leah's spine stiffens. She's up to date with her payments, she is sure of it. Or is she? Everything feels such a mess lately. Her head is lined with cotton wool, her usual organised thoughts disjointed, floating around in her head like confetti.

'My rent?' She is trying to sound nonchalant, undaunted by Grainne's unwavering gaze and rigid stance. Leah cannot let her see how susceptible and weak she is right now, how her heart has begun to pound in her chest and how her palms are suddenly slick with sweat. Whatever this problem is with the rent, she has to stand her ground. With no partner, no friends and a job she is currently not attending, this flat is the only steady thing that she has in her life. It's all she has.

'You're way behind with your payments, Leah. This month's rent is overdue and I still haven't had last month's money.' Grainne's hands are on her hips now. Her cheeks have coloured up and a vein is bulging in her neck, pulsating as she speaks. A fleck of saliva escapes out of her lips and bursts in the air between them.

This is not the Grainne Leah knows. Things have changed. She has changed. 'I'll get it to you, I promise,' Leah says, an element of panic creeping into her voice. She has no idea if she will be able to get the money to her or not. Her grocery shopping lately has consisted of packets of soups and loaves of bread that are past their sell by date. She doesn't even know how much money she has in the bank, if indeed she has any. The letters in her hand grow hot. One of them is a bank statement. She chose to ignore it, to pretend it wasn't there. She had hoped to sneak into her room to avoid bumping into Grainne. All these thoughts are in her head but there is no order to them, no cohesion or logic. Instead there is chaos and confusion, unwanted thoughts and distant memories crashing and colliding in her brain.

'I'll need it in a day or two. I've been fairly lenient, more so than many landlords, but I still have bills to pay. This is a big house and the gas and electricity bills are huge, not to mention the mortgage. And then there is the maintenance of it. I had to get the boiler repaired last week and I don't know if you noticed but this is a new front door as the other one had been leaking for quite a while.' She is short of breath after her diatribe. Poison drips from every word as Leah turns and heads to her room, hoping to blot it all out. 'Two days at the most, Leah, and then I'll have to find a new tenant. This is on you, not me. I've tried with you, I really have...'

Grainne's voice fades into the distance, a disturbing stream of disjointed syllables behind her as Leah shuts the door and perches on the edge of the bed, her knees trembling. How has her life come to this? Everything seems to be on a downward spiral and it's getting harder and harder to drag it back upwards, to put everything back in its rightful place.

She drops the pile of letters at her feet, keenly aware of their presence. It's as if they're glowing white hot, a stern reminder of her current predicament. She should open them, but then what good would it do? She would see that she is overdrawn at the bank, that she doesn't have enough money for this month's rent, let alone the month before, and seeing it all in black and white would make her even more depressed.

Her head feels heavy as she scrutinises the room, seeing it through clear eyes after a severe telling off from Grainne. It's an even bigger mess than she first thought. She has got to tackle it, to rid herself of all the unnecessary items that are cluttering up her space and her life, but everything feels like such an effort, such a gargantuan struggle, and she is beyond exhausted.

She lies back on the bed. All she needs is a few minutes. Just a short rest to gather her strength and then she'll set to and tidy it all up. She will. Then after that she will open the letters and get her life back on track.

Closing her eyes, she lets out a shuddering breath and imagines Jacob lying next to her, the heat from his skin merging with hers, the golden hue of his naked flesh as he leans over her and places his hand on her breast. She curls into a foetal position, a reassuring warmth flooding through her. This is better. Good thoughts, positive happy thoughts. If anyone can help her find her way through this tough time, it's Jacob. It's always been him. Soon he'll realise what he's lost. Soon he will see the error of his ways, realise the impact of what he has done and come around to her way of thinking.

All she needs is a little more time...

12

'Leah, open up right now! Open this fucking door or I'm calling the police!'

Leah sits up, her clothes askew, her hair sticking out at unnatural angles. She tries to fight her way out of the strangle-hold of sleep that presses down on her thoughts, muffling her senses.

'I need that key back right now! I know you got a spare one cut. Open this bloody door or I'll break it down!' Grainne's voice is piercing, almost a shriek.

Leah slumps back onto the pillow, closes her eyes, covers her ears. Wills it all to go away. Something stirs deep within her at what is happening, at the noise right outside her door – Grainne's shouting, talk of a key – it's a fleeting memory, a rogue thought, an unwanted recollection. The walls close in on her, the roof lowers, a pain slices across her abdomen, her windpipe snaps shut. She gags, splutters, struggles to breathe.

Then silence. All is quiet again. The pain has subsided, her throat is clear. Grainne is no longer screaming at her, hollering for her to open up. Leah looks around wildly, her eyes darting around the room. She jumps up out of bed, paces over to the door and pulls it ajar. There's nobody there. No Grainne, no Innes even. The hallway outside her room is empty. Her heart bangs around her chest, fluttering and flapping like a caged bird, pressing against her ribcage as she scans every corner for hidden figures. There is nobody.

At that, the front door opens and Grainne appears, holding an umbrella. She gives it a firm shake and drops it in the corner of the vestibule where it falls to one side, dripping water all over the tiled floor. She stamps her feet on the mat and turns to face Leah. 'The bus was late. Been stood waiting for the past twenty minutes in the rain. Sorry, need to get in and get dry.' She pushes past, leaving a trail of wet footsteps on the parquet flooring. Leah listens as Grainne bustles about, pulling off her coat, dropping it on the bottom of the stairs and cursing under her breath about stupid British weather and its unpredictable twists and turns. 'Hot as Hades one minutes and pissing down the next. Bloody sick of it. How are we supposed to dress for God's sake? For winter or fucking summer?' Her voice echoes down the hall, rattling in Leah's head. Grainne has been outside, not here in the house. She has been at work all day. So what in God's name has just happened and who was it that was banging on the door, demanding she open up and hand over her keys?

Nausea rises up from her belly, a swirling ball of acid that threatens to explode out of her if she doesn't sit down and dip her head into her lap. She feels herself being propelled forwards on legs that don't belong to her. She moves rapidly, reaching the toilet just in time. With a sudden desperate roar, Leah brings up the contents of her stomach over and over again. A trail of brown sludge fills the porcelain bowl, the stench causing her to retch until her sides ache and there is nothing left to bring up. She squats next to the toilet, holding her hair back away from her face, her innards growling and roiling. Breathing is a huge effort. She sucks oxygen in like a dying man desperate for his last breath, expelling it again in ragged chunks. In through her nose, out through her mouth. In, out. In, out. Her lungs are on fire, her head a jumble of insane thoughts. Once again, a sense of enervation pulls at her, threatening to swallow her whole.

She stands up, angles her face under the tap and rinses her mouth, spitting out trails of coffee-coloured slime that cling to the side of the sink.

Dizziness claws at her as she makes her way back to her room. Her legs ache and her muscles are as tight as knotted rope as she drops onto the mattress, her body feeling two stone lighter than it did five minutes ago. Despite feeling dog-tired, sleep is no longer an option. She is wide awake now with no idea of what time it is, what day it is. She knows where she is, however, and that's what worries her. As far as she can tell, she is travelling through hell with no means of escape and it's got to stop. She needs order in her life. She needs to know what is going on, not spend her days stumbling from one catastrophe to another. She needs stability.

Leah curls up on her side. A minute. She will count to sixty and then get up feeling better. She will tidy this room, open her stack of mail and then work out what to do about her unpaid rent. She needs to settle it. She has to live somewhere and until Jacob realises his mistake and lets her back into his life, she needs a roof over her head and here is as good as anywhere. It's close to his home and not so far from where she works. It's also affordable. With dwindling resources, money is suddenly very important. Her dip in salary has dictated she become thriftier and lower her expectations.

The thought of her job makes her head ache. It's imperative she call into the office, speak to her boss and explain her predicament, tell him about her medical issues. She's already lost one position. To lose this one would plunge her into an untenable situation. She wonders if she is actually in arrears at all. Did she imagine the confrontation with Grainne earlier or did it really happen? Time has no meaning anymore with events happening one after another, all piling up in her head. She visualises them as a mountain of rocks; impossible to climb. Completely impassable. Ready to topple down on her, flattening her body, grinding her bones into dust.

Reaching down to her feet, Leah snatches up the pile of letters and glances through them. She discards the junk mail and opens a bank statement, gulping down large breaths that feel solid and compacted, pockets of air sticking in her throat like gravel as she fights to swallow and control her breathing. She widens her eyes, blinking repeatedly as she reads the statement, sees the list of minus signs that scream at her. She's overdrawn. Badly overdrawn. Where is her money? Where are her wages? A stream of direct debits has been taken out but there hasn't been any money going in. She is entitled to sick pay. She has spent months paying into a scheme that should cover her for periods of protracted illnesses. So where is it?

The room swims; she is light-headed with fear and shock. The figure at the bottom of the page tells her all she needs to know. It reads -£482.76. And she still owes rent to Grainne. Or does she? Did that encounter actually happen or did she dream it? Her overdraft limit is £500 from the days when she had a decent job, money coming in on a regular basis. Back when she had a proper life and the bank trusted her.

Looking again at the letters, she sees one from her employer. Her stomach contracts. She's on the sick. She should be getting paid, shouldn't she? Her empty belly heaves as she opens it, ripping it apart with her long nails and holding it between damp shaking fingers.

The words at the top jump out at her – NOTICE OF TERMINATION

She shrieks, her hand flying to her mouth, then scans the

writing, checking for dates. This cannot be right. It just can't. This letter is from over a month ago. Or at least she thinks it is. Everything is too confusing. Time seems to have lost all meaning. She is living in a vacuum where nothing makes sense.

Tears blur her vision. She rubs at her eyes and reads the letter:

Dear Ms Browne,

We are writing to inform you of your termination at Timms & Co. with immediate effect for just cause due to poor attendance and gross misconduct that involved violence towards another employee.

Here at Timms & Co. we operate a zero-tolerance policy and put the safety of our employees above all else. Everyone, without exception, has the right to work in a safe environment and your conduct breached that policy and broke our company rules.

After much discussion, the employee in question and company directors have decided not to press charges but we feel that it would be irresponsible for you to enter the building, and remiss of us as courteous employers to allow it. Therefore, we have arranged for your belongings to be delivered to a PO box, the address of which is listed below. Please collect them as soon as possible.

Yours sincerely,

Marcus Frackett

Managing Director

A howl scrapes its way out of her throat, loud and feral. This can't be happening. It simply cannot be. She balls up her fists, pushes them into her eyes, pressing down hard, trying to suppress the river of tears that is bursting to be free. Her face throbs, her jaw aches. Everywhere hurts. She can suddenly recall what happened. It has come back to her like a punch to the gut, the memory of that day slinking into her brain, forcing her to see. Forcing her to remember.

That day. That awful fucking day.

Her dismissal.

She had arrived back late from lunch one afternoon. She would like to be able to use the excuse that there had been a queue at the sandwich shop or that the heavens had opened and she had had to shelter in a shop doorway until it stopped, but that wasn't the case at all. What she had actually been doing was standing outside Jacob's college hoping to catch sight of him, hoping to speak to him and talk him round, make him realise what a terrible mistake he was making. She had been standing there for what felt like an age and lost track of time. Before she knew it, over an hour had passed as she stood there staring, watching. Waiting. And that meant she was late. It was a good twenty-minute walk from her office to Jacob's place of work. When she finally arrived back at her desk, Gilly, the office manager was waiting for her, wearing an old-fashioned tweed suit and a deep frown.

Even though Leah knew she had made a grave error of judgement, arriving back at work forty-five minutes late, she felt immensely furious and had asked Gilly what she wanted. There was malice in her voice and she made no attempt to disguise it. Perhaps it was tiredness, perhaps it was the lack of food or perhaps it was spending all that time outside Jacob's place of work and not even seeing him, but regardless, Leah had rounded on Gilly. 'Go and pick your battles elsewhere! I'm perfectly entitled to take a longer break. I regularly get back to my desk before anybody else every morning so why don't you just leave me alone?'

Gilly had reminded her that they didn't operate a flexitime system and that she had missed a meeting with an important client. She then asked Leah to accompany her to the office.

And that's when it happened.

Leah had snapped. Fatigue, hunger and frustration overtook her, turning her into a raging monstrous being. 'You know what, Gilly?' she had shouted. 'You're nothing but an obnoxious odious bitch who lives to control people!'

She remembers the colour draining from the other woman's face, the greyness that replaced her normally healthy complexion spreading over her flesh as Leah continued with her tirade, shouting that she was frigid and would end up a lonely old spinster if she didn't start cutting people some slack and being nice to everyone around her.

Gilly had tried to take a step back, but in her confusion had stumbled and inadvertently moved closer to Leah, who in turn perceived it as threat and grabbed her arm before throwing her backwards with more force than was necessary.

She stares down at her hands, remembering the strength behind that shove, how she had actually wished Gilly harm. It wasn't an accident and yet it was. The older woman had stumbled and fallen backwards, hitting her head on the tiled floor and damaging her arm. It was twisted at a peculiar and painful angle. And there had been blood. Plenty of it too. Enough to cause a ruckus and for an ambulance to be called. People had gathered, shouts were heard. A hand was clasped around Leah's upper arm and a voice demanded that she go into the office of the managing director.

She had sat, head bowed, her stomach tight with worry. She hadn't meant for it to happen. It just did. Sometimes that was how life worked out for her. Trouble followed her around like a dark cloud ready to unleash a terrible storm upon her.

The manager had tried to speak with a modicum of reason in his voice and again, this set off a spark of irritation within her. His manner became more and more condescending with every sentence until she could hold her tongue no longer.

Standing up she had told him that he was a misogynistic waste of space who allowed male counterparts to get away with behaviour that was deemed unacceptable for female employees. It was true but possibly ill-timed. Only two weeks prior, two male colleagues had rocked in half an hour late and nobody had said a word to them. Not a damn thing. Yet when she did it, the world practically imploded.

'I beg your pardon?' Marcus had said, a tremble evident in his tone, his eyes wide.

'If I had been a man and had pushed somebody away, it would have been written off as laddish behaviour. Walking me to the office in view of everybody and sitting here speaking to me in that tone is discrimination.'

She knew then that the game was up. She was simply venting her spleen, trying to defend the indefensible. Without waiting for a reply, she turned and left his office, stepped through the crowd of gossip mongers who had gathered outside the door, and stopping only to grab her bag and coat, she left the building making sure she slammed the door on her way out.

Tears bubble up and escape, sliding down her face as she remembers that day, those few desperate hours she has tried hard to forget.

Her chest rises and falls, sobs catching in her throat as she stares at the evidence in her hands, the cold hard facts screaming at her that she is unemployed and broke with no means of keeping a roof over her head.

She stares out of the window, her mind throwing ideas at her randomly. All of this has happened since the break-up with Jacob – having to move house, losing her first job due to lack of concentration. Even the awful scene with Gilly only happened because she had been to see Jacob and lost track of time. This is what heartbreak feels like, she is sure of it. It isn't some undefinable ethereal condition. It is real, and she is suffering from it. It is an all-encompassing disorder that affects every aspect of her life, leaving her unable to function at the most basic of levels.

And there is only one person who is to blame for this.

Chloe.

Her last visit to Chloe's flat was just a warm-up, a prequel to the real thing. It's now time for Leah to up her game, to really start asserting herself instead of being the proverbial doormat. So far, she has taken the blows and done nothing about it except stand and stare in at the life that should be hers, the life that used to belong to her. She knows now that such action was a waste of her time; she has been passive for too long. More aggression is what is needed. Not too much, just enough to let Chloe know that she is onto her.

Just enough to scare her away and send her running back to wherever it was she came from.

Just enough.

Leah drops the handful of letters onto the floor, watching as they scatter onto the rug in a dishevelled pile. None of it matters anymore; her lack of money, having no job, being in arrears with her rent. None of it worries her anymore. Those things are just a distraction from what is really important, which is getting Jacob back.

And eliminating Chloe from their lives. For good.

13

2005

It didn't take them long to locate him. By the time he was found, dehydration and mild hypothermia had already set in requiring a short stay in hospital until his body temperature and fluids had returned to normal.

A part of him died the day they found him. He was supposed to feel grateful, to thank everybody who strapped him onto the stretcher, wrapping him up warm and inserting the cannula in his hand to fill him full of saline which would help keep him alive. But he didn't feel like that at all.

Resentment and disappointment had coursed through him. He had been made to go back home, to face his family, to live amongst the gossips who simply wouldn't let it go. As far as they were concerned, he was a cold-blooded killer. Despite the coroner's findings, despite his own parents dismissing the gossip, they all still believed the words of his younger sister, the girl who wore a permanent scowl and refused to engage with him in a polite, civil manner. It was easier for them to go with her lies. It provided them with a story, something to chat about. It provided them with someone whose name they could blacken without a shred of evidence.

His makeshift den in the woods will probably be found by local kids, used and wrecked before he can get back to it. He has nothing now. People who don't understand him took it from him; his own space, somewhere he could be alone and not be the young lad everyone believed had killed Lucy. They thought they were helping him when in fact, the opposite is true. His options are now limited. His life is being closed down.

School is impossible. Everyone stares, points, whispers behind his back. The first day back after being discharged from hospital was the hardest.

'Look who's back,' Anthony Robbins snorted as he made his way into the classroom. 'It's that mad murdering twat who showed his guilt by running away.'

The lad did his utmost to ignore the jibes, to walk away from the shoves and pushes as he made his way from class to class. He did his best to take them all, the jeers and insults, but everybody has their breaking point, including him.

It wasn't a particularly hard punch that he had aimed at Anthony Robbins, but the crack could be heard in all four corners of the room, even above the sound of thirty teenagers jostling and pushing their way into their desks. The blood spurted from Anthony's nose, a fountain of scarlet that dripped onto the floor and soaked through his shirt in seconds. People who previously had feared and secretly despised Robbins, suddenly stood close by him, aiding him, muttering false platitudes about how much they pitied him, being attacked by a suspected murderer, a child murderer at that. They closed ranks, shut him out.

The lad left the classroom, making a surreptitious escape while they all fawned over the victim, their voices loaded with faux concern at his predicament. Nobody tried to stop him. Despite the jibes and toxic comments, he wasn't really that important after all. His purported crime was forgotten and brushed aside, a non-event compared to the gushing and bloody nose of a notorious bully whose reputation was very possibly in tatters after being beaten by the surly quiet lad who always tried to keep himself to himself.

By the time he got to the reception area, word had already spread about the fight and the deputy head was waiting for him, arms crossed, a knowing look on his smug little face. 'I think you and me need a word, young man,' was all he said before turning and walking into his office, holding the door open for the lad to follow.

And that was when he made his decision. He wasn't prepared to live his life that way, to be labelled as a trouble-maker, as the boy who possibly murdered a small child. It wasn't who he was and he definitely wasn't prepared to live with it. They may have found him when he bolted into the woods but there was another way out of this mess. There is always another way.

He had sat, listening to the reproachful speech spewed out by the deputy head about how violence isn't the answer and that he would have to learn to rise above the taunts and insults, not get drawn into fights as that way lay trouble.

The words bounced off him leaving no lasting impression.

By the time he left the office, he already felt lighter than he had in months, as if a great weight had been lifted, his decision about his future allowing him a reprieve from the hell that was currently his life. There was a way out, a way to escape from the hatred. Everywhere he went he received those stolen glances, heard the lies, had to listen to the vile words of people who were convinced they knew everything but in fact, knew nothing at all.

His parents were going to be informed about the fight apparently. Not that it mattered. Not anymore. Mr Warwick's words were empty, pointless. He could tell his mum and dad anything he wanted. It wouldn't make any difference to anything and it certainly wouldn't affect the lad's decision.

There was a spring in his step as he left the main entrance. Was it his imagination or was the sun brighter? The clouds whiter and the grass just that little bit greener?

Everything was going to be just perfect. He could feel it.

The pale blue sky led him to where he wanted to go, the shadows of the sun pointing him in the right direction as he smiled and fixed his eyes on the road ahead, his body as light as air.

14

PRESENT DAY

'I can't tell you that, I'm afraid. I'm here to help you. That's all we need to focus on right now.'

Will watches Leah closely. She is feeling on edge today, more so than usual. Here she is, sitting in her usual seat opposite the man who seems to know so much about her when she knows so little about him.

'How did I get here? That's all I want to know. And why do I feel so confused and in so much pain?'

There are so many things she wants to ask him, a mass of jumbled words sitting there in the forefront of her mind, so many of them jostling for space that it's proving difficult to put them into an intelligible sentence, to say them out loud without sounding like she is losing her mind.

She wants to tell him that she has lost her job. She wants to ask him why her landlady was demanding unpaid rent and banging on Leah's door when the landlady wasn't even in the house at the time. She wants to ask him why time seems to slip backwards and forwards, events muddled and chaotic, out of sequence, jumping in and out of her life with frightening clarity. There doesn't seem to be any easy way to settle her fears without coming across as unhinged and it is starting to frighten her. Will claims he is trying to help her. So why does she feel so scared and alone, as if she is teetering on the edge of a yawning abyss with nobody around to stop her falling?

If she mentions any of these things, she will get told that it's all down to suffering a massive trauma and that her brain is struggling to comprehend what took place. That may well be so, but something about recent events has left her feeling unnerved, particularly these visits to Will. She has no memory of getting here.

She doesn't even know where *here* is.

Panic wells up inside her at not knowing her location, at not really knowing this man who delves inside her head and tells her over and over that he's trying to help her, to ease her suffering and assuage her many fears. The panic and dread expand in her chest, swelling and augmenting until breathing is no longer a natural process but a laboured effort that leaves her gasping for air.

Something changes in the room – a sudden shift in temperature, colours swimming and swirling. A movement close by, shadows dancing, flitting above her, next to her. Then a greyness, a body close by. It's Will. He is near, leaning over her, his bulk blocking out all the light, his eyes piercing, full of fire. She feels his hands on her sternum, pressing down on her ribcage, his face close to hers, his breath hot on her skin. She listens to him counting with each consecutive push, feels blood, slick and metallic gather in her throat, in her mouth, covering her teeth, coating her tongue. Choking her.

Breathe, breathe.

She blinks rapidly, rubs at her eyes and exhales, pockets of air punching at her lungs and bouncing in her throat as she widens her eyes and looks around the room.

It's back to normal. Everything back to how it was.

Will is still sitting in his seat, observing her like bacteria under a microscope, his eyes narrowed in fascination. Hot and frantic, she straightens her hair and attempts to regain some sort of semblance of normality. She is buying herself some time to clear her head, to work out what just happened. She stems the rising panic, telling herself it's just another unexplained occurrence in her upside-down life, the life that is rapidly spiralling out of control.

Will's body is rigid with what appears to be keen interest. His elbows are perched on the desk, his hands spread out over the mottled, grainy wood. The top half of his body is leaning forwards toward Leah as if he is waiting for her to move or say something of great importance.

She wonders if he knows what she has just experienced, if she unknowingly acted it out right here in front of him. The thought of it makes her skin burn, a wave of humiliation washing over her. She feels like a small child caught doing something reprehensible. Perhaps it's Will's unreadable expression or his permanently professional conduct, but she always ends up feeling foolish in his presence. It's as if he can read her thoughts and see right through to her soul.

She shivers and hopes not. He might not like what he finds there.

'As I said earlier, we just need to make sure you're safe. I want to help stop your pain.' His voice is calm. Always calm, always smooth, always measured. Will the rescuer, the helper of lost souls.

She is torn between feeling at ease, lulled into a hypnotic state by his ingratiating manner, and feeling angry at his lack of concern. She has just experienced a hallucinatory episode and yet Will remains unmoved, more concerned about her safety than her decaying cognitive state. Feeling safe isn't her priority. Making sure she isn't losing her mind is. She wants reassurances that all of this is if not normal then at least explicable, that there is a logical reason behind it all. She doesn't want to hear any more about trauma. She doesn't want to hear any more about the crash and its after-effects and how her conscious self is trying to adapt to what she endured. She wants tangible proof that she isn't going insane. And if he can't give her that, then she will go elsewhere for it.

Leah tries to stand up, to make a point that she no longer needs his services – services she can't remember requesting – but her legs are too heavy, a deadweight pinioning her in place. She stares at Will, trying to hold his gaze but her head spins and her vision mists over. The pressure on her body becomes unbearable. She closes her eyes, clenches her teeth together. The absurdity of it all makes her want to weep.

Thoughts of the past bleed into her brain, droplets of poison darkening her thoughts, seeping into the murkiest corners of her mind until she is saturated with them. It's impossible to shake them away. She is back there, back in her childhood home. It's all so clear to her now, so frighteningly clear.

Sitting on her bed, she is listening to her parents talking downstairs. Ellis is in his room. Ellis, the favoured one, their special child. The child who lived. Leah was simply Maria's replacement and yet never quite lived up to their expectations of her. She could never say she felt unloved, but neither did she feel particularly favoured either, not in the way Ellis was. He was the good boy, you see, the quiet boy. The one everybody fawned over. Ellis was good looking whereas Leah could at best be described as average looking. With her long mousy hair, poor eyesight and a dull complexion, she was the polar opposite of her brother. The Brownes were a handsome family. She knew from an early age that she wasn't one of them. And it stung. My God, did it sting.

The chattering continues below her, echoing up through the

floor of her bedroom. Her parents have been to visit Maria's grave, something they do every couple of months. Ellis went along but she, in her spitefulness, refused to accompany them, staying at home instead even though she was only twelve years old. They had relented and given in to her pouting and sulkiness. Had they not, the visit couldn't have gone ahead. And they never missed a visit. Ever. She knew that, played on it, wielded it in front of them, tapped into their misery and endless longing for their firstborn and used it to her advantage.

They had visited a café while they were out, spent time together as one big happy family. Without her. Ellis had told her this when they arrived back home, that he had had chocolate cake and a raspberry milkshake, that they had chatted, laughed, enjoyed themselves. Something else to feel aggrieved about. Something else to widen the chasm she felt between herself and the rest of her family. So she and Ellis had fought. She had called him a spoilt brat and he had responded by pushing her backwards onto the bed, reiterating how calm and peaceful it had been without her around to spoil it.

That's when the seed was planted. It took root in her brain, an unwavering idea that grew and grew, exciting her with its possibilities, firing up her senses. Making her feel in control. She could be charming when she wanted to be. She would use it to her gain, to get people on her side.

'Stay with me, Leah.' Will's words cut through her thoughts, his voice crisp and clean, authoritative. Solid.

She turns to him, somewhat alarmed by the look on his face. 'I'm here. Just thinking about things.'

He smiles, his eyes creasing as he gazes at her. Is she imagining it or is there a look of fondness in his expression? Or maybe it's just her madness, tricking her, fooling her into believing that he cares when in reality, Will is just another stranger, going through the motions, being perfectly polite and civil when in actual fact he couldn't care less about her. 'That's okay. Thought I'd lost you there for a minute.'

'Remembering things, that's all.'

'What sort of things?' He's interested now, his posture more relaxed. He leans back, twirls a silver pen between his fingers.

'My childhood. My parents.' Leah's face burns, her skin hot with anger and sorrow and shame. 'My brother.'

'Ah, yes,' Will says, his voice now quiet with just the tiniest flicker of interest that is also tinged with sadness, 'your brother. Do you want to talk about him?'

Leah shakes her head, a lone tear traversing down her face. She dips her head then looks up at him. 'Yes and no.'

'Why is that? Is it because he was so young when he died?'

She shrugs, sits for a few seconds, enjoying the silence in the room. It's too difficult a question to answer, too complex. Where would she start with her story about what happened to Ellis?

'How did he die?'

Blackness descends as she closes her eyes and lowers her head to block out that day. She can't go through it again. She just can't.

'No,' she says. 'I can't. I cannot bring myself to talk about it.' Her throat closes as she tries to speak. 'It's too difficult. Too awful.' She takes a couple of seconds to push away the dread that is closing in on her. She focuses on regulating her breathing, on quashing the buzzing that has settled in her brain, a deep desperate hum that knocks against her skull and fills her head. A thousand angry wasps rattling around in there.

'Why is that, Leah? Sometimes we need to face the things that frighten us, to look inward and start opening up about our past. Especially somebody like you who has something to hide, a guilty person who needs to unburden herself.'

Leah's head snaps up, a quick reflexive action that skews her vision, making her feel queasy and dizzy. She looks around, a thick pulse hammering in her neck. Will is nowhere to be seen. His place is empty. Those words. Did he say them or, like the other unexplainable things that happen in her life, were they only in her head?

She watches, her heart thudding as Will appears in her peripheral vision, floating ghostlike towards her. He gives her a warm smile, his eyes creasing at the corners as he speaks. 'Sorry about that. I needed to go and see a colleague. I thought it might give you some thinking time. Anyway, I asked you if you wanted to talk about your brother.'

Leah shakes her head. 'You said that we need to face the things that frighten us, didn't you?'

Will looks at her perplexed, bites his lip. A crease has set in between his eyebrows as he shakes his head. 'I think perhaps we've done enough for now. You're looking tired.'

She pushes the heel of her hands into her eyes until stars burst and a dull ache sets in. Will is right about one thing. She is worn out. Too tired to think straight.

'I need to go home, have a lie down. I'm not feeling too well,' she says feebly, her voice croaky with fatigue and humiliation. Ellis seems to be permeating her thoughts on a regular basis lately. She counts back. Fourteen years since he died. Fourteen long painful years of being haunted by his face, fourteen long years without hearing his voice. They were just teenagers for God's sake. It should never have happened. She was a bitter young girl and he – well he was just an ordinary kid. In her more lucid moments, she finds herself wondering why she hated him so much. If she is being perfectly honest, he didn't deserve her anger and wrath. He didn't deserve to die. Neither of them did. Poor Ellis and poor little Lucy. They were children for God's sake. Just children.

Sometimes we need to face the things that frighten us, to look inward and start opening up about our past. Especially somebody like you who has something to hide, a guilty person who needs to unburden herself.

Leah nips at the skin on her arms with her ragged nails, wishing she was in her room, lying on her bed, staring up at the ceiling. Anywhere but here. A shooting pain spreads over her abdomen knocking the breath right out of her. She stands up, her legs weak, her head light. The room spins, the brightly coloured artwork swirling and flickering like a sinister entity in the room, its vibrant colours taking on an ominous form. The devil. It makes her think of the devil and how hot it must be in the pit of hell with its raging fires, the air too hot to breathe as it scorches your lungs and strips your skin away leaving nothing but a pile of wet, blood-covered bones.

Leah lowers her eyes, watches as the ground comes up to meet her. Except it's not the floor in Will's neat office. It's a dark coloured carpet. She knows it, recognises it, thinks perhaps she is back in the carriage of the train, being tipped backwards, forwards, her body thrown about by a force too great to fight.

Then darkness descends, shutting her out of her own conscious thoughts, tipping her instead, into a welcome oblivion.

15

She wakes up in bed with no memory of getting there. Leah's hands trail down her body. Relief floods through her. At least she is wearing nightclothes. The thought of collapsing somewhere and strangers undressing her fills her with horror. Did she collapse though? Was it a dream or was she actually sitting in Will's office only a few hours ago? So many unanswered questions and they are piling up by the day, the hour, the minute, time no longer a tangible thing in her life. It spins away from her, refusing to adhere to the usual regime that she, at one time, lived her life by.

A dull streak of light filters through the curtains, filling the room with a triangular slab of ochre that spreads over the corner of the bed and the grubby rug on the floor, highlighting the ingrained filth lodged between the fibres. This place is such a terrible mess, just like her life. She is in a massive self-inflicted sinkhole from which there seems to be no means of escape. God knows she tries, clawing with her fingernails, gripping on, trying to get out, but every time she thinks she is free, down she goes again, back into the darkness.

She gets out of bed, pads over to the window, drags the

curtains open a fraction and stares outside. Half of the cars that are usually parked out in the street are not there. She looks at her watch, sees that it's 10am and realises everybody is at work. Exactly where she should be were it not for the fact she is no longer employed. Or was that a dream as well? She feels sure that awful incident did happen. The tight sensation somewhere deep in her belly tells her that it really did take place. She would rather it hadn't, but there it is. She is unemployed, accused of violent conduct towards another colleague and aside from turning back the clock, there's not a damn thing she can do about it.

With no idea of what the day will bring, she gets showered and dressed, aghast at how few clean clothes she has. Her laundry basket is overflowing and she hasn't any money to go to the launderette. Grainne is at work. The house is empty. A thought occurs to her. She will be able to get her laundry done in Grainne's washing machine without her realising. Grainne would possibly agree to it anyway. It's just a matter of her not being around for Leah to ask permission. Isn't that what friends do for one another? Ignoring the small still voice in her head that is reminding her that Grainne is her landlady and not her friend, she decides that needs must and attempts to wade through the mess in her room. She makes a half-hearted attempt to tidy it up on her way to the overflowing laundry basket standing in the far corner of the room but gives it up as a bad job.

She sighs, kicking items aside, tripping over mounds of fabric and discarded objects, thinking how utterly pointless it all seems, this tidying-up business, what a complete waste of time it is. Everything only gets messy and crumpled again anyway, so why bother? She gathers up armfuls of dirty clothes, wincing at the smell and turning her head away. A lump is wedged in her throat as a thought jars her, filling her head, her chest heaving as she tries to suppress an unexpected sob. How humiliating it is not having enough money to stay clean. She swallows down her misery, fighting back the tears. This is a low point in her life. The lowest. This time last year she had everything – Jacob, a decent job as an accountant with plenty of promotion opportunities, and now she is almost on the bones of her arse without enough money to wash her own clothes. A deep sense of shame eats at her as she leaves her room, makes her way into the kitchen and places the pile of clothes on the floor next to the machine. She picks up a box of washing detergent, eyeing up the brand, cursing at how rarely she can buy this type as it's way too expensive for her budget and then hears a voice from behind her, causing her scalp to prickle. She spins around.

Grainne is standing there, hands on hips, a smug expression on her pale, bony face. 'Can I help you?'

'Erm, sorry, I didn't see you. I thought you were out,' Leah says, a scarlet web forming on her skin, creeping up her neck, a crimson display of embarrassment. The room suddenly feels terribly hot. Her cheeks flush and burn as she tries to avert her eyes from Grainne's critical stare.

'Clearly,' the other woman replies, her gaze shifting to the packet in Leah's hands then back to the mound of dirty clothes piled in a heap at her feet.

'It's just that I don't have enough change for the machine at the launderette so I thought that if I could maybe...' She runs out of words, out of energy. She is spent, weak and wearied by poverty. Humbled and horrified by her life. She stares at the floor, indignity at being caught digging deep into the very marrow of her bones.

Grainne lets out a protracted grunt and shrugs dismissively, shaking her head like an exasperated school ma'am. 'Yes, okay, whatever. As long as it doesn't become a regular thing. And I'm only here because I've got an appointment. I'm at work later. I'm due at the dentist's in fifteen minutes. Just in case you were wondering why I'm still around.' She starts to walk away and stops, her face inscrutable as she speaks. 'By the way, Leah, your rent didn't go into my account. It was due last week. I didn't mention it before as I wanted to give you a few days to sort it in case there was a problem.'

Leah's breath catches as she loads the machine and turns it on, the slight whirring sound killing the tenseness of the moment. 'Sorry. I know I owe you some backdated money and–'

'No, not backdated. It's just this month that you owe. I'll need it in the next couple of days so I can pay what I owe to other people.' She stares at the washing machine then looks back at Leah, an accusatory tone in her voice. 'I've got a gas and electricity bill to fork out for, so if you wouldn't mind?'

Nodding, Leah stumbles away, her head full of cotton wool. She can't think properly. Yet again everything is askew, out of kilter; her life a series of unexplainable events, emotions, memories, all mixed up and out of sync.

She heads back to her room, mumbling her apologies to Grainne and thanking her for the use of the machine. Once there she slams the door behind her and leans on it, giving herself a couple of seconds to think.

A bank statement. That will solve it. She can check her balance again and work out what the fuck is going on. Throwing bags and bits of paper out of the way, she rummages through the detritus in her room, clambering over piles of discarded clothes and old newspapers and magazines until she finds it. Her most recent statement. Flipping it open she scans it to the bottom, to the most recent transaction. She's in the black. Just. £8.09.

She drags her fingers through her hair, thinking back to opening the other statement not so long ago, the one that said she was deeply overdrawn. The date. If she can find the other one then she can double check the dates. There has obviously been a mix up. The bank may have sent one of them out late. That's the only possible reason for the discrepancy. Nothing else makes sense.

Another scramble ensues as she searches for the previous correspondence. Drawers are pulled out and tipped upside down, wardrobes flung open and their contents dragged out. By the time she finishes, Leah is red-faced and almost in tears, frustration biting at her. Where the hell has that last statement gone to? She didn't bin it, that much she does know. Her room is a mess. She isn't even entirely sure where her bin is, if indeed, she has one at all. So where the *fuck* is that other statement? Not that it matters that much. Her current balance of £8.09 isn't enough to cover her rent and Grainne didn't look like she was in the mood for delays or excuses. Her rent is almost £400. How on earth is she supposed to find the money in the next few days? And why, only a few days ago, was she asking for rent dating back more than one month? Maybe she wasn't. Maybe it's another implanted memory cooked up by Leah's frazzled brain.

The dim light in the room suddenly feels unbearable, causing her to squint, to place her hand over her forehead to shield her eyes from the glare that is putting an ugly slant on everything.

There are a couple of options open to her, all of them unsavoury. This is a crisis. She hasn't seen or spoken to her parents in over two years, possibly even longer. Time is such a slippery thing lately, it's so hard to keep track but the one thing she does know is that approaching them and asking for handouts will be a humiliating and painful experience. And then of course, there is Jacob. As close as they were, turning up on his doorstep, cap in hand, is unthinkable. She simply cannot begin to imagine it. And yet she has nobody else. Those are her options, whether she likes it or not. The only other thing she can do is speak to Grainne and make promises she isn't entirely sure she can keep. It's a possibility, not a particularly appealing one, but neither are the other two choices.

She is trapped. Nowhere to turn. Thoughts of Jacob flit in and out of her mind, the sight of his face warming her cold flesh, tugging at her heartstrings. Making her wish she was back in his flat, back in his arms. Her life is cold and empty since their break-up. She is living a 2D existence in a pointless world. And now she is also unemployed and penniless. Her life is in tatters. Her mind lets her down every single fucking day. She feels certain she is going mad, losing her tenuous grip on reality. How much more is she expected to take?

With a headache creeping its way in, Leah lies back on the bed, doing her utmost to ignore the stale musty smell of unwashed sheets that wafts up from beneath her. How long has it been since she changed the bed linen? She has no clear memory of doing it recently. She has no clear memory of anything.

Despite oversleeping, the tiredness that seems to sit with her permanently these days, wins over. Her eyes are too heavy to keep open, the light fading as exhaustion drags her away once again, into the deepest, darkest corners of unconsciousness. First a floating sensation, next a heaviness too overwhelming to ignore. Then nothing.

~

She is standing, crying in Grainne's kitchen. Her shoulders are shaking, her chest heaving. Snot and tears are rolling down her face. It looks different to when she visited it earlier. The washing machine is empty. Grainne is wearing different clothes. Leah has no memory of getting here. She cups her hands and places them over her eyes, sobs wracking her body, convulsions rippling through her as she attempts to control her growing hysteria and pull herself together.

'I said last time that I needed the money, Leah. We're now nearly two months on and I've given you plenty of time. I realise you're having a tough time and I know you said you were waiting for your parents' inheritance to come through but I can't keep subsidising you! I'm not the cruel bitch you think I am. If that were the case you'd be out on the streets by now, but there comes a point when enough is enough.' Grainne is standing in front of her, hands on hips, her slim frame seeming to fill the entire room. Her shadow is an eerie elongated shape spread out over the floor, not dissimilar to the images Leah has seen of The Slender Man. She shivers and tries to ignore the monstrous silhouette splayed over the beige lino next to her, creeping its way up the bare wall. Thoughts wrestle their way into Leah's brain, one memory in particular standing out above the rest.

It was another rainy day. Grainne had once again asked for the overdue rent, yelling that she wasn't prepared to put up with any more late payments and was seeking legal advice on how to evict Leah, and in desperation, Leah had told her that she was grieving, that both of her parents had just been killed in a road traffic accident and she was struggling to manage. Silenced and remorseful for shouting, Grainne had hugged Leah, the colour escaping from her face in one rapid rush. Leah had even explained that she was on her way to the funeral home to make arrangements for their burials.

Grainne had looked outside to the dreadful downpour, pulled on her coat and offered to give her a lift. It wasn't often that she used her car as parking in the city was a nightmare but, on that occasion, Grainne had grabbed at the keys, linked her arm through Leah's and gently led her to the small white vehicle parked outside.

With a pounding head, Leah had climbed in the car, trying

to work out what to do next, desperately hoping Grainne wouldn't take it upon herself to accompany Leah into the funeral parlour. 'It's the Co-op,' Leah had said numbly, wondering why she had chosen to spin such a tale. 'The one in the city centre. So rather than park up, if you could just drop me off at the bottom of Gilesgate, I'll be able to hop out and make my way over from there.'

Grainne had looked at her, sympathy and compassion for Leah's plight obvious in her expression. 'I can come in with you if you'd like?' Leah had felt her heart start up in an irregular patter, bouncing around her chest; had sensed her eye beginning to twitch and blinked hard to stop it. Grainne going in with her to the funeral parlour to arrange a service for her parents who weren't actually dead was absolutely the last thing she had wanted.

'It's fine, honestly. Thank you anyway. For the lift and the offer of help. I really appreciate it.' Grainne had grasped her hand and smiled a warm, genuine smile that had pierced Leah's conscience and spiked her heart. Why had she told yet another lie? A dreadfully disrespectful one at that. It was as if she had no control over her mouth, over the stupid thoughtless things that came out of it time and time again.

'Well, you know where I am if you want me. Just shout.' Grainne had sat, watching her, waiting, smiling softly as Leah had crossed the road, weaving her way between the parked cars and the stream of pedestrians that snaked along the pavement, until she entered the building with no idea of what she would say when approached by the receptionist.

Leah had plonked herself in a chair in a thankfully busy reception area, watching out of the window until Grainne's car eventually moved out of sight. She then arose from her seat and left before the lady behind the desk had even had a chance to speak to her.

Sometimes, just sometimes, luck was on Leah's side. But only sometimes. And definitely not today.

Now Grainne stands, her face like thunder, anger pulsing out of her in great waves. Leah can't seem to think straight. She has no idea what to say, how to drag herself out of this situation with her self-respect still intact. Turning away, she focuses on staying upright, making sure her legs don't buckle and fail her as she walks back to her room and slams the door behind her.

16

2005

His mother had received the call from the school an hour before, telling her about the fight and now sits at home waiting for him to return, her stomach clenched, tight with fear and anxiety. Will this thing never end? That day, that bloody stupid, awful day at the beach is going to stay with them forever.

If they don't sort it out, it will ruin them all, tear their family apart, and she can't let that happen. She has to heal their rift.

It's an unspoken truth between her and her husband that their daughter, their troubled and permanently unhappy daughter, has unleashed a demon amongst them, doing what she does best – causing trouble.

Fighting back tears, Chrissie waits, watching the hands of the clock as the minutes tick by, second by painful second, until eventually the door opens and the girl spills in, her face set in its usual frown, her limbs locked in a stance of anger. She's alone. No brother with her. Just herself.

Disappointment undulates through Chrissie's body, her blood stilling as she suddenly realises her boy is over forty-five minutes late. It isn't unusual for the girl to come home at all hours after hanging around outside the corner shop but he is always on time. Always. Punctuality is his middle name. He would never not come home without letting them know where he is. Except for that time, that one godawful time, when everything became too much for him and he ran away. Chrissie shakes her head at the memory. And even then, he left a note. He didn't just up and go without a word. It was understandable after what he'd been through. Perfectly understandable.

They didn't shout or rant when he was found by the police and the mountain rescue team. They were just relieved he was safe and were desperate to have him back home, back in their family fold. So where is he now? What has happened to their son this time? Not another bid to escape. He can't have. His belongings are still here, his clothes still in his wardrobe, his travelling bag still there, his favourite watch given to him last Christmas still on his chest of drawers next to his bed. All there, all still at home. Unlike him, her beautiful boy, her sad, dejected boy. He is out there somewhere, on his own. And now she needs him back. Chrissie needs to have her boy home.

It was just a fight. All young lads fight at one time or another, don't they? It's no big deal. Except it is, and she knows it. It's a very big deal. Her boy isn't a fighter. Sometimes troubled, but never violent. He's a teenager after all. Aren't all teenagers full of angst?

This is different though. Something has happened, something to set him off. And now he hasn't come home after school. He could be anywhere, anywhere at all. The world is a big scary place and he is a vulnerable young kid. Not tough enough to cope.

'Where's your brother?' Chrissie tries to keep her voice calm, to keep her fears under wraps and not show her growing alarm to the girl.

'Dunno. How should I know? I'm not his keeper.'

Chrissie tries not to bristle at her daughter's words, at her harsh tone. She's just a child, hurting and currently disinterested in the world around her. One day she will realise how much time she has wasted on anger and resentment and hatred. And she will regret her brutality and black moods, she is sure of this fact. Since her discovery of that certificate, that damn certificate that should have been hidden away and not left lying around in the bureau, things have deteriorated. Her daughter (because despite what the girl thinks, she is their darling daughter and always will be) had been in there looking for a pen and stumbled across it. Since that time, she has felt marginalised, set apart from the rest of the family. And the mood swings. Dear God, the mood swings fuelled by hormones and a feeling of not belonging; they are so hard to deal with.

But they try. They try so much to make her feel loved, to let her know she is an integral part of their family and not an addition. She and Ralph were always going to tell her about the adoption but there never seemed to be a good time. And now it's too late. The girl seems to be on some sort of mission to become a juvenile delinquent. Sure, she is charming when required but something has changed. Or perhaps it has always been there, lurking, her darker side, waiting for an opportune moment to present itself. Like that day at the beach.

Chrissie knows it was a lie; she knew it then and still believes it now. She isn't stupid. Her daughter said it because she was still angry at them all, she felt like an outsider, an intruder in their family, which couldn't be further from the truth. They love her as much as they love their two other children but the girl is so wrapped up in her wrath and resentment that she can't or won't see it. She is hell-bent on revenge.

Chrissie fights back the tears. Everything seems to be unravelling; their lives coming apart at the seams. She has to do something to get it all back. Maybe a family holiday away from the gossips and the liars who grasped on to the story of little Lucy's death and refuse to let go, perpetuating the myth that their son is a murderer. People like nothing better than vilifying innocent folk, dragging their names through the dirt without a thought for how it affects both the person and their families. And it has affected them. They are on a downward slope and she doesn't know how to stop it, how to go back to the way things were. That's all she wants – to turn back the clock and be the happy family they once used to be.

But for now, she needs to know where her son is. She needs to know he is safe, not lying dead in a ditch or in hiding somewhere, far away from the taunts of those who choose to believe the lies said about him.

She just wants him back by her side.

Another hour passes with no sign. Phone calls to the school have proved fruitless. As far as they know, he left for home and can tell her nothing else about his whereabouts.

By the time Ralph arrives home from work, she is frantic, pulling on her coat determined to go out searching for him. Determined to get out there and find her boy.

'The police,' he says calmly. 'We need to call the police. He's run away again. He'll be out there somewhere, licking his wounds.' His voice has a slight tremble to it, the only sign that he is as anxious as she is. The only sign that he feels it too – the deep-seated worry, the terror that something terrible is about to take place.

As it turns out, there's no need to contact the police. The knock at the door only minutes after Ralph unbuttons his coat sends Chrissie into a near swoon. She knows then as any mother would know. She can tell by the heavy rapping, the dark shadows that their figures cast on the path, the silence in the room as she and Ralph watch each other cautiously, that the moment has come.

She just knows.

17

PRESENT DAY

Leah's eviction is imminent. Only yesterday, Grainne gave her just forty-eight hours to get her things packed and sorted before she is out on the street.

Leah scuttles around her room, kicking clothes aside, going around in circles, too tired, too confused to do anything constructive. Too bloody traumatised and shocked to do anything at all. It won't happen. She is not about to be made homeless. She won't let it happen. She's better than this. Everybody deserves a second chance, don't they? Even her.

She could go to her parents for help but isn't sure of the welcome she would receive. She thinks back to the last time she spoke to them. Tears prick at her eyes as she sits on the edge of the bed, her mind raking over those memories; memories she would sooner forget. She had visited them at home, doing her best to remain civil, but it didn't last long.

The subject of her brother's death came up and their conversation descended into chaos with insults being hurled around about how she knew that they had never really loved her and how she would have been better off with her biological parents. That one had stung. She could see it in her mother's face, in her eyes that had filled with unshed tears as the words hit her. Too late by then. No taking them back. Words once said, can never be unsaid. If only she had thought of that before she unleashed her invective on her already exhausted and permanently distressed parents. There was no need for it, she could see that at the time but felt unable to stop, standing there instead, spewing out years of bile that had festered deep within her.

She knew then that she was damaged goods. She still had enough insight to know that her behaviour wasn't driven by revenge or a sense of not belonging. It was just a part of who she was. Plenty of people were adopted, she knew that, and plenty of them, like her, didn't find out until later in life, but it didn't make them do and say the things that she did. Sometimes, she just couldn't help herself.

The growing ache in her abdomen causes her to bend double. She clutches onto her stomach, closes her eyes against the wave of pain that stops her in her tracks, preventing her from thinking clearly. This is her punishment. She is sure of it. A streak of never-ending pain that cuts her in half. She deserves this and more. It's a vicious circle. She is caught up in a perpetual cycle of anger, pain, resentment and more anger. It's pointless fighting it. It's like trying to stop the wind and the rain or attempting to catch air. Better to go with it than rail against it. Too exhausting to put a halt to who she is, who she has always been. She's hardwired to be mean and vindictive. It's embedded in her brain, the pathways well and truly furrowed, too deep to ever be erased.

Clutching her belly, Leah leans over towards her bedside cabinet and grabs hold of her keys. If Grainne thinks she is going to make her homeless, she can think again. Leah still has enough money to get a copy made of her own set of keys. There is no way Grainne is going to do this. Not a hope in hell. She will fight her every step of the way. There has to be a law against throwing people out on the street. Tenants have rights, don't they? And landlords have a duty of care to their tenants to make sure those rights aren't impinged upon.

Leah slumps back, her body weary, her mind sick and tired of all the drama. She is all out of energy and patience. Everything feels so fragile at the minute, her health, her mind, her very existence. There is one thing however that she is sure of, has never been more certain of actually, and it is that she is not going anywhere soon. There is no way she is leaving this flat. Not a chance. She may have her faults but she is not about to sleep in the gutter with the druggies and the alcoholics and the ne'er do wells. She is better than that, has more about her. She sits for a second controlling her breathing, steadying her nerves. Telling herself that this too will pass.

She closes her eyes, just for a second, to blot out the nasty stuff, to make plans for her future. The pain increases. She lets out a deep shaky breath, thinks about Will and Ellis and Jacob, about her place in their lives and what she means, or meant to them and whether or not any of them really care or ever cared about her.

Searing, eye-watering pain, a terrible noise, then more darkness.

~

She is standing outside Jacob's front door. As always, she has no memory of getting here. She just knows that she cannot stop thinking about him. Desperation and dread eat at her, gnawing at her insides, making her feel sick with the power they have over her. She has to see him, to tell him how much she misses him, to let him know that her life has collapsed since their break-up and that she can no longer function without him. He was the only stable force in her life and now he has gone and she is rudderless, staggering from one calamity to another. She needs his help. She needs him. She is frantic about the direction her life is taking and needs his solidity and guidance to help her through every day. She thought she was better than this, stronger, more capable, but obviously not. Without Jacob, she is nothing.

Raising her fist, she hammers at his door, not caring who sees or hears her. Sobs wrack her body as she prepares to see his beautiful welcoming face, to fall into his arms and spill out her story to him. Then he'll understand. Once he hears what she is going through he will relent and let her back into his life. She can sense it. His defences will be down once he sees her, every fibre of his being knowing, just *knowing* that they are meant to be together.

The door opens and through her blurred vision, Leah can just about make out the shocked expression on his face as he sees her standing there, distressed and dishevelled. She braces herself, waits for the inevitable backing down, the invitation for her to go inside. He will sit her down. They will talk rationally like the reasonable adults that they are and everything will be perfect again.

His brusque manner immediately bruises her already fragile state of mind. 'Leah? Jesus, not again. What now? What the hell do you want now?' His eyes darken, his brow furrowing into a deep, ugly crease.

More tears flow. Her body weakens, folding in on itself as she listens to his words. Words she didn't expect to hear. Words that cut her to the core. She thought he was better than this. She thought they were better than this. 'I need to speak to you, Jacob. We have to sort this out. I can't go on without you.'

He shakes his head. She watches aghast as he dismisses her so readily, so thoughtlessly. This is not how it was meant to be. She has plans for them both. Had plans. Judging by the look on his face, she can see that his mind is already made up. He is shutting her out, closing the door on everything they ever had.

A rasping hiccup escapes out of her chest. There's a reason for his manner, for discarding her so quickly, so cruelly. There has to be. And she knows exactly what it is.

Chloe. Again. Always Chloe. Always her.

She is the one who is driving him to act this way, the one who is behind his abrupt offhand manner. This isn't him. This isn't the Jacob she knows. He is under Chloe's influence and can't even see it for himself. He is blind to what she is doing to him. He needs Leah. She's the only one who can rescue him from that woman's toxic clutches. He just doesn't know it yet, can't see it for himself. But he will soon enough.

'Leah, this needs to stop. I'm busy. You're busy. We have lives. Please go away.' His words are cutting, his tone sharp and unforgiving.

Leah sobs once more, doing her utmost to control her weeping and failing miserably. She is under no illusions as to how dreadful she looks. Her hair is scraped back into a messy ponytail, strands escaping and hanging in front of her eyes. She isn't wearing any make-up and isn't even sure when she last washed her face or showered. Yesterday perhaps, or maybe even last week. Once again, her grasp of time fails her. No matter how hard she tries, it remains a slippery elusive thing, refusing to be pinned down.

'I need to speak to you, Jacob. Please. All I want is five minutes of your time. That's all I ask.' Her throat is sore, her head is throbbing. Can he not see how absurdly desperate she is? How so very close to the edge she is? Or is he so utterly devoid of emotion after pairing up with Chloe that all reason and humanity has deserted him? She would like to think not. That's not the Jacob she knows and loves. Her memories of him are of a kind, considerate man, a man who had time for others, always putting the needs of friends and family before his own. That's her Jacob, the one she wants back. Not this distant creature standing before her, his face creased with disgust.

'I have to go now. I'm working away for the rest of this week and I have stuff to prepare. Please just leave here, go home and do whatever it is you do in your spare time. Just leave me alone. I've had enough.'

The slam of the door is loud enough to put a stop to her crying, brutal enough to freeze her blood and make her heart jump around her chest like a rubber ball. She shivers, a chill settling on her exposed flesh, freezing her skin and causing her to shake uncontrollably. Shock. She's in shock. That's all it is. She has psyched herself up for a half decent conversation, one that could possibly even heal their relationship and now she has quite literally been left out in the cold by the only person she has ever cared about. This is not how it played out in her head. She had hoped for a positive outcome; something better than this. She hoped for warmth and understanding and instead has been subjected to a cold unfeeling dismissal.

Pulling her cardigan around her shoulders, she turns away from the door, the ground sloping under her feet as she makes her way back home. The laughter and cries of children from the nearby park catapult her back to her childhood, another miserable time. Apart from her time spent with Jacob, has there ever been a juncture in her life when she has been truly happy? It's as if she has been blighted from birth; a misfit, a social pariah. The unwanted. She doesn't want to wallow in self-pity – it's an ugly look – but whether she likes it or not, it's a fact. At one point she had Jacob and now there's just her. Leah Browne, wading through this shitty time, this low ebb in her life with nobody by her side to prop her up and keep her going.

She pushes her shoulders back and takes a few deep breaths. *Well, fuck them. Fuck them all.* All the people who have shoved her aside and trodden on her without giving her a second thought, they can all go to hell. The time has come for her to show some resilience, for her to scoop back some of her dignity. And she is going to enjoy it too. Jacob doesn't even realise it but he has just inadvertently given her the opportunity to turn this unholy mess around.

By the time she gets back home, she is practically bouncing. She had forgotten how it feels to be fired up with excitement as opposed to being permanently riddled with misery and shame. Nothing and nobody is going to blacken her mood today. She won't allow it. Even Grainne with her idle threats of eviction doesn't frighten her now.

She has something to look forward to, a task to be getting on with. And what a task it is. Fizzing with anticipation, she unlocks the door, flops on the unmade bed and lets out a bark of laughter that echoes around the room.

18

Will watches Leah carefully, his scrutinous gaze making her feel uncomfortable. She's never quite sure what it is he wants from her, or why she is even here. She tries to stand up but feels that weight again, pressing her back onto the chair.

She stays put, her body rigid, her abdomen once again aching, the pain cutting her in two.

'I'm trying to help you, Leah. We've spoken about this before, remember? Just try to relax and everything will be fine.' His soft reassuring voice travels across the room. It should soothe her but it doesn't.

Something isn't right. A thought won't leave her be. A memory that keeps on jabbing, poking, reminding her of what she did. How could she? *How could she?*

She tries to swat it away, the rogue memory, but it's a potent force, refusing to withdraw, prodding her, swatting at her, making her remember. Forcing her to. Leah shivers, shuts her eyes, swallows hard.

'Just stay calm, Leah. Stay awake and talk to me. What's troubling you?'

Her breathing is uneven, ragged, difficult to control. She's starting to hyperventilate and needs to stop it, to slow everything down. She needs to stay in control or she runs the risk of spilling all her secrets out to this man, this *stranger* sitting right here in front of her.

'Nothing,' she says, her voice a whisper. Every word she utters seems to come from the pit of her belly, scratching its way up out into the open. Her voice sounds hollow and distorted. And what is troubling her is anything but nothing. It is everything. What she did, what she said was, and still is, *everything* and now it is all coming back to haunt her. This is her time to repent, to apologise for all the bad things she has done. All of them.

'How are you feeling? Everything okay?'

She doesn't respond, is too frightened to do or say anything. Her throat tightens. Her head throbs. She thinks of Ellis. Everything is unspooling, coming undone. Her mind is falling to pieces.

And then it happens; the tears she has been holding back, finally fall.

'I was just thinking of my brother.' She lets out a strangled cry, rummages for a tissue in her pocket, finds nothing.

Will's hand looms in front of her as he gives her a large white handkerchief. She wipes her eyes, dabs at her face, pulls it away and lets out a guttural shriek. The handkerchief is covered in blood; thick globules of red liquid smeared over the linen, dripping through her fingers, splashing onto her legs. Small concentric circles of the darkest ruby, spreading across the fabric of her trousers, pooling on the seat beneath her. She can hardly breathe, her windpipe clasping shut as she stares at the growing scarlet shapes swirling in front of her eyes, like a flower in bloom, its petals slowly unfurling, their colours bright and vivid. Sickly red patterns that turn her stomach.

She lets out a choking scream, closes her eyes. Forces them open again.

To see nothing.

Everything is back to normal. No handkerchief and definitely no blood. Where are they – the bright smears, the trailing clots of cherry red blood. Where have they gone?

Leah glances over at Will who is still there, sitting in his usual position, watching her, observing her every move. Assessing her to see if she breaks. She says nothing, just watches and waits for him to speak first. She is afraid that if she opens her mouth, every secret she has ever kept will come pouring out, a stream of dreadful lies, a lifetime of repulsive deeds.

So she stays silent and concentrates on her breathing instead. She thinks that perhaps it's time to leave here, to stop the turbulence in her head before she breaks down and reveals one secret too many, her mouth refusing to stay shut as her brain unleashes her demons. The longer she sits, the more likely it is that she will speak without caution and those confidences, once cracked open, will poison the very air that they breathe.

'Do you want to talk about your brother? Are you ready for that yet?'

Leah's head throbs. She shakes it to indicate that she doesn't want to talk about him. About what she did to him, about what he did to himself. It's too painful. Even thinking about it hurts. A discomfort so strong, so overwhelming, it feels as if it has become part of who she is. It's there all the time, has taken root under her skin and is chiselled deep into her bones.

'How did he die, Leah? Tell me how he died. I think it's time now, don't you?'

She can't stop the tremble in her hands, her head, her legs. She is shaking uncontrollably. Is Will right? Is it now time to speak out about it? She wants to, she really does, but can't seem to find the right words. Even in her head they sound ugly, ill-fitting. How can she possibly go about telling him what happened that day up on the cliff? How she ruined everything.

She was angry. Always angry. Angry at her parents, angry at her brother, furious at the world in general. School was shit, with few friends. Home, after discovering that certificate, suddenly felt like a hostile place. She was disenfranchised, left out in the cold. All she did was lash out and it caused a deep dark vortex in their family, sucking them all under, dragging them down to the bottom of the earth, down with all the grit and mud and filth.

And then there was that day, that knock on the door. Those policemen standing there, telling her mother what no parent should ever have to hear. Losing Lucy was bad enough. Her parents and little Lucy's parents had suffered enough, but somebody somewhere decided that that was just the beginning and they kept the hatred and hurt going. There was no end to it. Still isn't. It just goes on and on and on.

And it's all her fault.

She knows that but can't seem to stop it. Hatred and hurt follow her about, straggling behind her like a thickset shadow, corrupting everything and everyone she comes into contact with. She's toxic. Always has been.

'How did Ellis die? You need to say it out loud, Leah, to get it off your chest. It's bothering you, we both know that. Since the accident everything you have ever done has preyed on your mind, hasn't it? Perhaps the time has come to clear the air, to start again with a clean slate.'

She looks at Will. Did he just say those words or was the voice only in her head? Her heart beats fast, too quickly. She feels dizzy, can hear her own blood as it rushes through her veins, roaring through her ears, gushing, pummelling against the thin skin of her neck.

'The police came,' she says, swallowing over and over, almost choking on her own saliva. 'He was late home from school. He'd had a fight. The school had called and spoken to my mother about it. She rang them back when he didn't arrive home and they assured her that he'd left at the normal time and that they hadn't seen him after that. She called his mobile, but it was switched off. I came in and she asked me if I'd seen him.'

'What did you say? Had you seen him?'

'I can't remember exactly what I said but I know that it was horrible. I was still furious with them all. And anyway, he was older than me. It should have been him looking out for me, not the other way around!' She's unsure how to handle this, this unplanned revelation and finds herself deflecting the blame away from her own failings.

That's what you do. It's what you've always done.

Leah spins around, searching for the voice. She sees nobody, holds her breath and stares at Will.

'And what happened next?'

'Next? I watched my mother open the door, saw the police enter, and I hid in my room. Then–'

'Then?' Will asks, a little too calmly. 'What happened after that, Leah? What happened next?'

'Then they spoke to my mother and said those words that no parent should ever have to hear. There was a couple of seconds of silence, maybe longer. It felt like it went on for forever. Then she screamed. My mother screamed and screamed and screamed. I stayed in my room, hiding from it all, and then I heard it – the sickening bang as my mother fell to the floor and sobbed.'

19

2005

He empties his mind on the way there. It's the only way he can go through with it. He doesn't want his brain to be filled with the clutter of everyday life. What he's about to do is a significant thing. It warrants a period of quiet reflection. It's critical that he does this thing with a clear head. No distractions. Nothing that may force him to change his mind.

The sun's weak rays warm his back as he passes through the park and heads over the bridge, stopping to listen to the hiss of the vehicles below. Even the thunderous roar of rush hour traffic doesn't displease him. In fact, he rather enjoys standing there, watching cars passing underneath his feet. He ponders over where they are all going to, where they've come from, what their lives are like, whether they are happy with their lot in life or whether, like him, they are entrenched in an existence of complete misery. He hopes not. He hopes they are happy. Despite not knowing any of them, he wishes them happiness and a good life. Everybody deserves contentment and a certain amount of joy in their lives, don't they?

Looking down over the edge to the dark asphalt beneath, at the traffic that pounds it relentlessly, he feels a bout of dizziness begin to muscle its way in. So many cars, so much speed. A snaking line of lights, brightly painted metal, road markings and tarmac that blur and twist as he watches from above, his eyes locked on the traffic, mesmerised by the energy and momentum. People holed up in cars, trucks, buses, all on their way to somewhere else. People clutching steering wheels, children in the back seat, arguing, crying, laughing. Truck drivers fighting exhaustion, bus drivers trying to stick to a rigid timetable. Car drivers desperate to get back to their neat little homes and their families and pets, more than ready for their evening meal, perhaps a beer or maybe a glass of wine. People, just ordinary people, that's all they are. All crammed together, and yet all very much alone.

Despite the initial dizziness, peering down over the side of the bridge doesn't frighten him. He relishes it, is giddy at the sight and sensation it gives him. When he and his sister were younger, their mother wouldn't allow them to walk over this way. She said that the handrails on the bridge weren't high enough and that the sound of the traffic below and the speed at which the vehicles travelled made her feel as if she was about to pass out.

He takes a deep breath, leans farther over and thinks about how it would feel to do that – to pass out right here, to lose control and fall onto the tarmac beneath, to feel the crack of your bones, the almighty smash of your skull as you hit the deck, to be pummelled and knocked about by car after car after car until there is nothing left of you but bits of torn and bloodied skin and a pile of broken bones, unrecognisable, even to those closest to you.

He smiles, picks up his pace and walks to the other side, safely away from the height and the speed and the noise and the danger. He stops at the end of the bridge and looks back. Not there. He wouldn't do it there. It's too obvious, too predictable.

He has other plans.

Instead, he walks into town, finds a bench and sits down. It's busy, everywhere crammed with commuters and shoppers, folk bustling past him, their faces lined with worry, their features creased with anger and exasperation. So many broken, miserable people. All in a hurry, no time for anything or anybody. Is this what life is supposed to be about? People simply finding a way to get by, a way to get through each day without giving up, only to go to their beds at night, blot it all out, then arise eight hours later and face the same problems the next day, their lives on repeat, their daily routines continuing ad nauseam. Misery heaped upon misery. Not a chink of light to be seen in their dark, forlorn existences. Isn't life supposed to be better than this – more fulfilling, more pleasurable? More frigging rewarding? And if not, then why not? Even with his problems, he looks happier than this lot. What is the matter with them, all these stricken people? Why don't they smile, nod at passers-by, do anything at all to look as if they're actually glad to be alive? He focuses on one lady, sees her as she moves past, her head dipped, too low to acknowledge anybody around her. He tries to catch her eye, to smile at her, show her a friendly face but she is oblivious and rushes past, gone before he can say or do anything. Do these people not realise how lucky they are, how easy they have it, how fucking privileged they are to actually be here? There are hospitals full of ill people – patients dying, children with terminal diseases, grasping onto life for as long as they can and yet these people stagger around town as if they're carrying the weight of the world on their shoulders.

He thinks of his sister and her permanent frown, her own dark cloud of misery that follows her wherever she goes. Maybe that would be the kick up the arse that she needs – to visit a hospital ward for the chronically ill, make her realise how lucky she is to have the life that she does. Then he thinks that perhaps it would make no difference to her, that she is probably beyond redemption, her blackened heart too stone-like to ever soften to the woes of others. She's too wrapped up in her own little cocoon of discontentment and anger, blind to the needs of anybody else to ever care.

He sits, watching, thinking, working it all out. Life is a tricky path to navigate, there's no denying that. It's a mish-mash of everything – people, emotions, events. And there are no set rules, no handy guidebooks to help people work their way through the shit that gets thrown their way. No wonder they tear about in their cars trying to escape it all, crazed, desperate people, looking for somewhere to hide, somewhere better than where they actually are.

A pigeon struts near to where he sits, pecking the leftovers of somebody's lunch – a half empty sandwich packet and a handful of stale crisps. His heart surges, feeling a flutter of joy as a smaller bird lands next to him and joins in the feast. He's always loved animals and has wanted a pet for as long as he can remember. Possibly a dog even though he knows his mother wouldn't ever entertain the idea. Too messy, too much fur. Too smelly. It's good to dream though. He'll definitely have his own when he's older and gets his own place, and he'll call it Gandalf. The dog that is, not the house. He chuckles softly to himself, the sound of his own laughter feeling good in his throat. He doesn't care what type of dog; he isn't fussy. It would just love him and he would love it in return. That's what life is supposed to be about – love and compassion and being happy and making others feel the same way. He knows that now. He's always known it. It's just that sometimes things get muddled in his head, everything too difficult to fathom.

He sits for a while longer, thinking, watching. Something happens; a twist in his gut, an about-turn in his thinking. A full 360 degrees. Like an epiphany. He isn't sure what has caused it.

Maybe it's sitting observing the world go by or maybe it was the walk over the bridge, or maybe it was thinking about nature and animals and the love they give freely and unconditionally that has made him think again, made him value life and everything it has to offer. Perhaps it was all of those things, seeing birds sharing their food, seeing all the pained expressions of the people passing by, scrutinising their features, the features that displayed nothing but torment and sadness and misery. It has unexpectedly transformed his outlook, completely altered his thinking.

Life isn't that bad. He isn't that bad, despite what friends and neighbours may think of him. And more importantly, he doesn't want to be like the people he has seen today, to be a part of that sea of miserable faces. He wants to be happy, to be free of worry and guilt. Ending everything isn't the answer. Staying to make this life better, is. If he runs away from every problem that he encounters then how will he ever be able to move on from this, grow into a better person, a more rounded person? He needs to face this head on, prove to the world that he isn't a bad person, that he is resilient, compassionate, caring. That he is all of those things and more. Which he is. What he isn't, is a murderer. Far from it. He is a young man with feelings and needs and thoughts and ambitions who is trying his best to fit in.

The waning heat still warms him through, caressing the skin on the back of his neck. He stands up, startling the birds who flap their wings furiously heading for the sycamore trees that frame the perimeter of the park.

He walks on, enjoying the moment, thinking how strange life is, that one minute he is about to give up to end all the misery and heartache he has endured and now here he is, glad to be alive, consumed with relief. He feels as if he has been led to the gallows only to be given a last-minute reprieve. He isn't one of those commuters, wracked with misery, unable to get off the hamster wheel. He has options. How he chooses to deal with the hand that life deals him is completely down to him. That's what he didn't realise earlier. He is the one in control. He is the master of his own destiny, and boy does it feel good. A weight has been lifted. He is lighter than air.

He heads down Sutton Street, onto Station Approach stopping to listen to the rattle of the trains as they enter and exit the platform. That was his original destination – those tracks, those cold, hard, unforgiving lengths of metal – they were his plan, his way out of this mess, to lie down there and let the darkness consume him. That was where he could have ended up. But not now. Now he will head back. Back to his parents, his sister, his friends. Back to his home. That's where he belongs. Not here in the middle of the city amid flocks of angry strangers, all desperate to be on their way to somewhere else. He is struck with an overwhelming desire to simply go home.

~

There were no witnesses, that was the problem. Nobody who could say what actually took place that afternoon, so assumptions were made. More tongues clacked, putting two and two together and once again being completely incorrect when they came up with five. They all thought they knew. They had the backstory; a young lad accused of a terrible crime, coming to terms with his guilt. What else was there to say? There would be talk that he had been unable to live with what he had done, that the guilt became too much for him to bear. And that is exactly what did happen. They went ahead with their vicious stories without any credible evidence. Evidence is for forensic teams. All they craved was gossip and tittle-tattle. What they didn't know, they managed to fill in with their own suppositions and lies, blanks in the story filled by the loose lips of locals.

It happened as he took a different route back. Drawn to the station by the hiss and screeching of the trains, the slightly rubbery smell that permeated the air, he decided to take a quick look. He had loved railway stations ever since he was a young kid. They reminded him of holidays with his family. He remembered the excitement, the butterflies in his stomach as they boarded, bustling their way down the narrow aisles to their seats, having a table between him and his sister, his father pulling out a pack of cards to keep them entertained on the journey, his mother opening the foil that contained their homemade sandwiches.

Even the CCTV footage couldn't determine the truth of the events of that day. He was just a shadowy figure, a silhouette who fell. Another tragedy. Another body. Another light snuffed out.

Stepping onto the platform, he felt positive, buoyed up by the thoughts that had settled in his brain; good thoughts, happy thoughts. Not the blackness he had become mired in of late. He had seen a chink of light, been given a helping hand out of the shadows and back into the sunshine.

'Not here to see The Flying Scotsman, are you lad?'

He felt his heart soar, nodded and widened his eyes. Talk about good luck. He had no idea it was passing through. The man standing next to him patted his arm, smiled and shook his head. 'You've just missed it I'm afraid, laddie. Sorry about that.' The man gave a weak, apologetic smile and started to walk away, then turned and spoke once more. 'You might catch it next week on its journey back.'

A hammering filled the lad's chest. Next week. He would do that. It would be worth the wait. He could walk into town and stand on this platform with his camera, watching, waiting. He would be prepared. It was something to look forward to. A reason to keep going. A reason to be here.

He watched as the older man exited the platform, trailing behind the crowd of camera carrying people, leaving him alone. In the distance, he heard the familiar rush of metal against metal, the sound that sent butterflies spinning in his belly, and stepped forward to catch a glimpse of the oncoming train. Not The Flying Scotsman but a fast moving train nonetheless. If he got close enough to the edge of the platform, he could capture it as it passed through and hopefully get a good shot of its sleek body, that gleaming paintwork that never failed to make his skin prickle with delight. His love of photography had fallen by the wayside since that day, swallowed up by the misery and the accusations. Anything worth doing, all the things he used to love, crashed and burned once his life took on this unexpected turn. He had no interest anymore, no energy for them. He would turn all that around. Once he got back home, he would go back to playing football, going out with his camera, downloading music. Back to doing anything he wanted.

Fuelled by a sudden surge of adrenaline, he dug into his pocket, fumbling around, trying to free his phone. They weren't allowed mobiles in school, but nobody ever took any notice. They were only phones, for God's sake. He had hidden it in the lining of his old school trousers, deep in his secret pocket, switched off unless he wanted to take a picture or send a message. And now the damn thing was stuck, snarled up in torn fabric and strands of cotton.

Tugging to retrieve it, he took a step forward, aware that time was against him, aware that the train was just passing through and not stopping to pick up passengers. He took one more step closer, wanting to be at the edge of the concrete platform when it passed, then another, staggering as he lunged, his feet becoming tangled together, a sheen of sweat coating his skin as he realised what was happening. What was about to happen. His hand was lodged in his pocket, trapped between the lining as he tried to extricate his mobile from the snarl of cotton. He tried to right himself, struggling to regain his balance as his feet locked together and twisted beneath him.

Too late. His hand sprang free from his pocket, his fingers slippery with perspiration. The phone remained hidden deep within his clothing. As if pushed by an invisible hand, he was propelled forwards, unable to control his own body movements, unable to stop the fall, his unwanted descent into a world of nothingness.

He didn't feel anything. It was all too fast, his bid to stop his staggering movements all too late. The metallic screech of brakes as the train ground to an unplanned halt was a sickening sound, filling the emptiness of the station, reverberating and bouncing off the bare brick walls. The echo of death.

Afterwards, police scrutinising the footage simply saw a lone figure, a silhouette struggling at the edge of the platform before jumping close to the edge and tipping forwards into the path of the oncoming train. Nobody knew what was going through his head before the impact. But people guessed, incorrect theories were tossed about, lies told, stories made up to feed the frenzied masses. They thought they knew, were convinced of it. They knew nothing.

The funeral was a private affair. His family gathered in the church, heads bowed, tension rippling through them. Grief tearing them apart. It was their lowest point. They thought that Maria's premature death then Lucy's horrific demise was as bad as it could get; yet here they were again, in the same church, seated in the same pews, listening to yet another eulogy of a child who should be at home with his family, not lying cold and alone in a stiff oak casket.

His parents held hands, unable to think, unable to voice their grief, their terror at spending the remainder of their lives without their son. Another child lost.

They still had a daughter. A troubled daughter. But they clung onto the fact that they still had a child. She was difficult, damaged; yet still easy to love and hard to dislike despite all her issues and anger. She was theirs and always would be.

The boy's father squeezed his wife's hand. Just the three of them now. They would make it work. They had to. No choice now their boy was gone. The girl was all they had. She was their life, everything they ever wanted, even though they didn't feel as if they were a part of hers. Soon she would come round, soften, her fury dissipating as time moved on. She couldn't stay angry at them for forever, could she? At some point she would weaken, her hatred for them melting away to reveal her softer side. The part that used to love them.

It was time to start again, to forget the past, to move on, wipe away all the grime and rage that had festered for so long in their little family unit. It was all behind them. A new fresh wind was blowing through the cobwebs of their past and they had to embrace it or crumple under the strain.

They knew what choice they would make. All of their love would be directed towards their remaining child.

Whether she wanted it or not.

20

PRESENT DAY

Leah is lying on her bed listening to Grainne screeching outside her door. It's easier to pretend she can't hear her. That's the only way she can deal with it – by blocking it out. Pretending it isn't happening is far less stressful than trying to dig herself out of the hole she has found herself in.

Grainne kicked her out three days ago. The backdated rent Grainne requested didn't magically appear so she did some poking around and exposed Leah's lies. Her quiet, middle-class landlady was quite the detective and confronted her over the purported death of her parents. Leah winced as she listened to Grainne's outburst. Hearing her own terrible, desperate lies thrown back at her wasn't the easiest thing to stomach. She had watched and waited, meekly handing over her keys as Grainne finished, her face flushed with the effort of being so angry, so completely out of control.

'What sort of sick fuck would tell people her parents were dead when they're still alive? What the hell is wrong with you, Leah?' Grainne had shouted, her usual poise absent. For all she was prone to swearing and cursing, Grainne still had a way about her that exuded charm, precision and reserve. That had evaporated as soon as she discovered Leah's lies. She insisted that Leah pack her belongings while Grainne stood over her, watching her throw a few measly items into a bag. Leah owned more things than she had realised, most of them unnecessary which made loading up her bag a lot easier. She only took what she needed and left the junk for Grainne to sort out. Served her right for being such a cold, calculating bitch.

Leah hadn't intended to use the extra keys she had had cut to let herself back in the house, but sleeping rough was far worse than she ever anticipated. She spent the first night with an old acquaintance who offered her the sofa after Leah knocked on her door tousled and distraught. She and Daisy had worked together for a few years and occasionally kept in touch. They weren't exactly friends but neither were they enemies. Daisy had a kind heart and even as she knocked at her door, Leah knew that Daisy would let her in. Telling her that she had had an argument with her boyfriend and just needed a warm bed and friendly face, Daisy had cocked her head compassionately, offered her sympathies and stepped aside to let Leah into her house.

The next morning, Daisy had explained that she was having family over to stay and had stood, watching Leah as she lay on the sofa, waiting for her response. That was her cue to go. Leah doubted the story about the family visit but wasn't about to challenge her. The sofa had been appreciated and she left, thanking Daisy, insisting they meet up for a drink, knowing it would never happen. It was a weak platitude, a way of thanking Daisy for giving her a roof over her head on a cold wet evening.

The second night, she spent wandering around town, waiting for the sun to come up. Every shadow, every sharp movement of the local wildlife had had her nerves jangling, her brain screaming at her to move away. And so she had walked and walked and walked. That was the only way to stem her innate fear of being attacked while she slept, the only way to stop the lethargy from setting in. By the time it was light she had a blinding headache from lack of sleep and her mouth felt like somebody had tipped the contents of a dustbin into it. She washed in the local public toilets and swilled her mouth out with cold water.

Rummaging in the bottom of her bag, she had discovered a £20 note. Her stomach had flipped with excitement at such a lucky find. She bought herself a toothbrush and toothpaste, and managed to book a room in a hostel, shutting out all thoughts of what she would do once the tiny amount of money ran out.

The hostel smelt like a discarded old shoe and had a stream of undesirables trailing in and out at all hours. The room was £8 a night and the mattress felt and smelled like there was a decomposing body tucked inside it. Sharp lumps and bumps dug into her spine every time she turned over. But it was better than a park bench, better than wandering around the town in the darkness praying for daylight to break.

She knew the next morning after spending a night in a noisy, damp room that bordered on squalid, that she would use her key and let herself back into her old room. Grainne was at work. She could salt herself away, make as little noise as possible, be the soul of discretion. It was doubtful there was a new tenant living there in such a short space of time. All she needed was a few days until she sorted herself out, just a few days to get her problems fixed.

And now here she is, being abused and hollered at for simply wanting somewhere to sleep at night. Curling up on her side, Leah closes her eyes, squeezing them shut against Grainne's constant haranguing. She places her hands over her ears and rocks backwards and forwards, unsure what to do next. Would Grainne really do something as drastic as removing the door and dragging her out into the street, or worse still, calling the police and having her arrested for trespassing? Somehow, Leah can't see any of that happening. For all of her threats, appearances still matter to Grainne. She has boundaries and levels of decorum to maintain.

Unlike Leah, there are certain depths to which she refuses to stoop. They may not be friends but Leah knows Grainne, knows her standards of etiquette and social graces and screaming at people in the street and having the police call around to forcibly haul somebody out of her house isn't something she would do.

She continues to ignore the wall of noise, to slip into a state of unconsciousness where nothing and nobody matters or exists. Only darkness, a dense blanket of nothingness.

~

'Do you blame yourself for what happened?' She is in Will's office, uncertain of how she got here but then, isn't that always the case? Being on unsure ground is who she is lately. Her life is a see-saw, her mind unable to grasp the simplest of concepts. She oscillates from one thing to another with no idea of how the transition occurred. She is a traveller moving through time and space with no sense of direction, unconstrained by the usual binds.

Perhaps she is losing her mind? Perhaps in reality she is safely locked away in a mental health unit and this is her subconscious self, attempting to make sense of it all. The thought makes her shiver.

'Sort of,' she replies, her voice croaky as she finds herself opening up to ideas and thoughts that she has had locked down for so many months and years that allowing them to be free is like a physical blow to her body.

'Okay, this is good. You're making progress but we still have some way to go before you're completely better.' Will's voice is gentle and comforting. For once she feels relaxed, not trapped in some sort of feverish state, worried that her life is about slip away from her and that she has to grip on to it with both hands so she doesn't lose it. Opening up to this man suddenly feels like the right thing to do.

'Ellis was only a teenager when he died. Far too young. It was beyond traumatic for my parents. They died along with him.'

'They still had you though, didn't they?'

Leah's heart crawls up her throat. Why has he made that comment? It has so many connotations and possible meanings behind it. Then she remembers that he doesn't know. Will has no idea about her secret, her dark rotten secret. The one she created herself that has her in its clutches, refusing to let her go.

She sighs, tries to stop the quiver in her fingers, hoping for the searing pain in her abdomen to subside. 'I wasn't the best daughter to them. Hardly a model child and not much better as an adult.'

Will nods as if he understands when Leah knows that he doesn't. He can't. How can he possibly understand what she is saying or understand how she functions as a person when she doesn't even understand it herself?

'I'm a bad daughter,' Leah whispers, her throat closing with the effort of speaking. 'A bad person all round. I say and do horrible things and I have no idea why.'

The air in the room is thick with anticipation; her flesh crawls and chills. This is who she is. Time to own up to it. No more hiding, no more pretending to be somebody she isn't. Her mask is finally slipping to reveal the real Leah Browne underneath.

She looks over at Will who appears to be immersed in his own thoughts. Did he hear what she has just said? Is he even remotely interested in her admission or is this scenario just some sort of warped role play they go through to make her feel better? More tears gather. She squeezes her eyes shut, trying to stop them from falling. Her efforts are useless. Hot tears cascade down her face as she speaks, warming up her cold flesh.

'My brother took his own life and I'm to blame for it.' She drags her gaze away from Will, suddenly too embarrassed to see his expression as she reveals what she did. 'There was an accident. We were on holiday, having a picnic up on the clifftop and the daughter of my parents' friends fell over the edge. I told everybody it was Ellis, my brother, who pushed her. I said he had shouted at her and that he did it deliberately.' Leah wipes at her eyes with her sleeve, rubbing at her face fiercely with her fist. 'Lucy was a little girl. Just a kid. A small helpless child and I told everybody that Ellis, my fifteen-year-old brother, had killed her.'

She is sobbing now, her face swollen and red, blotchy with remorse and humiliation. Will is a blur in her peripheral vision, his features indistinguishable amid the unrelenting flow of tears. She can't stop. So many years of holding them back and now the floodgates have opened, she is drowning, struggling to stay afloat in her own tsunami of misery.

Leah stops, waiting for him to interject, to come out with something that will make her feel better, a pearl of wisdom designed to heal her gaping bleeding wounds, but he says nothing. His silence is worse than any words of retribution or anger or judgement. His silence says more than any words ever could.

She keeps her gaze fixed on the picture on his wall, knowing the next part of the story is the worst bit. As if anything could be worse than blaming her own brother for the death of a small child. But it is. It's far worse and she doesn't think she has the strength to even think about it let alone say it out loud. Instead, she sits, allowing herself to cry, allowing herself to feel regret and mortification at her actions instead of the hatred and resentment that has lived inside her for so many years. It's exhausting being permanently angry. She feels a hundred years old after everything she has endured, after everything she has put her family through. Too late now, though. It's all too late. Ellis is dead, Lucy is dead and she is the one who is responsible.

21

Leah had moved out of the family home at eighteen. Her mother and father didn't want her to go. She was too young, too naïve to cope with the many trials and tribulations of the world. She had neither the ability nor the resilience to cope on her own. Chrissie and Ralph had begged her to stay but their daughter's mind was made up. She had a decent brain and some good solid A-level results, but nothing else. And they couldn't let her leave with nothing. They just couldn't. They were her parents, she was their daughter, their baby. None of them deserved this outcome. They needed to soften it with something, make the move a little less painful. When they looked back at this moment, they wanted to be able to say that at least they tried.

On the day she left, they transferred £10,000 into her bank account. She never acknowledged receiving it, showing no gratitude, giving no words of thanks. But then, that was Leah all over. Not that they expected anything in return. Only her love, something she hid and displayed rarely. It gave them a small amount of comfort knowing that she had money enough to find somewhere to live. Chrissie and Ralph weren't wealthy people, but they had savings for a rainy day and with only one child, no Maria or Ellis, they were in a position to assist her wherever possible.

As far as they were aware, she stayed local, finding a flat somewhere in Durham, only a few miles from where they lived. They hoped to see her from time to time but weren't surprised when she didn't show her face. She broke any dates they made with her for lunch or an evening meal at their house. That's just how she was. Chrissie liked to believe it was because she was busy making a life for herself and was working or seeing friends. They could but hope.

Over ten years, they saw their daughter less than six times. Her final visit was the worst. Chrissie did her best to remain cheerful and upbeat despite it being the anniversary of Ellis's death. It was just bad timing, that's all it was. Leah had chosen to call around and see them uninvited. Not that she needed an invitation, but they simply weren't prepared and Leah took their surprised expressions and dour mood as an insult and was immediately slighted. Chrissie and Ralph had been getting ready to go to the graveyard to see Maria.

Venturing out to the beach to see Ellis was out of the question. It was a blustery day; the tide was in and neither of them was getting any younger. The walk up to the top of the cliff to pay their respects would have proved too much. They had the memory of their son tucked deep in their souls and that was enough for them. He was never far from their thoughts and always in their hearts. Ellis would have understood their absence on that day of all days. He had always liked visiting Maria at the cemetery and they kept that in mind as they got ready to go.

Leah walked in just as they were buttoning up their coats and the look on her face said it all. The fact that they dared to consider leaving the house just as she had arrived was enough to turn her mood around. She made a barbed comment about never being made to feel welcome and the conversation pretty much descended into the gutter from that point onwards.

Chrissie had tried to talk Leah around, calm her down and assure her that she was always welcome but nothing she said seemed to help.

'Do you know what?' Leah had shouted. 'I've spent my whole life on the sidelines of this family.' An interloper in her own family was how she described herself even though it couldn't be further from the truth.

Chrissie had tried to explain while Ralph had sat shaking his head, unable to take it in, wondering what they had done to deserve such venom and vitriol, wondering why their daughter hated them so much. There was no easy answer to that.

Leah always did have her own reasons, her own agenda. She danced to her own tune giving no thought to those around her. As a small girl it was one of her defining features and gave her a unique quality that people admired and found endearing, but as she grew older and became more resistant to change and to the ideas and thoughts of others, what began as a cute characteristic rapidly transformed into a stubborn streak that was increasingly difficult to deal with. And increasingly hard to forgive. Leah was anything but malleable.

'She's such a strong character,' Chrissie would say to friends. 'Somebody who knows her own mind, and that's just the way we like her.' But deep down they knew that their daughter was a difficult person with few friends.

That afternoon after many cross words, Leah stormed out, refusing to accept their explanations and requests for tolerance and forgiveness, and they didn't see her again.

Chrissie had, on occasion, spoken to Ralph about going to visit her, but they had no forwarding address after she moved flats. She considered transferring more money over to her daughter in the vain hope it would soften Leah's steely resolve but even that could have been taken as an insult. There was no knowing with her, no set rules. She was their daughter and they loved her, but she was an enigma and, most of the time, a complete stranger to them.

22

The front door is locked. Leah tries again to get her key to fit, pushing it in with sweaty trembling fingers and twisting the cold tiny piece of metal, but to no avail. Her head spins, panic gripping her. The ground is unsteady beneath her feet. Everything is coming apart, her safety net disappearing. Her life separating and unspooling. A spasm takes hold in her gut. Pulling at the handle is pointless. It's patently obvious that Grainne has kept good her threat and changed the locks.

Leah purses her lips, leans back on the big oak door and stares down the street. No sign of Grainne or Innes. As far as Leah can recall, she has only been out of the house for ten minutes. Maybe she's got that wrong. Perhaps it's been longer. It probably has. How would she know? Time is a hollow meaningless construct in her crumbling world.

She turns around, tugs at the handle, pulling and twisting, giving it one more go even though she knows it's futile. This is a pointless exercise. She is locked out. Exasperated, she throws her key into the tangle of shrubbery next to the bay window. It lands with a dull thunk in the deep undergrowth.

Damn, damn, damn!

Grainne has thrown Leah out on the street. The cold-hearted bitch has done it. The unthinkable has happened. She is homeless.

A rush of anger causes her chest to tighten and her head to ache. There are laws against this type of thing, there has to be. Leah thinks of the homeless people she passes, the ones slumped in shop doorways with their ragged sleeping bags and mangy looking dogs. The ones with skin like parchment, their bones protruding from their flesh, eyes sunk deep into their skulls; haunted and desperate, ghosts of their former selves. She is not one of them and never will be. She doesn't deserve this. Or maybe she does. She swats such thoughts away. A hundred ideas and thoughts race around her brain. She tries to grasp at them, to catch one that will help her out of this corner she has found herself in but nothing works. Perhaps this is it. Perhaps this is the part when everything comes to a painful juddering halt.

A thick low cloud scuds past, darkening the horizon, casting a grey shroud over the landscape and chilling the air. The tip-tap of raindrops echoes around her as the impending storm gathers momentum, bouncing off the tarmac like sharpened bullets.

She is soaked through within seconds, her clothes clinging to her skin. Still fighting back tears, Leah shivers violently, huddling for cover under the small canopy over the front door, wondering where the remainder of her belongings are. She has a memory of Grainne placing them next to the wheelie bins in the back garden with the threat of them being taken away if Leah didn't move them within the next few days. She has no idea what's in the bags, and has no desire to find out either. If she has managed without them for the past few months then they are obviously surplus to her needs and she can live without them. Those bags however, contain evidence of her life. What if somebody finds them and decides to have a rummage? They are her personal effects and although most of them undoubtedly contain nothing of any interest, some of them may reveal things she would rather stay hidden.

She stands, waiting for the rain to ease up, holding her hands out from under the canopy and up to the sky until she is sure it has stopped, then steps out and makes her way through the small, damp alleyway to the back garden.

Halfway down she stops and takes a few deep breaths to steady herself. She isn't, and never has been, prepared for this moment. She should have been, she knows that now, but her mind has been so fragmented, so hung up on Jacob and Chloe that she didn't see it coming. And now she has been caught on the back foot with no contingency plan, nowhere to go. Apart from one place, that is.

She grits her teeth, pursing her lips into a tight, thin line. This has been thrust upon her, this thing she is about to do. If somebody, months from now, were to ask her why she did what she did, at least she could lay bare her problems and say, *You see? This is what they reduced me to. They gave me no choice. They made me do it.*

Balling her fists, she makes her way into the back garden, a long stretch of lawn surrounded by neat borders filled with low-growing flowers and shrubs. It's typical Grainne – immaculate, tidy, perfectly manicured. On impulse, Leah strides over to one of the flower beds and tramples on the spread of small pink flowers that are just coming into bloom. Leaning down, she grabs a handful of petals and tears at them, ripping them apart with her wet fingers, enjoying the sensation of the damp silken petals as they mash together in her palm. With each consecutive trample and tear, she feels some of her dignity being restored. It's the only bit of power she has left. She is determined to use it well.

By the time she finishes, Grainne's perfect garden is ruined.

Leah stops, catches her breath and surveys the area. Her heart begins to patter around her chest, moving up her throat as she inspects the damage. She hadn't meant to do so much harm and destroy so many of the plants and flowers. She was upset and now look at what she has done. Once again, she has lost control without realising it. Swallowing down her fears and any thoughts she has of Grainne sending her a bill to replace her precious plants and shrubs, Leah walks over to the neat line of wheelie bins and peers behind them. Her things are still there – everything she owns slotted into black bin liners, tied up in a neat tight knot. This is the sum total of her life – her belongings, everything she owns, dumped outside with the rubbish, exposed to the elements and left to rot.

She looks at her possessions. It's pointless grabbing them. She doesn't have anywhere to take them. Once she has sorted out a place to live she can come back, pick up the bags. She only hopes Grainne doesn't dispose of them. Leah takes a glance at the garden she has just decimated and feels a flutter in her chest, knowing she can kiss goodbye to everything she owns once Grainne sees this mess. Anything of any value, she'll have to sell to pay for this damage.

Wiping her wet palms down the side of her trousers, Leah leans over the top of the bins and attempts to push her things farther back, well out of view, closer to a large bush where they will be concealed. If she can shove them into the shrubbery, perhaps Grainne won't see anything untoward and she can come back for them another time when she's ready.

Only one particularly bulky bag doesn't fit. Leah leaves it alone, slumped against the wheelie bin. Placing it next to the shrubbery will make Grainne more inclined to start rummaging, giving her the chance to discover the rest of Leah's things. Next to the bin looks less suspicious, unmoved and untouched.

She unties it and peers in, a smile spreading over her face.

Inside is a pile of old clothes she no longer wears and a couple of battered handbags that have seen better days. If Grainne decides to throw this one out then so be it. It won't be missed, and Grainne, automatically assuming that she has collected the other bags, is less likely to go searching for them.

Feeling smug, Leah makes her way back out to the front of the house and heads to the park. She can sit on a bench, give herself some time to think, to decide what she should do next. A vision of her parents' faces flits through her head, a fleeting idea that she should pay them a visit, attempt to heal old wounds. It's a last resort but not something she can rule out completely. Not just yet anyway. She has another idea already formulated in her head. She will see how it pans out then consider going back to her childhood home, cap in hand. But not at the moment. All in good time.

The bench is wet after the downpour but she sits down anyway, ignoring the dampness that seeps through her trousers, settling on her skin. Leah manages a weak smile despite her predicament. There is something about this bench that makes her feel tired. It has a soporific effect on her every time she visits, forcing her eyelids down, filling her limbs with lead until she can't stop it and sleep wins over once more.

It's windy up on the clifftop. The sun beats down, stopping the chill from setting in. Leah wipes at her neck, shields her eyes from the glare overhead and stares out to sea. The crashing waves in the distance mesmerise her, the ebb and flow of the expanse of azure water, the swell of the horizon, the way the barely discernible flecks of white foam roll over the surface of the sea; they all keep her rooted to the spot. And yet despite this calming sight, still she feels a creeping anger deep within her veins, a white-hot fury that refuses to leave.

She peers down over the side of the cliff. The tide is out. She has no idea why they can't just go down onto the beach with the other people. She is bored and apart from the picnic, there is absolutely nothing to do up here. Her parents harped on about having the best view in the whole of the north east but as far as she can tell, the people playing in the sand have the same view, so why stick them all up here away from the fun? They can't even go for a paddle. Not that she would want to anyway – paddling in the sea is for kids – but it would have been nice to have the option. And what about little Lucy? Surely, she would love a dip in the sea like all the other little ones down there? None of it is fair. Her parents are the most selfish people ever.

She moves closer to the edge, peering down at the craggy boulders jutting out beneath her, imagining how long it would take to climb down to the bottom, working out whether it could be done without slipping and falling.

Behind her she hears a noise. She turns to see Ellis and Lucy playing, tumbling around like toddlers. Beyond that, her mum and dad and Johnny and Petra are setting out the food on a large blanket. Leah rolls her eyes. The whole thing is such a fucking cliché. Here they are playing at Happy Families when they all know they are anything but. Ellis only came here because he was forced to and she would rather be anywhere but in the presence of the people who call themselves her parents.

Closing her eyes, she dreams of another life, another family, another home. One where she is appreciated, surrounded by people who actually care about her, not stuck here with the Browne's and their stupid friends high up on a cliff overlooking the freezing North Sea. She can think of a million other places she would rather be. Ellis didn't want to come either. He was way too busy waiting for a call from Lauren Bixby. Leah smiles.

She never called him back. He stands no chance with somebody like her. With her long legs and tumbling blonde hair, Lauren has the eye of every boy in school. Why does her stupid brother think a girl like that would ever be interested in him? It's ludicrous. Ellis might be fairly nice looking but Lauren is in another league entirely.

The sounds behind her grow in volume. She turns to see Ellis scowling at Lucy. She is goading him, wanting him to continue playing with her when it's obvious he has had enough. Leah laughs. It lifts her spirits to see him cornered by a six-year-old.

She heads over to where they stand, sees Ellis's face grow serious as she approaches. Anger seeps into her bones like molten metal. Fury lines her stomach and scorches her innards. 'What's that face for?' Her voice is sharp, accusatory.

Ellis shrugs and turns away, angering her all the more. Lucy pushes past Leah's legs, knocking her off balance. She watches as Ellis sniggers at her stumble, a glint in his eye that infuriates her. *Who the fuck does he think he is? And as for that spoilt little brat hanging around – well, she can piss off as well.* Leah has had enough of all of them – the adults, Lucy, her twat of a brother – they can all take a running jump.

'Come on, Lucy, let's play a new game. It's called "Annoying Leah". All you have to do is breathe in her presence and then watch her nostrils flare and her skin turn red. It's the easiest game ever!' Ellis laughs and grabs Lucy's hand.

The little girl giggles and jumps up and down. Ellis picks her up and pretends to tickle her before swinging her around. Her shrieks of delight echo around the clifftop before being swallowed up by the roar of the sea and the howl of the warm summer wind that pushes at their backs and messes with their hair. Leah stomps away from them, closer to the edge of the cliff where they can't be heard.

Bollocks to Ellis and his stupid loutish behaviour and damn that brat of a kid as well. Neither of them knows anything about her or what it feels like to be on the periphery of life, to have no control over anything and be excluded, squeezed out of their own family. Ellis is the golden boy and Lucy is a spoilt princess who only has to snap her fingers to get whatever she wants. One bat of her eyelashes and her parents run to her like a pair of slaves, making sure her every wish is granted, her every command swiftly met.

Leah stands, listening to the screech of the seagulls, watching the crowds below, wishing she was down there, closer to the water. The gulls circle above the throngs of people, waiting, watching, diving down and coming back up with whatever they can, small scraps of leftover food clutched between their long yellowy cream beaks. A sudden gust of wind catches her unawares, making her lose her footing. She steps back from the edge, amazed at how tiny everybody looks, how insignificant they all appear to be from this height, like ants scurrying about, each of them focused on their own activities, locked into their own little worlds unaware that she is here, above them, staring down, thinking how pointless they all are. How unimportant and worthless their lives are.

'Your turn to amuse her now, misery guts.' Ellis is behind her. She spins around to face him. Lucy is standing next to him, looking up at his face, smiling inanely. She is so innocent, so completely unaware of anything that it almost makes Leah laugh out loud. People are idiots. Her parents, her brother. Even this blameless little girl. They know nothing about her. Nothing at all.

'I don't think so, Ellie boy. She's all yours.' Leah watches as his face clouds over, his eyes growing dark with undisguised irritation. 'You're the golden boy, the chosen one. Weave your magic spell and make the child dance, why don't you?' She can't help herself. Her laugh scatters through the air like a shotgun, a rapid stream of noise, caustic and deprecating.

He shakes his head at her, his mouth set in a firm line. 'Sad really. Is there any reason for you being such a bitch? Or were you just born that way?'

Leah spins around, looking for some sort of backup from her parents but the adults are all too busy sorting out picnic rugs and chairs, too busy opening bags of crisps and slicing boiled eggs, too busy pouring out tepid tea from flasks to notice what is happening.

'Okay, Ellis, I'll play with her. Just you watch. I'll show you how little kids are meant to have fun.'

Her voice is sharp as granite as she grabs Lucy's hand and drags her close to the edge of the cliff, ignoring the little girl's resistance. 'Come on, Lucy. Why don't we play near the edge and pretend we can fly?'

'No!' Ellis shouts, leaping forward, reaching out towards them. Leah curls her lip into a sneer as Ellis tries to pull the little girl back from the precipice.

The next part is a blur as they both struggle with the girl wedged in between them although the final section of the story is now crystal clear in Leah's mind. She has denied it for so many years now, pushed it away, refusing to acknowledge her part in Lucy's death but it's there, an unshakeable truth, unwavering and solid as the rotation of the earth, constant as the onset of each new season.

The struggle continues until eventually Ellis manages to move Lucy towards him away from the dangerous drop beneath. And then seeing that she has lost, that yet again, she has been humiliated, Leah sticks out her foot causing the child to stumble. All it takes to complete the process is one small secret kick, a hidden push, and Lucy's fate is sealed.

Realising the enormity of what she has done, Leah panics,

makes a snap decision and thinks up a story to exonerate herself. A twisted story that once told, can never be untold...

~

'So, it was all your fault?' Her head snaps up. She is sitting opposite Will. His face is blank. Her heart is pounding, stampeding around her chest. She is sweating yet feels so very cold. She swallows, looks around, tries to drag herself back to the present. This is the part where she feels sure she is locked away in some asylum, her mind gone, destroyed by her past, by what she did, by what she is still doing, day after day after day. This is the final part, the bit of the story where she loosens and comes apart, pieces of her falling away.

Covering her face with both hands, she places her head in her lap and weeps.

23

Will is silent, watching Leah through narrowed eyes. He is probably trying to figure out what goes on inside the head of somebody like her. She shivers, pulls her sweater tighter around her shoulders. There's a sudden chill in the room, a cooling of the air around them. Leah shuffles down in her seat, weary of being here in this place, weary of Will's probing questions. Weary of life. She is running on empty. Nothing in reserve. She visualises herself as a half empty glass, slowly being drained until there is nothing left. What then? Who will step in and help her when she is a husk, a dried-up shell of a person with nothing to offer?

'Stay with me, Leah. Try to focus on your breathing.' Will's voice reverberates in her head, a distant sound coming from somewhere she cannot reach. 'Come on, Leah. Try to concentrate.'

She stares over at him, at his hazy outline. Her vision is blurred with tears, her eyes swollen and sore. Everything hurts. Her abdomen, her head, her entire body. 'I can't do this, Will. I just can't. I'm too tired. Really really tired. I just want to go to sleep. Please let me shut my eyes and rest.'

Leah thinks back to that day at the beach, that argument, the moment Lucy fell. The feeling of the child's soft skin against her leg. The look on Lucy's face as she toppled backwards into the waiting abyss. Then Ellis's crumpled expression as she spat out those words, those accusations that she was unable to retract. The words that sealed his fate making sure she never saw him grow up into the kind generous man he would be today. Who knew that being a liar and being so horribly and utterly deceitful would be this exhausting? It's gruelling being dishonest. Look where it's got her. Look at what she has become.

'Try to stay awake, Leah. Talk to me. Tell me about your family, your friends. Tell me where you work. Just keep talking.'

She blinks to clear her vision and sees Will's face in front of her. Has he moved closer or is she hallucinating? She wants to tell him that she doesn't see any of her family and has no friends, that she is out of a job after an altercation at work, is now unemployable and has no money to live on but it's all so difficult to voice out loud, the words sticking in her throat, sharp and cumbersome. The truth is so often the hardest thing to say. Lies have always come so much easier to her, like water gliding over a worn pebble – smooth and effortless.

'My Aunt Mary,' she says eventually, 'I sometimes keep in touch with her. She lives in London. We used to visit her when I was little.'

Will nods and smiles. She doesn't even attempt to work out what he might be thinking. It no longer matters. Dealing with her own thoughts is hard enough. She has neither the energy nor the inclination to deal with anybody else's.

'She's my mum's sister and has always been kind to me.' Mary used to sit next to Leah when she was a child and tell her tales of what it was like when she first moved to London on her own, how she used to wander the streets alone, in awe of how magnificent and scary it was being a young woman in the big city on her own. Mary always seemed to understand Leah, was tolerant of her moods and sullen ways. She knew everything about Leah; her strange ways, her unfathomable thoughts and mannerisms. Somehow, Mary just knew.

'She once took us on a tour around the city. I thought I'd died and gone to heaven. It was like nothing I'd ever experienced before. So many cars and so many people. All the busyness and the noise. It was like another world.' She allows herself a slight chuckle as she recalls the time that she and Ellis thought they had got lost only to realise that they were being tricked by Mary who had hidden around a corner. Ellis had taken Leah's hand and promised her that he would keep her safe and find his way back. He had told her that all they had to do was look up to the sky and keep an eye out for Big Ben and it would guide them back to Aunt Mary's house.

More tears flow at the thought of Ellis and how he only ever wanted to be a decent brother to her. He was a good person, a kind person. He was everything she wasn't. She sniffs and wipes at her eyes, dabbing them dry with her sleeve. The lump in her throat aches as she swallows it down. She would cry again if she could but it's too painful. Everywhere hurts, her head, her eyes, her abdomen, her limbs. Everywhere. So much pain. Why is she in so much pain?

Will's face appears over her, his breath on her skin, his eyes locking with hers, his dark pupils searching hers for something she simply cannot give.

She lets out a small shriek, tries to edge away from him, blinks and sees that he's in his chair watching her, his hands resting on his lap. Another hallucination. That's what it is. There's no other explanation for it, is there? She should be accustomed to them by now yet they still terrify her. They're inexplicable. Frightening, making her feel as if her tenuous grip on reality is slipping away out of her grasp.

'Am I dead?' She has no idea where that question came from. No idea why she is even asking it. Perhaps she is right. Perhaps she has died and is stuck in a terrible limbo, suspended between heaven and hell. She remembers being taught about purgatory at school and wonders if she is in a spiritual holding bay waiting for somebody to decide whether or not she deserves to have her soul cleansed and purified before moving on to her final resting place. Her soul is too filthy to ever be properly cleaned. It's dark and rotten and nobody will ever be able to help her or rescue her now. Everything is too far gone. Sullied and beyond redemption, that's how she would describe herself. She deserves to be relegated deep into the bowels of hell.

Will doesn't answer her question. He leans across to her instead and rests his hand upon hers, tapping it lightly before speaking in a low whisper. 'Let's just get you sorted, shall we?'

She's not dead. That's all she can focus on as she rubs at her eyes and thinks about what she is going to do next.

'I'm not dead,' she mumbles, a slight smile forming at the corners of her mouth. 'I'm not dead.'

Will nods his head and clears his throat. 'You're not dead, Leah. You're definitely not dead.'

She closes her eyes and leans her head back, thankful that she's still here, still alive. Her body is hurting, battered and broken but in time, can heal.

Her mind is another matter entirely.

24

Leah's heart thrums in her chest as she stands outside Jacob's front door, fist raised in the air, ready to knock. Ready to do what should have been done a long long time ago. She has no real plan. Nothing concrete in her head. That's not entirely true. She has half a plan of sorts with no contingency if it all goes horribly wrong, and half a plan has got to be better than no plan at all.

Jacob left just over forty-five minutes ago. Leah had huddled at the end of the road, tucked away between two houses, watching him as he loaded up his car with bags and briefcases. It's a fortunate turn of events him being away this week but even more fortuitous Chloe being here at his flat while he's gone. Leah wonders if she has moved in permanently. She seems to spend an awful lot of time here. Too much. The thought of it pulls at her guts sending a series of sharp pains up through her chest. She imagines the pair of them, Chloe and Jacob, draped across one another on the sofa, Chloe's personal belongings dotted about, a precursor to her moving in for good. It was bad enough being forced to watch as the two of them stood for a good three or four minutes before Jacob left, locked in an embrace, smiling and cooing over each other. They continued for what felt like an age, whispering and fawning, stroking one another's backs until eventually he managed to extricate himself from her grasp, waved goodbye and got into his car whereupon Chloe turned and headed back into the flat on her own.

On her own.

That was when things started to look up.

Leah's skin prickles with excitement. This is it, her moment. Her time has come and it feels damn good. She's nervous. Of course she is. That's to be expected. She is about to confront the girlfriend of her ex-partner and the whole episode may prove to be less than pleasant but by God it will be worth it. She's waited so long for this moment. It feels as if she has been waiting her whole life for it.

Leah lowers her fist, deciding knocking is too intrusive, too public, and tries the handle instead, hoping Chloe was too wrapped up in thoughts of Jacob to drop the latch. This is a nice area, high property prices, low crime. People aren't on the lookout for intruders, are less likely to fear for their safety and more likely to be lackadaisical when it comes to security.

She pushes at the handle and smiles. For once luck is on her side. An excited thrumming beats in her neck as the door opens with ease and she can step into the hallway that leads to Jacob's flat.

With stealth-like precision, she shuffles through the long vestibule and creeps up the stairs; quietly, carefully. She has made it thus far, which is further than she ever expected: she had imagined having the door slammed in her face or being threatened with the police. She cannot afford to lose this chance. In the past few weeks, she has tried to speak with Jacob and Chloe and been thwarted at every turn. This is a golden opportunity and she can't let it pass her by.

Reminding herself to stay calm and keep a clear head, she

gets to the top stair and tiptoes across the landing, avoiding the parquet flooring and keeping to the thin length of matting that runs across the middle of the tiles. Perspiration bubbles up on her forehead. She stops and tightens her jaw, her skin tingling, a frisson of excitement shooting through her veins, quelling her fears, pushing her on. She has to get inside that flat.

This visit has been a long time coming.

She wipes her fingers over her face, wishing it were cooler, wishing she could stop the myriad thoughts jostling around in her head and just get on with it.

Standing still, she takes a few deep breaths and tries to focus and not come undone before she even gets inside. *This is ridiculous. All I have to do is stay calm and appear confident and unruffled and in no time at all Chloe will be putty in my hands. It's all about bluff and poise*, Leah thinks. It is those qualities and attributes that top everything else. Superior intelligence and knowledge play no part in getting what you want; it's confidence and self-assurance that do it, grabbing people's attention, scaring them even. It's a kind of psychopathy, making people cower in your presence, getting them to co-operate. It's the behaviour of winners.

A creak from the floor below forces her to stand still, oxygen exiting her lungs in short gasps. A door somewhere in the lower hallway is opened, followed by the echoing click of footsteps, then the closing of another door. Leah lets out a long breath, air whistling through her pursed lips. Had she turned up just few minutes earlier, she would have been caught sneaking in here. She's been given a chance here, luck playing a big part. She has to use it wisely, not end up frazzled, unable to function. Chloe is alone in the flat and all Leah has to do is get her to open that door and the rest will fall into place.

With a feeling of foreboding still fluttering in her belly, she strides towards number eighteen and gives the door a light push. It stays put. She clenches her jaw, bites at her lip, tugging and nipping at a loose piece of skin. Perhaps her luck has run out before it has barely begun. Maybe this is it and here is as far as she will get. She places her fingers around the handle and gives it a shove, pressing her body against the wood for extra momentum. It opens with a soft shush, a triangular crack of light appearing on the mat as she pushes the heavy door ajar and slips inside, a slight quiver running under her skin.

How stupid and thoughtless, leaving it unlocked so she can sneak in and challenge her nemesis. How fortunate. And how utterly and deliciously marvellous.

All is silent inside as she pads through the long hallway, her ears attuned to every little sound, every beat of her heart, every tiny breath. She stops, steadies herself and looks around, squinting, trying to orient herself to her surroundings. Keeping her eyes focused on the door to the living room, she continues walking, delicate steps that make no noise, stopping only when she hears the sound of trickling water coming from the bathroom closely followed by a woman's voice. A wave of heat crawls up her neck as she listens to Chloe's one-sided conversation, her voice echoing around the bathroom, bouncing off the tiles and porcelain.

Leah imagines Chloe languorously perched on the edge of the bath, wrapped in Jacob's white robe, her hair in a turban-style towel as she casually trails her fingers through the water, watching while bubbles rise and the bathroom fills with steam. It is sickening, absurd even. Leah's skin tightens. Fury courses through her. She should be the one who is in there, wearing Jacob's gown, helping herself to his creams and lotions and bath oils. She has been rudely elbowed to one side; her identity stolen. Her life crushed beyond recognition. Chloe is a calculating slut, pushing her fist deep into Leah's chest and ripping out her beating heart. She has taken everything from her. Everything.

It's now time to even up the scoreboard and take it all back.

The living room has an orderly silence about it as she pads through, looking around at the pictures and photographs and the objets d'art dotted about. It's a minimalistic regimented space, unfeasibly neat and tidy with muted colours and carefully selected trinkets strategically placed for maximum effect. Chloe's tastes it seems, are modern with an eclectic twist. She has heavily influenced Jacob with his choice of décor. A weight presses down on Leah's innards, disappointment rippling through her. This isn't him. He has had his head turned by this woman, giving in to her wants and needs to the detriment of his own. Jacob prefers objects that exude class and style, things of beauty that have provenance and patina, not these mass produced soulless items. Leah knows this. She knows him; knows what he wants, what he needs. And he doesn't need Chloe, never has.

She glances to her left and hanging there, pride of place on the main wall is a Hockney print framed in cheap ornate gilt. Leah recognises it from her time spent studying art at school. She knows that Jacob desires the impressionist movement, particularly Degas and Cézanne, and is again disheartened that he has allowed himself to be so dominated by this woman, to have his tastes crudely ignored and cast aside in favour of fashion and cheap imitations. Chloe is a philistine; all eyelashes and nail varnish. More interested in the price of lipstick than the value of art. No real substance or depth to her at all.

A fake vintage musket is laid across the mantelpiece, sleek and smooth, the grain of the wooden handle and the gleaming metal trigger an incongruous sight against the bleached stone fireplace. Leah isn't sure what message they are sending out by having it on display. It's an ugly piece. She allows herself a wry smile as she picks it up, brings it up to eye level, aims it at a photograph of a grinning Chloe on a nearby shelf, and softly pulls the trigger with a muffled click. She sighs and lays it back down then turns, surveying the room once more with a critical eye, her gaze sweeping over every surface, across the walls, trying to commit it to memory. This isn't how it would look if she lived here. Jacob has allowed himself to be manipulated and moulded by somebody who knows nothing about anything and it has shocked her, a small amount of despair settling deep inside her. She has a lot of work to do around here, many bad habits to undo.

The sound of running water stops, the thump thump of Leah's heart the only sound to be heard. There is a growing sense of exhilaration coursing through her, pushing her on. This is what it feels like to have ultimate control. She has spent so long now being jealous and frightened of the woman in the room next door and now feels nothing but pleasure at the thought of catching her unawares and scaring her. This moment has been a long time coming. Too long. All the things that have happened in the past few days and weeks – losing her job, having no money, getting evicted – they all pale into insignificance because this is the pivotal point in her life, the part where everything comes good and she gets exactly what she wants.

Jacob.

He is all she has ever wanted. Jacob isn't suited to Chloe. They are a mismatch. It's just that he doesn't realise it, but he will in time. Leah is going to implement changes, make him see where he has gone wrong. He'll thank her for it. Maybe not now. Maybe not tomorrow, but soon.

Somewhere deep inside her chest, she can feel it, the slowing of her heart, the cooling of her blood, the heightening of her senses as she prepares herself. She is aware of the sound of Chloe climbing into the bath; noises deadened by the thick walls that separate them, yet still audible. The squeaking of skin against enamel, the idle sloshing of water, even her soft sighs as she slinks down under the bubbles, hot water lapping against her body. Leah is sensitive to each movement, each sound, imagining Chloe's features, the look of relaxation as she lies back in the bath, then the look of horror when she realises that she isn't alone.

She stands, wondering if the time is right or thinking that perhaps she should wait. Confronting Chloe right now will give her an advantage. Chloe is naked, vulnerable, unable to defend herself. Nothing too drastic – just enough to frighten her, just enough to make her think about what she has done, how she has disrupted Leah's life. Just enough to send her fleeing back to her own flat leaving Leah here, in Jacob's home. The thought of it makes her giddy. She will double lock the doors, throw Chloe's belongings out of the window and make herself at home.

Because this is, after all, where she belongs. Always has. Grainne throwing her out suddenly doesn't seem so distressing. Not now she has a new place to live. The thought of spending time here makes her shiver, goosebumps prickling her skin, forcing the hairs on the back of her neck to stand to attention.

Her back is rigid, shoulders thrown back as she marches over to one of the shelves and picks up a heavy ornament – a small stone lion – for no other reason than to protect herself. She holds it aloft as if grasping a trophy. This small object is the thing that will save her; light enough to wield as a weapon and heavy enough to break bones should she need to. The floor is soft underfoot, a carpet of quicksand, swirling and undulating beneath her as she shuffles towards the bathroom grasping the object tightly in her hand, stopping every couple of steps to catch her breath and steady herself. Then gently, so very gently, she pushes at the door and steps inside.

Lying back in the bath, her hair twisted up in a messy bun

with a wet towel over her eyes is Chloe, oblivious to Leah's presence, unaware that there is somebody else in the room with her. It takes an inordinate amount of strength to not laugh out loud at her ignorance, at her ineptitude, at the lack of security in the flat but most of all at how ridiculous she looks, splayed out across the porcelain looking like somebody who is trying too hard at being hip and fashionable. She has, Leah thinks, modelled herself on one of the lithe, smooth-skinned individuals that adorn fashion magazines, lying there with her legs dangling over the side of the bath and her face tilted upwards in a contrived pose.

Despite the heat and steam that billows around her, Leah's flesh is suddenly cold, like winter. She remains still, unwilling to announce her presence before she is ready to act. That would be a tragedy, to blow everything and never again have this chance. She has dreamed of this moment for so long now it makes her quiver, her body almost convulsing with the anticipation.

Just a few more seconds and Chloe will realise. She will sense that somebody is close by. She will panic, sit up in the bath sending water everywhere as she attempts to cover her nakedness and protect herself. Perhaps she will scream, alerting the neighbours who will come running and possibly even call the police.

That's not going to happen. Leah won't allow it. She clutches the lion tighter, her knuckles white, her skin taut.

Chloe's phone lies on the floor next to the bathtub. Leah bends down and silently removes it from her reach, sliding it across the bathmat before plucking it up and clasping it tightly between her fingers. The black case is hot and sticky, moisture clinging to it. On impulse, she slips it into her pocket pondering over its contents; all those messages and names and secrets. Later, she will search through it, gain some insight into Chloe's life, discover who her friends are, find out what sort of a person she really is, glean as much information as she can from this device. Knowledge is power.

Leah glances at the heavy object clamped in her hand. This is her protection, the only way she has of silencing Chloe. She will use it to threaten her and if that doesn't work – well if that doesn't work she will have to think of something else. After all she's been through in the past few months, she is nothing if not resourceful. There is an endless well of ingenuity stored deep inside her that she can draw from. She has a keen eye for detail and can pre-empt Chloe's every move. She is going to be fine. Everything is going to be absolutely fine. It has to be. She's here now; there's no going back. No way to suddenly disappear without causing a major ruckus. This is her moment, her chance to put everything back to how it was, to make everything perfect again.

The sound of splashing and the slight breeze of a nearby movement makes her head fizz with desire. She purses her lips, bracing herself for the ensuing chaos as Chloe sits bolt upright, eyes bursting out of their sockets as she spots her intruder, registers who it is standing there next to her. Leah lets out a sigh of satisfaction that borders on sexual. She leans forward towards the startled naked woman, their faces almost touching, Leah's skin burning, her pupils dilated with expectation.

A thrill runs through her, an electric pulse. She smiles, presses her free hand over her victim's mouth and whispers softly, so very softly that her voice can barely be heard above Chloe's muffled scream, 'Well hello there. I didn't bother knocking, I just let myself in. Guess who?'

25

The emotional pull of power and control Leah feels is like nothing she has ever experienced. She sucks in her breath, keeps her feet planted firmly on the floor, thinking that doing this sooner would have stopped her life from spiralling out of control and ending up in the gutter. She wouldn't have lost everything she held dear, including Jacob. Perhaps she would be the one currently lounging around in this bathtub like a lady of leisure, taking everything for granted, always assuming that life will go her way, forever thinking that the good things in life will naturally fall from the sky into her perfect little lap.

Chloe has had such an easy ride, such an easy fucking time of it while Leah's life has turned to shit. Well, not anymore. That is about to come to an abrupt end. Chloe's days of having Jacob all to herself are over. This is Leah's time to shine.

Having the advantage and feeling Chloe slip and struggle under her grasp has pumped her full of adrenaline and she is high on the sensation, her head spinning, her body trembling. It's better than any drug or substance designed to give thrills. Her skin is on fire, her muscles tight and hot with pleasure. She can do this. Chloe is remarkably weak despite Leah holding her still with only one hand. She is using minimal force and hasn't even broken a sweat. She giggles, an unintended high-pitched screech. This is going to be so easy.

'Lie still and I won't hurt you,' she says, suddenly serious, her voice a hiss through gritted teeth and laced with menace. 'Just listen to what I have to say and you won't get injured. Do you understand?'

Chloe nods, her eyes wide, brimming with tears. Leah presses her hand down harder, applying more force, just to show that she is serious. Just because she can. It's a warning and Chloe ignores it at her peril.

'I'm going to give you a set of instructions and you're going to follow them. In a minute you will be told to stand up. I will remove my hand and you will step out of the bath and put on your dressing gown. You won't scream or make a noise or even whisper, because if you do, I will bring this down on your head and I can assure you, it weighs enough to do an awful lot of damage to your fragile little skull.' She leans forward, her voice sibilant in Chloe's ear, 'And think of the state your pretty little face will be in afterwards. All those scars. Your flawless skin battered and bruised and torn to shreds. What will Jacob think of you then, eh?'

To prove the point, Leah lifts up the solid cream-coloured lion and brandishes it like a weapon, twisting it in the air, visualising the bone and blood splatter that would spread far and wide if she were to bring it down onto Chloe's face. 'I don't think I even have to tell you how much it will hurt, do I? You've probably dusted this old thing a hundred times, so you know exactly how much it weighs, don't you?'

Leah smiles, her eyes as cold as steel as she continues to speak. 'By the way, you've done a fine job of keeping house for me. I'm not so keen on your choice of colours. Bit bland for my tastes but I quite like the musket. Not so sure about the Hockney print though. I doubt Jacob approved when you brought that nasty piece of artwork into the flat. Bit obvious, don't you think? You really need to educate yourself when it comes to choosing pictures, Chloe. Pop art is for boors and barbarians. Anyway, I might have to redecorate and replace some of the knick-knacks once you leave here. They're a bit twee. But then I suppose somebody as uncultured as yourself wouldn't know any better, would they? I'd like to say I forgive you for stealing Jacob, for worming your way into his life and living here in my home, but that would be a lie. A big fat fucking lie. I have nothing but contempt for you and your weaselly little ways. Now do exactly as I say and stand up.'

Wide-eyed and nodding furiously, Chloe gets to her feet, her legs shaking and bending like a young foal, soap suds clinging to her reddened flesh. Leah stands back, still grasping the heavy lion, watching the dripping terrified figure as she stands in the bath, immobile aside from the involuntary tremble of her slim, soap-covered thighs. The horrified girl bends over slightly, one arm strategically placed over her breasts and the other across her midriff. Leah smiles, leans forward, moves Chloe's arms away, pushing them down to her sides before standing back to look at her properly.

'It's a funny thing,' Leah murmurs, her eyes sweeping over Chloe's naked body, 'seeing you completely nude like this, I suppose I can see why Jacob took a fancy to you. You've got the perfect figure – slim, nice arse, pert tits.'

She stares at Chloe's toned physique, at her small perfect breasts, her narrow hips and the thin line of dark hair that runs between her legs. She mentally compares it to her own shapeless body, to her loose breasts and flabby backside, to her chunky thighs and not so perfect stomach and thinks how shallow Jacob must be to be attracted to such things. Surely he is better than that? He's an intelligent, well-educated guy who should be above being magnetised to such superficial traits and features. Leah tightens her jaw, grinding her teeth together, wondering how long Chloe would take to drown if she held her head under the water, how much she would fight and struggle to stay alive. Then she thinks about Jacob, visualises his smile, remembers his sweet scent, his twinkling eyes and softens at the thought of his beautiful face. He may well be an intellectual but he is also a young man in his prime, driven by lust, and for that reason alone, she is prepared to forgive him.

'Right, now I want you to listen very carefully to what I'm telling you. Don't scream because if you do, I will cave your skull in. Are you listening to me?' Leah moves her face closer to Chloe's, leans into her ear and hisses once again, 'Are you sure you're listening to what I'm saying, you sad little bitch. Are you?'

Chloe nods furiously, tears running down her cheeks, her chin wobbling as she looks to Leah for the next instruction. She wants to comply. Leah can see that. At least she is being pliant and not railing against what is happening. *This is good. It's a positive start. It's going to make everything so much easier.*

'Right,' Leah says briskly. 'Step out of the bath and put this on. We're going into the bedroom and remember, one word, one sound, even if you breathe too loudly, I will hit you so hard you won't have time to wonder what happened.' She hands Chloe a white towelling robe and watches as, shivering, she climbs out of the water and wraps herself in the thick robe. Chloe pulls the belt around her middle and ties it tight with trembling fingers that lack basic dexterity and are clearly struggling to co-operate with her brain.

Leah grips Chloe's upper arm and guides her into the bedroom. Once again, Chloe's influence is everywhere. At the foot of the bed is an ottoman covered with a cream satin fabric. The headboard is a huge tangle of ornate wrought iron and on the opposite wall is a large mural of a Victorian Parisian street scene complete with flower sellers, ladies carrying parasols and the Eiffel Tower protruding into the distant sky. It is beyond hideous and possibly the worst vintage urban image Leah has ever seen, so crass and ugly she laughs out loud, the sound of her voice bouncing around the room.

'God, this place is a mess,' she says, her laughter abruptly stopping, anger now creeping in as she tries to suppress the sight of Chloe and Jacob lying in this bed, devouring each other, Chloe flaunting her body in front of him, knowing she has to do very little to arouse him. 'All you need is a neon light above the door to tout your wares and this room is complete. Jesus Christ, Chloe, this place is disgusting. I pity Jacob, having to relent to your demands, decorating this room like a whorehouse and tearing the very soul out of it.'

Chloe lets out a whimper of protest and cries some more. Leah tightens her grip on her arm, feeling solid bone beneath the layers of flesh, muscles and sinews.

'Stop it. Stop crying and whining or things will turn nasty, and you don't want that, do you?' Another shake of the head and more tears. Leah smiles, satisfied she's in control. How wonderfully gratifying it is to see the tables being turned, to have her power restored and watch this person crumple under her influence. This is what winning feels like. This is what ultimate dominance is. For the first time, Leah is the powerful one, the person making all the decisions. Chloe is a nobody. She'll do exactly as she is told without question.

'Lie down, don't move, don't whimper. Do absolutely nothing, do you understand?' Leah pushes her down onto the bed. Chloe suppresses a sob, biting at her lip with force, her small white teeth digging into the soft pink flesh of her mouth.

'You and I are going to play a little game. We're going to pretend that you no longer want to be with Jacob. You're going to send him a text message explaining that you need some time apart because you've found somebody else. And you will do it without any resistance or crying and whining, d'you hear me?'

Chloe lets out a small moan of desperation, more tears spilling out and pouring down her face. Leah cannot help but stare and smile at her, marvelling at how weak and helpless she is. From a glamorous confident woman, in a matter of minutes, Chloe has been reduced to a blotchy-faced gibbering wreck. Oh, how the mighty fall. And how glorious it is to observe, to be a witness to their long-awaited demise. It feels amazing to be back in control of her life. For a time, she was sure that nothing was ever going to come right again, but now here she is, with Chloe as her little servant, doing her bidding, and it feels glorious.

On impulse, she crouches down and places her hands around Chloe's throat, enjoying the sensation of the thin pliable skin under her fingers, elated by the fact the small delicate bones in Chloe's neck twitch and shift as she begins to apply more pressure. She watches fascinated as Chloe's eyes bulge and her nostrils begin to flare. Leah smiles, shakes her head dismissively and then lets go. She didn't have any intention of going through with it but it was worth it just to see Chloe's reaction. And she didn't disappoint. Her response was everything Leah ever hoped it would be. It's obvious she's terrified about what the next few minutes hold for her.

This is perfect. Everything is perfect. Things have never been better. She imagines Jacob's face when he receives the text and then thinks how delighted he will be to come home at the end of the week and find Leah waiting for him. He'll soon forget all about Chloe and everything will go back to how it was before she came on the scene. Once Chloe has fled, Leah will spend all week putting the flat back to how it should be. She knows exactly how it will look, can visualise it already. The fake antique trinkets will get bagged up and every single photo of Chloe will get stacked on a bonfire and burnt.

Leah lets out a quivering breath. She's going to savour every moment of this time and one day she and Jacob will look back on it and shudder at how close they came to losing each other.

She stares around the room, at its ghastly décor and is struck by an idea. The curtains are pulled back using tiebacks made from a strong corduroy material. Keeping her gaze fixed on Chloe, she heads over to the window, drags the curtains closed and unhooks the tiebacks, pulling them tight between her fists to test them for strength and durability. Perfect. It would take an inordinate amount of strength to break free of these beauties. Just goes to show that this room isn't as bad as she first thought and does have its good points despite it looking like a prize whorehouse.

Resting her backside on the edge of the bed, Leah rolls a subservient Chloe over onto her front, places her knee in the small of her back and pushes her face down into the pillows. Chloe responds with a muffled cry but makes no attempt to escape. Grabbing her hands, Leah roughly wraps the corduroy ties around them and pulls tight until she hears a squawk and another cry. Making sure they're properly knotted and as taut as they can be, Leah does the same to Chloe's feet, relishing the element of control it gives her. Who knew being cruel could be so much fun?

Only when she is satisfied that she has eliminated any chances of escape does she drag Chloe back over. The pillow is damp with her tears and sweat and snot. Feeling repulsed, Leah drags it out from under Chloe's head and holds it aloft, her face creased with revulsion. 'This is disgusting. What is wrong with you? Is this how you live? Like some kind of filthy creature?'

On impulse, she lowers the pillow and places it over Chloe's face, pressing her palms down onto the soft white cotton, watching as Chloe bucks about, her hips and chest thrusting and twisting as she tries to break free and gasp for breath.

'Oh, relax,' Leah says sullenly, removing her hands and throwing the pillow to one side. 'I'm not going to kill you for God's sake. I'm just trying to teach you a lesson, that's all.' She lets out a hollow laugh and kicks the pillow away to the other side of the room. It lands in the corner with a soft thump and sits there in a stout crumpled heap. 'Now,' she purrs as she reaches into her pocket and pulls out Chloe's phone, 'this is the good bit. This is the part where Jacob finds out about your cheating and how you're leaving him for another man.'

Moving closer to Chloe's tear-stained face, Leah hisses in her ear, 'Password, Chloe. No messing about, now. No lying or refusing. Just give me your password and let's get this thing over with, eh?'

Chloe trembles and shakes her head repeatedly, her eyes wide and unblinking. She reminds Leah of a cornered animal. Soon she will whimper, beg for leniency, maybe even lash out in desperation. Who knows how she'll react when the pressure really starts to kick in. Leah watches her, a furrow beginning to gather on her brow, her patience waning. She sighs, rolls her eyes and presses her lips together, the force of it causing her skin to tingle. She has neither the time nor the temper for these sorts of delaying tactics. The sooner this whole thing is done, the better for everybody.

'Can I just remind you that you're not in any position to refuse?' She can feel the heat pulsating from Chloe's face as she closes the gap between them once more and raises her voice a notch. It has an edge to it, is sinister in its strength and ferocity. 'Give me the fucking password or that statement about not hurting you gets cancelled out. I'll do whatever I have to do. You know that, Chloe. You've always known it. Now, tell me the password or I will do something to that pretty face of yours that will leave a scar for the rest of your life.' Her jaw aches with the effort of containing her temper. She moves back, surveying Chloe's sprawled and weeping body like a scientist assessing its specimen ready for dissection.

'No, please. Don't hurt me. Don't make me give you it. I can't,' Chloe manages to blubber, her chest rising and falling rapidly. She looks like a small child, a useless sobbing youngster who is incapable of taking care of herself.

'Okay,' Leah replies calmly as she picks up a nearby nail file and casually inspects it, running her finger up and down its edge, testing it for sharpness. She covers Chloe's wet mouth with her hand and brings the sharp metal object down onto her cheek, dragging it across the soft skin under Chloe's twitching eye. A faint pink line appears almost immediately, a thin reminder of what she can do, of who she really is.

A muffled scream comes from behind Leah's hand. She presses her palm down to stop the noise and digs the sharp implement into Chloe's skin, pushing down, sharp metal against soft young flesh.

Now Chloe knows. Now she will assist her.

'Relax,' Leah sighs, her patience beginning to wear thin. 'I haven't drawn blood but there is a mark. Let's call it a deep scratch. Whether or not I have to do it again and whether or not it will leave a permanent scar is completely up to you. Now,' she says icily, rolling her eyes and removing her hand, staring long and hard into Chloe's bewildered face, her dilated pupils as black as night, 'what did you say that password was?'

26

'The year you were born. How original.' Leah punches in the number, grinning wildly as the phone springs to life, a garish swirl of brightly coloured apps catching her eye.

She mumbles under her breath, her gaze flicking back and forth between the list of recent messages on the phone, and Chloe who is lying motionless, tears streaming down her face. She wonders if putting something over her mouth would be advantageous. Chloe screaming for help could bring this whole thing to a halt. Having got this far, the thought of it makes her concerned enough to consider rummaging through drawers to try and find a piece of fabric long enough to serve as a makeshift gag. Anything that will stop Chloe from screaming for help once Leah sends this message to Jacob. Which she will.

She stands up, opens a chest of drawers and pulls out a tangle of fabric.

Funny how being attacked and tied up hasn't been enough to really send her into a frenzy, yet the thought of sending a final goodbye message to somebody she thinks of as the love of her life is enough to tip her over the edge. Leah supposes that everybody has their weaknesses, their snapping point, and losing

Jacob is Chloe's. *Well, welcome to the real world*, she wants to say to her. *Welcome to my life.*

'Ah,' she says huskily, pulling out a pink silk belt. 'Bingo.'

Leaning over Chloe's face, Leah lays down the silk belt on the bed and picks up the stone lion, brandishing it above her head. 'Just a reminder as to who is the boss around here.' She places a finger to her own lips and makes a shushing sound, her expression threatening, eyes narrowing to tiny dark slits. 'We don't want any unexpected screaming now, do we? This is a quiet neighbourhood. We wouldn't anybody hearing you and getting upset.'

Leah moves farther forward, close to Chloe's face. She wants to see the fear in her eyes. She wants to see Chloe squirm, feel the heat of her terror. Leah thinks she has earned this. She deserves it. Her body is next to Chloe's, their skin almost touching. Her hand hovers over Chloe's hair. She inhales, savouring the moment. She can almost taste the scent of her, can sense her distress and helplessness. The room is thick with it, the air sharp with the sour tang of her dread.

And then it happens. The sharp stab of pain takes her by surprise, travelling up the soft flesh of her inner arm, increasing by the second, intensifying and bringing tears to her eyes. She lets out a yelp, tries to move away and sees Chloe's face, her frenzied expression, the glint in her eyes, her manically wide mouth and a sliver of pink gum visible as she hangs on to Leah's flesh with her teeth, grinding and clamping, refusing to let go.

'God almighty! What the hell are you doing?' Leah lets out a roar of protest and places her hand over Chloe's face, pushing and gouging at her eyes, at her nose, at anything she can grab hold of, trying to release the vice like grip that Chloe has on her arm. 'You stupid bitch. You stupid fucking bitch!'

Confused and in pain, she drops the lion, cursing as she attempts to reach it with her free hand, bending and groping while Chloe clamps onto her arm. This isn't how it's supposed to be. Chloe is restrained, immobile. She's the prisoner here, not the aggressor. It's she, Leah who purportedly has the advantage. She's the one with all the power and yet here she is in pain and unable to shake off this demon of a woman who is tearing at the flesh on her arm with such ferocity that Leah can barely breathe.

Using her fingers to defend herself, Leah holds them down on Chloe's eyes, pushing and gouging, pressing and scratching; using all of her strength, doing anything she can to shake her off and release the grip that Chloe has on her skin. Chloe responds by throwing her body around, twisting her head and champing at Leah's flesh with teeth that feel as sharp as razors.

Slippery with perspiration and weakened by the pain, Leah begins to lose impetus. She wonders if there is blood and if so how much she is losing. With one final thrust, a sudden surge of energy she didn't know she possessed, she pushes at Chloe's face, forcing her palm down over her nose, her eyes, tearing at skin, nipping, clawing, scratching, doing all she can to make Chloe stop, until eventually, the tugging on her arm ceases.

Blood is smeared over the bed sheets, a ruby stain that slowly bleeds into the cotton, tiny veins of scarlet, growing and blooming, curling like tendrils, red and pink strands slowly unfurling like the first flowers of spring. Leah stares down at the stain, keeping her eyes diverted away from her arm, too wary, too frightened to look at the gaping wound that will infuriate and sicken her.

She turns her attention instead to Chloe and suppresses a low gasp. Her nemesis is lying on the bed, a vision from a horror film, her eyes wide, glinting and unseeing. Chloe is aware she is being watched. Her expression is one of knowledge, and growing power. Her mouth turns up at the corners, her skin stretches over her prominent cheekbones, over her slim face.

Slowly, so very slowly, she turns her head to the side, opens her bloodied mouth and spits out strings of saliva. Globules of viscous fluid streaked with pink hang from her lips, thin strands of spittle flecked with Leah's blood and tiny pieces of her flesh. Trying to stop herself from retching, Leah moves away from the bed holding her arm, still unable to look at the damage.

'You're a psychopath,' is all she can say. Leah's voice carries over the room, piercing the sudden silence that has settled over them. Everything feels dulled. Time has slowed down. They're suspended in a moment, unable to break free. The throbbing ache in her arm has skewed her perception, stopped her from reacting properly. She needs a couple of seconds to right herself, to make sure she stays on top of this situation, not buckle and lose her grip.

Chloe doesn't reply. She continues spitting and drooling, her mouth hanging open, pink saliva dripping from her slack jaw.

'If you think this is going to stop me, then you're sadly mistaken,' Leah says with a drawl in her tone. 'This is just a blip. I'm going to make sure you pay for this, you stupid cow.' The final words are spat out, laden with loathing. Because she does truly loathe her. She has never hated anyone as much in her entire life.

Leah grips onto her damaged arm, feeling for the slickness of blood and is surprised to find some but not the amount she was expecting. She had prepared herself for a deep open wound in need of stitches. A mirror opposite tells her all she needs to know – Chloe has inflicted damage but it's minimal. She'll cope. It's painful but nothing that requires hospital treatment. It's not quite a graze but neither is it bad enough to slow her down. A small fold of skin shifts beneath her fingers as she massages at her own flesh. It hurts like hell, making her eyes sting and burn, but she's not about to bleed to death. Far from it.

The belt has slipped down onto the floor and is sitting next to her feet. She bends to pick it up, watching as Chloe begins to buck about again, writhing and bending feverishly. Soon she will exhaust herself. She'll get thirsty, a headache will set in. She will become sapped of energy. Then she'll stop. She will realise that her efforts are futile and will lower her resistance, conserve her strength, be her biddable self once more. The urge to whip the belt over Chloe's face consumes her. She deserves that much.

Leah kneels on the bed, watching Chloe's every move. A vindictive sneer sets in on Chloe's blotchy face. Gone is the terror, replaced now by a swathe of anger that is evident in her body language, in the way she thrashes about. In the way she meets Leah's gaze, refusing to look away.

'Don't you dare touch me. Come near me with that thing and I'll scream the place down.' Her voice has a richness to it, a confident inflection that almost makes Leah laugh out loud. Poor little Chloe has finally grown teeth. No more the quivering wreck, no more the blubbering terrified victim. She is starting to fight back.

Leah takes a couple of steps away from the bed, holding the belt between both hands, pulling it taut and snapping it with a twang. 'Really?' She bends down, picks up the stone lion and curls her fingers around it, appreciative of its cool surface, of its smoothness against her hot palm, of the reassuring heft of it. 'How will you scream when you're unconscious? Or maybe you'd forgotten about this little beauty.'

Chloe sees the lion, her eyes twitching and blinking, her mouth trembling. Leah watches, delighting in the moment, knowing Chloe will have to relent. Knowing that she, Leah, will win this particular little game. This is what she enjoys – controlling Chloe, having the upper hand. Her life so far has been a series of monumental fuck-ups. Never before has she felt the ease of being the victor, the effortless luxury of knowing, just *knowing*, that everything will go her way. Well, now it's here. Her time has come. And she is going to make the most of it.

Grasping at the opportunity, Leah takes the belt and drapes it over Chloe's mouth, pulling it tight around the back of her head and knotting it, making sure she is silenced before any screams or noises can filter through. She can't have that – being caught out, having neighbours calling around, hearing the telltale sound of sirens outside that would indicate that her time is up, that her lovely little game is over before it's barely begun.

'There you go,' Leah whispers into her ear, her lips brushing against Chloe's hot wet skin, 'made the decision for you. We're all sorted now, aren't we?'

She watches, emotionless, mildly curious, as tears bubble up and spill out of Chloe's eyes. Leah shakes her head, her voice suddenly easy and gentle. 'You really are a strange one, aren't you? Terrified and weepy one second, angry and violent the next, and now you're back to being a big cry baby again. If I didn't know better, I'd say this was all one big act, a charade to get me to set you free.' Leah places a finger on Chloe's arm, trailing it up and down, up and down, then up over the papery skin of her neck before resting it eventually on Chloe's sodden cheek. 'Well, well, well. What a thoroughly wicked little creature you are, Chloe. Such a naughty person. Who would have thought it, eh? Little old Chloe with her big innocent Bambi eyes and baby soft skin. You're not the person everyone thinks you are, are you? Not at all. You're wicked through and through.'

~

Scrolling through Chloe's phone proved less stimulating and interesting than Leah had hoped. Sending a message to Jacob and watching Chloe struggle and writhe about trying to stop her, lightened her spirits somewhat. It took just seconds to destroy Chloe's little world. The biggest disappointment is the fact that up to now, Jacob hasn't replied.

She stares down at the message, willing an answer to appear, willing the love of her life to reply.

Jacob,
This message has been a long time coming. It may come as a bit of a shock to you but you need to know that I've found somebody else. He is everything to me and so I've decided to move my things out of your flat.
Please don't come looking for me when you get back from your conference. I don't want to discuss it any further.
Sorry to do this to you when you're away but it's easier this way. I'm sure you'll get over it soon enough.
Chloe

The sobbing when Leah read it out to her, showing Chloe the message after she wrote it, and watching as it disappeared into the ether and winged its way to Jacob, was intense. Chloe wept and wailed, her cries muffled behind the makeshift gag, her eyes distended and swollen as she tried to voice her disdain and disapproval. The air was thick with her anger. But it didn't matter. It was all too late because those words were already out there, on their way to her lover. Ex-lover.

The weight on Leah's shoulders eases, the invisible pain she has been carrying around for what feels like an age, begins to dissipate. This whole thing has been far easier than she anticipated. She hopes it's an omen of what lies ahead. Trying not to think too hard about Jacob's reaction when he arrives home, Leah stands up, looks around the room and focuses on other things.

There are too many photographs in this place of Chloe and Jacob locked in each other's arms like a pair of star-struck teenagers. Leah stands and strides around the room, gathering them up before flinging them in a bin, the glass on the frames making a satisfying crunch as they collide in the bottom of the metal container.

Behind her, she can hear Chloe's strangled cries, her high-pitched stifled howls of protest. 'Shush now,' Leah murmurs, turning briefly to glance over her shoulder. 'You always knew this was going to happen. It was only a matter of time, wasn't it? If I was you, I'd take a nap. You need to conserve your strength. You can't keep on fighting me. I've got the advantage here. I'm going to win Jacob back, Chloe. I was always going to win.'

She continues around the room, eyeing up trinkets and the numerous knick-knacks that are dotted about, all of which obviously belong to Chloe. There is nothing of Jacob in this place. Chloe has inched her way in until she is so entrenched in here that it's impossible for Jacob to remove her. It's a ploy used by many women; manipulative, scheming women like Chloe who have only their own interests at heart.

Leah opens a jewellery box and takes out an expensive gold necklace, draping it over her fingers. She holds it up and smiles, seeing the look of distress on Chloe's face. It's a treasured item then. Something special. Hopefully something irreplaceable. Perfect. Grasping it between two hands, she pulls, snapping it in half. The slight metallic click it makes as it breaks and comes away in her fingers, fills her with glee. The dulled grunt from the bed is enough to tell her that this was Chloe's favourite piece of jewellery, perhaps even bought for her by Jacob. A series of fireworks explode in Leah's head at the thought. She shivers and closes her eyes.

Today is turning out to be a very good day.

'What a terrible shame,' Leah murmurs as she drops the necklace to the floor and stands on it, grinding the small chain under her heel. Such an exquisite sensation. Such power. She is fuelled by a strong sense of revenge and can't seem to stop herself. Grabbing handfuls of gold and silver jewellery – earrings, bracelets, necklaces – she pulls and tugs, tearing and stamping on them until all that remains is a pile of knotted and broken jewellery at her feet, dulled and tarnished by her violence.

The squirming and contorting from Chloe as she attempts to free herself is worth the effort. Leah stares long and hard, her expression one of curiosity as she assesses her victim, wondering how long she will continue with this rebellious streak before realising how pointless her efforts are. Thrashing about will only exhaust her. It certainly won't stop Leah inflicting more damage and it definitely won't bring Jacob back. It's all a waste of time.

Chloe's face is crimson, her eyes shiny with tears. Beads of perspiration have formed on her face. Her hair is plastered against her scalp, the towelling robe she was wearing having long since fallen. She slumps back on the bed, a dry heaving sound emanating from her throat. Leah grins. All of Chloe's dignity, her natural grace and self-confidence have vanished. Lying on the bed is a worthless individual who has nothing, and is nothing. Funny how a bit of trauma can bring out the worst in people. Their ugly underbelly is soon revealed. This is the true Chloe, the person who stepped in without a second thought and stole Leah's boyfriend. She is no more than a common thief.

And this is her punishment. Chloe deserves everything she gets.

27

Chloe is sleeping. Being imprisoned and her attempts to writhe free have finally exhausted her. Leah sits on a chair by the bed watching, too careful and too damn anxious to move away. Not that Chloe could get anywhere with her hands and feet tied together, but you never know. She may be slim and supple and those knots are as tight as Leah could possibly get them but all it takes is one small mistake and she could lose everything, including her freedom. The thought of being locked up in jail terrifies her. She needs to be vigilant, be on her mettle at all times. It would be foolish to have come so far and then fail because of a silly oversight. Chloe could still possibly manage to crawl to the door on her knees and grunt for help. She could do lots of things to free herself. She's terrified and desperate, and terrified desperate people do impossibly insane things.

Leah chews at her nails, already ragged from years of biting and nibbling, an outward sign that she is not all she claims to be, that she struggles with her confidence. People think they know her, understand her. They don't. She sighs, knowing this is the tricky part, the bit she hasn't fully thought through. Anger and a need for vengeance drove her to do this. Her thoughts were muddied with plans and ideas of how to get revenge and it has clouded her judgement somewhat, driving her on without any real inkling of what she will do with Chloe after her little game is over and she has relieved herself of her fury.

She has a person here that she needs to remove and silence. If she throws Chloe out onto the street, the first thing Chloe will do is go to the police claiming Leah tortured her. Of course, they only have Chloe's word for it. By the time they arrive, Leah will have removed every trace of Chloe from the flat. And she will have the text that Chloe sent to Jacob as evidence that she was planning on leaving anyway. What sort of police officer is going to take her claims seriously when presented with evidence to the contrary? Leah will say that she and Jacob are old friends and he asked her to call round and look after the flat while he was away.

The problem is, one call to him will shoot that particular lie down in flames. No, best to not be here when the police arrive. She will wander around town. She's done it before after Grainne threw her out. She can do it again.

Her stomach flips at the thought of it, at the sickening reality of having nowhere to live. She is not prepared to sleep on the street again. She needs to think of something else, another way of ousting Chloe and having this place to herself without being questioned. Lots of things can occur in the space of a week. Miracles can happen. At least she hopes so because right now, that's what it's going to take to get her out of this sorry little mess. But what were her other choices? It was either this or sleep in a shop doorway or on a park bench or, God forbid, another seedy little hostel with the dregs of society. She doesn't know which is worse, a flea-infested mattress in a damp squalid room or sleeping under the stars with passers-by glaring at her as if she has just attempted to eat their young. Leah looks around. Here is better. This flat will give her the comfort she needs until she works out what to do next.

Chloe's low breathing seems to fill the room, echoing off every wall, bouncing off every surface. Even when she's asleep she has to take centre stage. Always the drama queen, thirsty for attention.

The room is warm – too warm despite there being no heating. Leah suppresses a yawn, her eyes suddenly heavy with the exertion of getting in here and doing what she had to do. Perhaps the mental effort is catching up with her. It's difficult to fight the deep-seated exhaustion that has taken root in deep inside her. She won't fall asleep. All she needs is a couple of seconds to restore her energy. Just a few seconds and she will feel better, her battery recharged to full capacity, her mind refreshed and renewed, and ready to tackle whatever comes next.

The service for her brother has finished. Everyone is filing out of the church. They left Ellis behind at the crematorium, his coffin disappearing behind the sweep of a thick velvet curtain, his broken remains ready and waiting to be scorched and turned to dust. Leah tries not to think about her brother burning in a furnace so hot it grinds his bones, leaving nothing behind but a pile of ashes.

Her parents are barely holding it together. Aunt Mary is by Leah's side, their arms linked in solidarity. Mary is her mentor, her rock, the only one of her family with whom she ever formed a bond. Mary was always able to see Leah's need to belong, her desperation to be anybody other than who she really is. Mary also knows the other side of her; the real Leah, the hidden identity that even Leah herself has tried to ignore. The other Leah.

The dark one.

She first saw it when they stayed over at Mary's on one of

their annual family holidays to London. Tired of trailing around the city looking at sights that held no interest for her, Leah had decided enough was enough and refused to accompany her parents on any further visits, staying home with Mary instead. Bored, a young Leah had slunk off into one of the many rooms in Mary's big old Victorian townhouse, deciding to find other ways of amusing herself.

Hearing the noise and the squawks and the laughter, Mary had joined Leah in the bedroom to see what was going on. She caught her holding the guinea pig in one hand, and a pair of scissors in the other. The squirming animal was hurt but, fortunately, lived. It had a scar on its back where she had traced the sharp edge of the scissors up and down its spine, giggling and bouncing up and down excitedly as the stricken animal writhed and twisted its small body, trying to free itself.

That's when Mary realised. She discovered Leah's concealed self. The bit that nobody else knew about. Their eyes had met and Leah saw the recognition there. It was their secret. Both she and Mary hid it well over the years, Mary insisting that she speak to Leah every few weeks, questioning her over how she was behaving and what was going on in her life; trying to instil a sense of morality into her, explaining that being kind and thinking of others was an important part of growing up. And sometimes it worked and sometimes it didn't.

Mary and her mother hold one another as they slide out of the pew and make their way outside. Nobody speaks. A grief filled silence hangs over them all. What is there to say? Ellis is dead, her parents are inconsolable and she is to blame. This is all her doing.

At times like this, a part of her thinks that there is no point in trying to do the right thing by people. They rarely notice or give thanks. It seems that it's easier to take your own track in life and do whatever the hell you want. Being the good girl becomes too difficult a path to walk. Nobody expects anything from bad people except heartache and bouts of trouble. There is less pressure, fewer expectations to do anything of any value, however when you do, the reception is greater. It is met with an overwhelming sense of gratitude. People are caught unawares, receiving your small acts of kindness with such enthusiasm it almost makes the bad times feel so much more worthwhile. This is what Leah tells herself. Because she is so terribly damaged, acts of hurt and destruction have become part of who she is. It's a rigid unbending path she is on and she doesn't know how to deviate or turn around and leave.

There is no gathering afterwards, no meeting of family members and close friends. Emotions are raw, words too hard to speak. Nothing anybody can say will ever make any of it better. Easier to say nothing at all than say the wrong thing and make it even worse. People slink away until there is only herself, Mary and her parents left. They slide into the waiting car and travel home in complete silence. The quiet weeping of her mother as they round the corner to their house pierces the deathly hush. Leah's spine stiffens. The thought of going back in there, into the stuffiness of the house with its bare dark corners fills her with dread. Passing her brother's still and silent bedroom is more than she can bear. The very thought of it makes her queasy. She can't. She just can't do it.

Writhing at the handle, Leah wrenches it open and all but falls out of the car, her legs scrambling for purchase on the pavement. She can hear her mother's crying, her father's pleas for her to return, Aunt Mary's whispers for her to come back, telling her everything is going to be just fine, that she needs to be here for her parents. She ignores them all.

Nothing stops her. Pushed on by fear and anger and isolation so deep and so strong it tears at her insides with claws of iron, she keeps on moving, just walking, stumbling, running until the voices have faded and she can no longer see their house or the street on which it stands. She has no idea of where she is going. All she knows is, she has to get away.

It's dark by the time she arrives back home. She has spent the day wandering around town and is now hungry and tired and cold. Mary has left for the station and her parents are sitting in the darkness when she marches back in feeling blackened by the day's events. Charred by what she has done.

The feeling in the house is oppressive, the atmosphere as heavy as lead. She tries to inject an air of levity into it but can tell by the reception her chirpy manner receives that it is ill timed. She realises then that this is how it is going to be now Ellis has gone. The light has escaped from their lives and the darkness is all pervading. He was their sunshine. She is their storm.

She slips upstairs, her footfall light. She wishes she could be spirited away and find somewhere new to live. A place where she can start again, be a new shiny version of herself and begin her life all over again.

A new life with Lucy and Ellis in it.

Chloe is laid on the bed staring at her, an accusatory expression on her face. Leah shakes herself awake, wonders what time it is and how long she has been asleep for. She is disorientated, slightly dizzy. She needs to stay awake, have her wits about her. Chloe escaping is out of the question. She can't allow that to happen. Everything has gone too far now to turn back or pretend none of it has happened. There'll be no happy ending to this scenario, she knows that now, no way of escaping her actions.

'Right, at some point you're going to need to go to the toilet.

I'm warning you,' Leah says slowly as she glares at Chloe, trying to regain control, 'if you try anything untoward when you go, I will break your skinny little neck.'

Chloe nods, the brightness fading from her eyes. Bit by bit, the fight will leave her and will be replaced by physical and mental exhaustion. The biting was just a kickback, an unsuccessful attempt to break free. Chloe isn't a fighter. She is neither strong enough nor powerful enough to plan a sustained attack.

'I'm going to stand you up and you're going to hobble to the bathroom, sit down and have a pee. Then we'll come back through here and you're going to lie back down on the bed.' Leah raises her eyebrow, waiting for a response from a suddenly placid Chloe who nods miserably as more tears cascade down her face.

Dragging her up off the bed is easy. Holding her up while they both shuffle to the bathroom proves more difficult. Fortunately, Chloe complies with Leah's wishes, sitting on the toilet, releasing a stream of urine before standing back up and slowly padding her way back onto the bed. She slumps down, her body not quite the lithe fighting figure of just a few hours ago. She is hunched, a little broken. Not the same person at all.

'Right,' Leah says quietly, voicing her own thoughts whilst looking around the room, 'now that we've got the ablutions out of the way, I need to decide what the hell I'm going to do with you.'

28

The pain is excruciating. Leah can't see straight, think straight. She is incapacitated, unable to do anything at all. The light is fading, her eyes too heavy to stay open, dead-weights on her lids, forcing them shut. She focuses only on getting enough oxygen into her lungs, to do what is required to stay alive, but everywhere hurts. Everything hurts. Even breathing.

She moves her hands, spreads them out in front of her, her fingertips creeping around, feeling for something – anything that will give her a clue as to where she is, something that will help her to find out what has happened. She stops, touches upon something solid. Something broken and twisted. Metal, or plastic. A hard surface where there should be air and space. This is wrong. Where is she? Why can't she move?

A face looms over hers, a blurred silhouette. Something touches her, pressure being applied to her face. She shrieks, recoils, tries to move away, to shift her position and free herself from the compression on her skin but the bulk bearing down on her is too great, the pain too intense. Everything is useless. She is useless.

'We need to move. We have to move her.'

A voice, more than one. People passing her. Shuffling, pushing, creeping through debris.

The silhouette comes into focus. A man. There is a man staring down at her. She knows him. She knows this face. He speaks again, his voice familiar, comforting.

Behind the face, a spread of colour. She recognises that too. She knows those colours, the ones she despises so much. It's the painting, that ghastly garish picture.

She is in Will's office. The weight on her torso and face eases, the pain in her stomach dulls. The artwork behind him fades, his blurred features coming into focus, becoming sharper, more recognisable. He reaches over to her and taps her hand, his fingers clutching hers. She is too weary to stop him, too scared to move away.

'I'm dying,' is all she can say, her voice croaky, her throat thick with blood and tears.

'Not if I can help it,' Will replies with a smile. 'Not if I can help it.'

'Where am I?' Her words are slurred, her mind slow, clogged up with pain and tiredness.

'You're safe with me,' Will replies. He gives her one of his broad warm smiles and clutches her hand as if they are old friends. Perhaps they are. Perhaps they have known each other for the longest time and she has forgotten, the memory of how they first met erased from her brain. Anything seems possible. Her world has shifted, an imperceptible tilt in its rotational spin and now everything is askew, back to front, upside down. The normal rules no longer apply.

'I want to be safe. Please help me.'

'I'll do my best, Leah. I'll do my best.'

He turns away from her. She wants him to turn back. She needs to see another face, to know she's not alone.

'I'm frightened.' Her voice is shaky, slowly fading into obscurity. Everything is diminishing, disappearing out of view. She closes her eyes and sighs, then takes a rattling gurgling breath and waits for the darkness, welcoming it.

29

Chloe is looking at her, a pleading expression in her eyes, creases of sadness on her brow. Leah swallows down the unease that has begun to burrow under her skin. She has to do something. They cannot remain here indefinitely. Something has to give.

She lets out a breath, her throat dry, her stomach hollow with hunger even though she feels quite sick. Everything is so terribly delicate, ready to blow apart at any moment. Their existences depend on her next move, on the decision she makes regarding what she is going to do with Chloe. Where is she going to take her? What on earth is she going to do next? Perspiration breaks out on her top lip, a thin film of sweat that sticks to her flesh, bleeding down into her mouth. She traces a line around the perimeter of her lip, salt coating her tongue. Sitting here is futile. She must do something, has to make a move otherwise she will lose her nerve. She will forget how to react, then everything will come undone and all of this will have been for nothing.

Standing up, she heads for the door, glancing behind her to the gagged and bound Chloe who is still staring at her like a small child reprimanded, desperation etched into her features.

'Don't worry, I'm coming back.' She stops, cocks her head to one side and smiles. 'Aw, did you think I was going to leave you here tied up and gagged with nobody to keep you company?'

Chloe's eyes bulge. Her skin turns grey, the colour of ash. Leah watches her, sees death sitting on her shoulder, nipping at her, reminding her to acquiesce, to be the subservient individual Leah needs her to be. Both their lives depend on this, on how Chloe chooses to react.

'I'm getting you a drink of water. I'd say don't go anywhere but that would be a tad insulting now, wouldn't it?' Leah smirks, buoyed up by her sudden ability to see beyond the present and keep a level head. She leaves the room and heads into the kitchen, opening cupboards, rummaging for a glass, inspecting the things she finds there. She pulls out various pieces of crockery and, for no other reason than she can, drops them on the floor, watching gleefully as they shatter at her feet, an explosion of white porcelain littering the tiles and spreading across the kitchen floor.

Only when she has smashed over a dozen cups and expensive plates does she reach in and locate a tumbler. She fills it with water, takes a slug, refills it and leaves the trail of fragments behind, stopping just once to view the carnage on Jacob's floor. She will clear it up later, once she has dealt with Chloe. It's not important. Not at the moment. She has other things to consider, more pressing matters to attend to.

'Right,' she declares loudly as she appears in the bedroom holding the glass of water in front of Chloe. 'I suppose you'll be ready for a drink. You see, here I am, thinking about your needs. I'm not the cruel bitch you think I am.'

The chair groans as she sits down. Her eyes are drawn to the colours on the wall, the hue of the crimson and the mesmerising greyness that reflects her mood. This happens sometimes. Something changes inside her head, a switch gets flicked and life suddenly becomes overwhelming, the smallest of problems taking on gargantuan proportions. Perhaps it's the shadows in this room or maybe it's this current situation. Perhaps it's just how she is and no amount of trying to work out what the trigger is for her downward drag will ever alter her thinking. She doubts that Chloe has ever had to suffer episodes like this, to fight the demons that do their level best to pull her off into the shadows, hollering at her, telling her repeatedly what a terrible person she is, how everybody hates her and wishes she didn't exist. Chloe has led a trouble-free existence, skipping from one blissful day to the next, never having to worry or fret, never experiencing the crushing loneliness that has been a part of Leah's life for as long as she can remember.

'I wish it hadn't come to this but I was left with no choice.' Her gaze locks with Chloe's. They stare at one another, the palpitations of Chloe's heart visible beneath the thick fabric of the dressing gown, the pulse on her neck a fluttering movement. 'I don't suppose you would understand. I'll bet you've had such a lovely life, haven't you? Everything falling from the sky straight into your lap. That's how it is for girls like you. You don't know what it's like to have to try really, really hard, do you? To do your best to fit in and yet still fail at everything you do time and time and time again. No doors have ever been slammed in your face. I can tell just by looking at you that you've had an easy time of it, such a fucking blessed existence, that you have no idea where I'm coming from.'

The veil of darkness in Leah's head drops another fraction, blocking out any remaining light. 'I'll bet you have loads of friends, a gang of girls you can call on to tell them your latest purported dramas. I can see you all now, you and your empty-headed little pals, trotting off to your Pilates lessons, bleating and complaining because you've broken a nail or your highlights are fading and your hairdresser is too busy to fit you in.' Leah lets out a hot unsteady breath, rubs at her eyes wearily with the heel of her hands. 'Do you know how many friends I have, Chloe? Any idea? No? Well, I'll tell you. None.' She is shouting now, her pitch belligerent and hostile, a climax of the hatred and resentment that has been held captive in her for so many years, suddenly released into the open.

She stands up, the water in the glass sloshing about as she shouts, her voice bouncing off the walls, filling the room. 'I have nobody. Not a single soul. The one person I had has gone. You stole him from me. You fucking well stole him!' A single tear rolls out of the corner of her eye and down her face unchecked. 'You could have had anyone, Chloe. Anyone at all, but you had to have Jacob, didn't you? It had to be him.'

Chloe writhes about on the bed. She is frightened by this outburst. Leah allows herself a small smile. So she should be. So she fucking well should be. She hopes Chloe is fearing for her life. Because this is Leah's time. This is the moment she has waited for, for so long. It's here. It's finally here.

'How many boyfriends have you had?' Without waiting, Leah holds up her hand and begins to count, bending her fingers as she reels off the numbers, her voice a loud bark; sharp and caustic, like the crack of a whip. 'One? Maybe two? I'm guessing three, four or five. Probably more than five. I'll bet I can double that and still fall short of how many men you've had. I've met your type before – women who will spread their legs for anybody as long as they're getting attention, as long as they have a man on their arm.' Water splashes at her feet, the glass wobbling about, her fingers bone white as she clasps it tightly. She should stop now but can't. It's all too late. 'Do you know how many boyfriends I've had, Chloe? I'll give you a clue. You know him. You know him intimately.' She cocks her head and widens her eyes. 'That's right. Just the one. Jacob.'

More water dribbles out of the glass, large orbs wetting the carpet and dampening her clothes. 'Jacob was my life and now I have nothing!' She lowers her head then looks up again, her eyes narrow, dark with bitterness and recrimination. She wants to curb her hate, to keep it in check but it's a wild beast within her, mewing and howling to be free. 'And you know what that means, Chloe? It means I have nothing to lose. Whatever happens after today doesn't matter because our lives are worthless. Yours and mine. We're invisible, of no use to anyone. And if that doesn't scare you, then I don't know what will...'

She sits down on the bed, chilled and spent, and holds up the glass with the remaining water, gripping it tightly. Leah watches, waits, hoping Chloe will cry or sob or at least look scared or marginally grateful for the favour Leah is doing for her. Many would leave her to choke and dehydrate, but not Leah. She's better than that. For now.

The glass rocks slightly as she places it down next to her feet before turning her attention to Chloe, who shrinks away, her eyes wide with terror. The mattress tilts and compresses as she attempts to shuffle her body away, a muffled shriek coming from behind the gag.

'Don't be scared. Come on now, if I was going to do anything bad to you, I would have done it by now, wouldn't I?' Her head shakes, her lip pouts. 'You never fail to upset and disappoint me, Chloe, do you know that? Just when I think I can't hate you any more than I already do, you go and do something stupid, something that insults my intelligence. Is it any wonder I've had to tie you up and threaten you? If you do end up getting hurt, you'll only have yourself to blame. I can't be held responsible for what happens after you disobey me, can I?'

Leah moves closer, so close she can smell the fear emanating from Chloe's skin; an odious combination of urine and sweat so powerful and pungent it almost makes her gag. She recoils, shifts her body away, her face wrinkled with disgust.

'Right, as much as I don't want to do it, I'm going to remove your gag and allow you a drink of water because I'm a kind person. Better than you'll ever be. Don't think of doing anything stupid now, will you? Because you'll regret it. I swear to God you will regret it.'

She reaches over Chloe's head, tucks her fingers behind her hair and removes the belt from around her mouth. Chloe responds by contorting her lips, stretching and gurning to allow the feeling to return to the lower half of her face.

'Here,' Leah says as she tilts Chloe's head forward and brings the glass to her mouth. 'Don't gulp it. Just a few sips and then this belt is going back on. And remember, do anything stupid and you run the risk of being hurt.'

Chloe smiles, her eyes soft with gratitude and acceptance. She takes a mouthful of water, then another.

'That's it,' Leah whispers, relieved she's co-operating. 'One more and you're done.'

It takes her by surprise. She tells herself later that she had no option and was forced into it, cornered into doing what she did. It was all Chloe's fault.

A coldness hits her as a stream of water is directed at her face, Chloe's mouth pursed into an O-shape as she spits it at Leah's eyes. She lets out a shriek, brings up her arm to dry herself, but it's too late. Too late to stop Chloe's unearthly scream that shatters the silence, bouncing off every wall, every surface. It goes on and on and on, the screaming and the cries for help.

It's instinctive, what Leah does next. Something that is out of her control. She just wants it to stop. She wants the noise and the screaming to stop. Reaching down, she picks up the stone lion, holds it tightly and brings it down on Chloe's face as hard as she can. The screaming continues, muffled, distant, but still there. She raises her arm and brings it down again and again and again, raining blows on her, hitting and hitting until the screaming becomes subdued, turning into a wet muted moan before stopping completely.

Spent and wracked with a sudden inertia, Leah stops, turns away, keeping her eyes diverted from the body slumped next to her on the bed. Splatters of blood on her hands, her clothes. Smears of thick scarlet spread over the bed sheets and the carpet. She stands up, backs away, stumbling and falling, her breath coming out in short bursts. She didn't mean for this to happen. She had to do something to stop the noise. Anything.

It was Chloe's fault. All that screaming. She had been warned. She had been warned and yet she still went ahead and made that awful racket. And now she is lying here, not moving, probably dead, her face bashed in, and all because she wouldn't do as she was asked. All because she screamed and screamed and screamed and just wouldn't stop.

Leah sobs, tears blinding her. She heads into the bathroom and pulls off her clothes, throwing them into the tepid bathwater. Shivering and staggering, she fills the sink and washes herself, up her arms, over her face, across her abdomen. She empties the sink of the rose-coloured water, refills it and repeats the process until it runs clear and no longer streaked with pink.

Her clothes are still sticky with blood and heavy with water as she pulls them out of the bath and shoves them into a black bin bag that she found in the kitchen. Perspiration coats her as she realises that she has to go back into the bedroom. She needs some clean clothes. She and Chloe are different sizes. Chloe is at least two sizes smaller than her. There must be some old item in the wardrobe that will fit. There has to be. Even if it's one of

Jacob's shirts, a pair of his old jeans even. There *has* to be something that will fit.

Treading lightly for no other reason than she is hyper aware of the fact she is about to enter the room that contains Chloe's body, Leah walks back in, her eyes fixed straight ahead. She refuses to look at her, at her blood-splattered body, at her shattered skull and crushed face. She won't look. She can't.

Opening the wardrobe door, she rummages through the hangers, searching for something suitable, anything that will fit and doesn't look too out of place. She doesn't want to draw attention to herself. That's the last thing she needs right now. Pulling out a hanger that has numerous pairs of trousers slung over it, she frantically tears at them, searching for a pair that look as if they will fit. So many clothes. Too much to choose from. Plucking at a faded pair of cream slacks, she pulls them on and is pleasantly surprised to discover they sit perfectly on her hips. She grabs at a plain white shirt and puts it on, fastening the buttons with trembling fingers. She is lacking in deftness, her co-ordination absent as nerves begin to get the better of her.

A buzzing from somewhere in the room stops her, causes her skin to prickle, her back to become clammy. Cold water fills her veins. The thumping deep in her chest makes her woozy, forcing her to hold on to the nearby wall for balance. It's the phone. A message is coming through. In her peripheral vision she can see the bright colours of the screen and feels nausea take hold in the base of her belly as she stands, frozen.

Then a continual ringing. It's a call. Somebody is trying to get through.

As unobtrusively as she can, Leah edges her way over to the bed, leaning down to pick up the mobile, making sure her eyes are averted away from Chloe's body, from the blood and the pulpy mess that is now Chloe's face.

Her fingers shake violently as she clasps it, waiting for the noise to stop before opening the text. Her heart thumps about her chest. She swallows, saliva choking her, as she scans through the message, trying to digest the words dancing about on the screen.

It's Jacob. He's finally replied. It's a desperate missive. He's cancelling the conference and driving straight back home. There's a missed call from him.

Leah lets out a hiccupping sob, unsure of whether to feel elated or terrified.

Her skin turns icy, her blood runs hot and cold, merging in the middle with an explosive fizz.

Jacob.

He's on his way back.

30

What the hell is going on? I've tried calling you. Please answer me. I have no idea what is going through your head or why you're saying or doing this. Is it some kind of joke? Just told my colleague I've got a family emergency. I'm on my way back home. The drive will take me about 2 hours. Please don't leave until I get there.
I love you. Please please don't leave. See you soon. xxx

She has to get out of here. And quickly. It might be a two-hour drive but every second counts. She has to clean up, cover Chloe with a sheet and dispose of any evidence. So much to do.

Her gaze creeps over to the blood-stained lion on the floor next to the bed. She needs to move, to get cleaning and scrubbing and tidying, and yet she can't seem to move. Her limbs are solid blocks of stone, panic and terror consuming her, gripping her, nailing her feet to the floor. She can't think straight, can't function properly. Her mind is fogged up, stripped of logic and instinct. And yet time is of the essence here. She has to move. Has to.

Snapping out of it, she suddenly breaks into a run, tearing

around the room, searching for a sheet with which to cover Chloe. The ottoman. That's where they'll be. Her hands are shaking violently as she opens it and drags out a large white quilt cover. Without looking too closely, she throws it over a still, bloody Chloe and bends double, clutching her stomach to stop herself from retching. She has got to sort herself out and not unravel. Not now. Not here. She doesn't want to go to prison. This was an accident. A terrible accident, that's all it was. It's not how she planned it. She has no idea what her plan was, but feels sure it wasn't this. She's better than this. Misunderstood, prone to outbursts when provoked but she is not a murderer. This was a horrible accident; an unfortunate meeting that went terribly wrong.

In the kitchen she finds a pair of latex gloves stashed in a cupboard alongside some cleaning equipment; scrubbing brushes, a bottle of detergent, bleach. Suddenly she is thinking clearly, her brain kicking into action. She pulls on the gloves, the snap of the rubber as it hits her skin causing her to jump, and goes about cleaning up the kitchen, picking up the shards and fragments of ceramic scattered all over the floor. It suddenly feels as if there is so much to do, so many places to clean. Her fingerprints will be everywhere; in the kitchen, in the living room, all over the bedroom. Even the bathroom where she washed herself down. She has just two hours in which to rid every trace of her DNA from this flat. An arrhythmia takes hold in her chest, her heart bouncing and thumping, shifting around under her sternum at the thought of what lay ahead, what she has to do. What she has already done. Yet again she has made a mess of things, burning everything within her reach, turning it all to ash. How did it come to this? Destruction follows her around, always has, trailing in her wake, ruining her life.

She picks up piece after piece of the shattered porcelain, stopping suddenly as she hears a sound. Her blood freezes.

Somebody is knocking on the door. Jesus Christ, of all the times for somebody to call. Her breathing becomes amplified, roaring in her head as she listens to somebody banging their fist against the wood, calling out into the silence.

'Hello. Is everything all right? Jacob? Chloe? Are you okay? It's Collette. I hear things through wall, screaming and shouting and worry that you are hurt.'

Leah doesn't move. She holds her breath, feels the dull thud of her heart, the pulsing and throbbing of her nerve endings as they respond to the call of this woman. The woman outside that Leah wishes would go away and leave her alone.

'Hello, Chloe? Are you fine? Shout if you fallen and not able to get help. I help you. I am a nurse. Or call me on phone, yes?'

She listens to the voice, to the strong Eastern European accent, and wishes her away, closing her eyes like a small child, willing everything to disappear. Why can't this person just piss off and mind her own fucking business?

The breath she is holding bursts out in a low steady rush as she hears the footsteps moving away. What if this interfering woman calls the police? Leah begins to shake. She has to hurry. She has to clean up and get out of here as soon as she can. Her hand automatically flies up to her head where she rubs at the small bald patch, her latex covered fingers impulsively grasping at a clutch of hair. She tugs at the strands, wrapping them around her fingertips before leaving go. No time for such things. No time for self-pity. She has to get a move on and get out of here.

An impromptu thought jumps into her head; a random yet vaguely promising idea. Something that this Collette lady said that has set her thinking. This could buy Leah some extra time, stop the neighbour from making any unnecessary calls.

Spinning around, Leah pulls off the gloves, grabs the phone and tries to unlock it. She lets out a small moan of frustration as it falls to the floor, watching as it spins round and round on the tiles before snatching it back up. Exasperated, she clutches it, her hands slippery with perspiration. This lady, this Collette woman mentioned Chloe giving her a call. Tapping in the passcode, Leah scrolls through the list of contacts, grinning inanely as she sees Collette's name there with her address printed underneath. God, Chloe has made everything so easy for her. Simple, pathetically naïve Chloe has just saved Leah from possible arrest. Suddenly emboldened, she sends a short text.

Sorry I couldn't get to the door. I was in the bath having a soak. The noise you heard was just me screaming because I dropped my nail varnish all over the floor. Everywhere was covered! Bright red too. Thank you for being concerned but I'm fine.

She clicks send and watches as the message disappears, hoping Collette sees it before she takes it upon herself to call 999.

Time is still against her. She needs to hurry, to rouse herself and get this place cleaned up. Jacob is currently somewhere on a motorway heading back here, his foot pressed to the floor. She can't afford to hang around. There isn't any time to waste. She scoops up the rest of the fragments of broken pottery and stops only to glance at the phone as a message comes through.

Hello Chloe.
That is good to hear. Not about the nail polish though! I was worried for a short while. Hope you clean it up well enough. Stay safe and see you soon. Xx

Leah laughs, her voice ringing in the still air; a combination of relief and dominance. So many stupid gullible people out there. A sea of idiocy. She thanks God she isn't part of it, that she at least has enough intelligence to see beyond the obvious and to question everything and everyone. She may have her faults but she is nobody's fool.

She finishes sweeping up, pulls on more gloves and uses a cloth to wipe down surfaces, spraying detergent liberally, hoping to eradicate every last sign of her fingerprints before moving on to the bathroom where she sets about cleaning, wiping furiously until her arm aches. The bath, the sink, the toilet, the floor; they all get thoroughly cleaned and rinsed before she backs out and closes the door behind her.

In the living room she wipes down shelves and ornaments, carefully putting them back in the same place at the same angle, acutely aware that in such a neat and flawless environment every little detail, every little change will be obvious to the trained eye.

Opening cupboard doors, she locates the vacuum cleaner and runs it around the carpet, getting in every corner, every little space, before replacing that too, making sure her clothes don't brush against anything. Every stray hair, every fibre can lead back to her. She has to be scrupulous, to leave no trace and exit this flat leaving it immaculate, as if she has never been here.

She glances at her watch and sucks in her breath. Jacob will be back in two hours, possibly less. Trepidation nips at her as she thinks about the final room, the one that still needs to be cleaned, the one she has been putting off until the end. Her guts coil and curl as she heads into the bedroom. Keeping her eyes averted she steps around the bed, refusing to look at Chloe, at her white body-shaped shroud that makes her weak with terror. Spots of scarlet are beginning to bleed through the thin cotton, small red blossoms unfurling and spreading. She won't look. Instead she pads around the carpet, spraying and wiping, picking up the pile of broken jewellery and throwing it into a bin bag with a distant thin clatter.

An unpleasant odour has filled the room. Leah belches, suppresses a gag, swallowing down vomit. She fights to keep it at bay but the smell is unbearable; the stale stench of sweat combined with the tart metallic tang of blood. It assaults her olfactory system, making her nauseous and dizzy. Using a gloved hand, she props herself up against the nearest wall, fighting the sickness. She closes her eyes, hoping to stem the sensation, waiting for it to pass. The contents of her stomach bubble and swirl until she can hold it back no longer. Hands clutched over the belly, she leans forward, heaving and retching into the black bag, warm bile splashing into it, spreading and dispersing, sliding over the bits of broken and twisted jewellery.

Leah moves back, her face twisted. She is panting and gasping, using the back of her latex covered hand to wipe at the gelatinous strings of saliva that hang from her mouth. They smear over her chin, thick and warm, causing her to shiver as she wipes at her cold flesh. She swallows repeatedly, all the while attempting to regain some sort of normality, to restore her dignity and keep herself upright when the floor has increased its gravitational pull, doing its damnedest to drag her down, beckoning her to drop to her knees and curl up in a tight foetal ball.

She checks herself. This needs to stop. No time for regrets or fear or contrition. She has to get going, to clean up in here before leaving the flat for good. Her breathing is laboured, anxiety rising within her. Leah counts, her voice a whisper in the silence of the room. She will give herself until ten, and then she will move, forcing herself out of this stupor, her body springing into action. She will clean this place and get out of here, close the door for good and never return. Not to the house nor to this street. This is it. It's over, her obsession, her desperation to get Jacob back. It's at an end. All she needs is a few seconds to gather her strength.

The room is deathly quiet as she stands, waiting for her own body to respond. That's when she hears it. It weakens her, the sound, cuts her in half.

A low moan, a whisper of breath, a rustle of fabric.

Her skin contracts, fine hairs raised on her flesh as she turns, blinking repeatedly, and forces herself to look at Chloe's body, to stare at that bleeding battered mound on the bed. There it is again. A sound, a tiny murmur. The ambient temperature in the room plummets. The floor tilts. She gasps, presses her back against the wall. Then another noise. A low sound, a small quiver from underneath the sheet. The tiniest of movements but enough to make her bend double, to clutch her stomach and cry out before slapping a hand on her mouth to stem it.

Another movement. A twitch underneath the sheet, then a soft breath followed by a whimper, faint but there all the same. She isn't imagining it. This isn't a shock induced hallucination. It's Chloe.

She's still alive.

The sound of Chloe's soft desperate sighs, Leah's proximity to the bleeding body, the stench of blood and sweat, make Leah dizzy with guilt. Shame and fear bites at her. She clutches her chest, doubles over, retches again, bringing up nothing but belches of warm foul-smelling air.

Leah sobs, a quiet release of pent-up terror. Emotions that have been sitting in her gut for as long as she can remember come spilling out until she is howling, unable to stop the outpouring of every emotion she has ever experienced; primitive and powerful feelings that render her incapable of doing anything at all.

She stops, her chest heaving, her eyes reluctantly drawn to Chloe who is still twitching, her movements so slight, so very faint that Leah has to concentrate to ensure she isn't mistaken. In the few minutes that she stands and watches, the sheet covering her rises and falls with growing regularity, Chloe's breathing becoming more consistent, stronger and worryingly robust.

Leah's head spins, she senses her own breathing becoming shallow and rapid. She is unsure what to do next. She didn't want to kill her. That was never the plan, but now Chloe is sure to pass Leah's name on to the police and a national manhunt will take place.

Unless Chloe dies before any help arrives. Before Jacob arrives back at the flat. Or unless she suffers massive memory loss and is left with permanent damage to her brain, unable to recall anything about the incident. Leah exhales, her breath hot, her mouth gritty with dread. It's possible. She remembers reading about it once. It's called retrograde amnesia, a condition that leaves sufferers unable to retrieve memories before the event that caused the damage. Perhaps Chloe will wake up with no idea of what happened by which time Leah will be far away from here.

She has already made up her mind to go to London. She will stay with Aunt Mary, tell her she is out of work and looking for a job in London. Except she needs to finish cleaning up in this room and she hasn't any money to get to London. She bites at her lip, tugs at her hair until it hurts, pain screeching over her scalp.

She could make certain that Chloe will never identify her by lifting that stone lion once more and finishing what she has started. The thought of it is too much to bear. Another death. More shame. More terror. She isn't sure she can take any more, is able to shoulder any more blame. This was an accident. She did it in a moment of confusion and panic. Doing something drastic now would be premeditated and that would make her a murderer. She isn't a killer. This whole thing was an accident. Every stupid thing she has done has always been borne out of anger, not because of a need to spill blood just for the sake of it.

No, she must leave Chloe alone, clean up and get out of here.

Spurred into action by her diminishing options, Leah uses the detergent to clean every surface she has touched, ignoring the small sighs and groans of pain coming from under the blood-stained sheet. Her jaw clamps shut as she squats down to grab at the blood-smeared stone lion. Refusing to look at it directly, she drops it in the bag and knots it tightly. She'll take it with her and dispose of it in a wheelie bin somewhere along the way – not Jacob's bin. That's the first place the police will look for evidence. She will spread pieces of herself far and wide and hope some unsuspecting neighbour doesn't spot the extra bag stuffed deep within their bin.

Back in the kitchen, she pulls off the gloves, rinses her hands under the tap and stares at the handbag on the counter. How did she not notice it earlier? Pulling at it feverishly, the bag sits wide open like a hungry gaping mouth, its contents visible. She delves inside and brings out a purse stuffed with notes. Chloe's purse. Leah's face heats up as she quickly glances at the amount – at least a couple of hundred pounds, probably more. She quickly flicks through the notes, counting, stopping when she gets to 300. There's more still, maybe another two hundred. Enough to get her to London. Her pulse quickens, her flesh warms. This is it. This is all she needs. This wad of cash is her ticket out of here. More than enough to get her to Aunt Mary's and far away from here. Far from the trouble that this situation will undoubtedly invite.

Relief and euphoria washing over her, she whips up the bag and throws it across her shoulder. Once she has finished vacuuming and removing as much of herself as she can from this flat, she will be out of here, on her way to somewhere else. On her way to the safety of Aunt Mary's – her sanctuary. Somewhere hardly anybody knows about. This time next week, the whole incident will be out of her mind, just another blot in her ragged copy book.

Heartened by her find, she finishes cleaning, a fresh surge of energy pulsing through her. She needs to get a move on, to get out of this place, to breathe clean air and leave this fucking awful mess far behind.

31

The stairwell and hallway are empty. Leah half expected to find Collette the nosy neighbour nearby, spying on her, peeping through her letterbox, then creeping out of her door and asking what she was up to; poking and prying until Leah finally comes undone and spills her darkest secret to a perfect stranger, but there is nobody about. Not a sound to be heard apart from the low shuffle of her own movements.

The urge to keep looking behind her is overwhelming but as far as she can tell Collette has stayed firmly put. Still unsure, she creeps and tiptoes until she is out of the front door at which point she begins to pick up her pace, fists clasping the bin bag tightly, holding it to her chest like a mother protecting her newborn.

The street is thankfully empty, everyone at work or busy in their homes, going about their daily business, their lives too full to take notice of some strange, frazzled young woman clutching a bin bag full of evidence tight to her body.

The walk is an onerous task. Her breathing is laboured, her skin both hot and cold at the same time. She has to keep a level head, not melt into a puddle of nervous desperation. She's come too far now to slacken and come undone. It would mean losing everything – her life, the last fragments of her family. Jacob. She would lose him completely. That is, if she hasn't already. He will discover Chloe, feel duty-bound to stay with her, to protect her, keep her from harm in the future. He will be wracked with guilt at not being there for her. This happened in his flat. He left her there, alone and exposed to danger. What Leah has done inadvertently is form a bond between the pair of them. They share a common tragedy and are now inextricably bonded. What started off as a bid to get Jacob back has driven him further away. Even this has gone terribly wrong. Leah has fucked up yet again.

She's useless. A damaged human being, a pathetic individual who can't even wreak revenge properly.

What a stupid awful fucking mess.

Clutching the bag even tighter, Leah bites at her lip until she can taste blood, and breaks into a run, desperate to be out of this street. Desperate to be away from everything.

32

It's busy at the station, the platform filled with people.

Leah stands, shivering. It's not particularly cold but her body is like ice, her flesh tingling, her extremities numb. She thinks that perhaps she is in shock, unable to come to terms with what she has just experienced; what she has just done.

Maybe once she is settled in her seat, things will seem different, she will start to think clearly, to calm herself and get a grip of her senses. She can't allow herself to fall apart. Not now. Not after all her efforts, not after the amount of energy she exerted to remove all traces of herself from that flat. The worst is over. That's what she keeps telling herself. The alternative, owning up to what she has done, handing herself into the relevant authorities and accepting the consequences, is unthinkable. Perhaps she should have done things differently, left Jacob alone, gone to her parents for help, but it's too late for that now. It's too late for everything.

The sound of a train in the distance rattles her bones, regurgitating memories she would rather stayed hidden. Despite trying to suppress it, despite thinking of other things, filling her head with ideas and thoughts of more pleasant times, the image of Ellis catapults into her brain. What was he thinking that day before he lunged forwards onto this track? What sort of things were going through his poor tortured brain? Did he think of her, what she put him through? How she tried to ruin his life.

She allows herself to glance at the lengths of metal just for a few seconds, recalling that evening when the police called at their house, saying those words, telling her parents what no parents should ever have to hear, cracking their world in two. A streak of sunlight catches her eye. It spreads itself across the tracks, a ribbon of yellow, glinting, daunting, mocking her. Refusing to leave her alone. She forces her gaze elsewhere, swallowing and rubbing at her eyes.

She can't begin to imagine how he was feeling, how desperate he was, how fragmented his thoughts were. Why didn't he come home? Why didn't he come home after school and speak to their parents about what was going through his head? They would have helped him. They would have protected him, kept him safe from all the insults and the jibes and the hurt. That's the type of people they were – it's who they were. Still are. Decent people. Caring people. If only she had realised it earlier.

A spark of irritation flares under her skin. A flamethrower burning at her insides. This is her fault. Even when it's about Ellis and little Lucy, it all comes back to her, what she did. What she said.

It always comes back to her.

Perhaps she is cursed, blighted from birth. She has always felt like an outcast, an imposter. Maybe her brain is wired up differently to other people. Maybe she has every reason to feel permanently angry.

Or maybe she is just bad through and through.

The weight of Chloe's handbag digs into her shoulder. It's full of Leah's belongings. After leaving Jacob's flat and dumping the bag in a bin on a neighbouring street, she made her way back to her own place and crept around to the back garden where she rummaged through her belongings, the ones Grainne had thrown out. Ignoring the ripped flowers and the garden that she had ruined, she managed to salvage some of her own things which she then stuffed into the leather handbag she had stolen from Chloe; a change of underwear, her glasses and her purse with her bank cards still slotted inside. Not that they would be of any use to her now. Her account is empty. She is completely broke. Still, having some form of ID with her makes her feel a little less empty, as if she is a somebody, not just a criminal running from her past. She is a person – Leah Browne, and despite her anger issues, despite what she has just done, she deserves to be recognised as such.

A muffled voice over the public address system announces the arrival of the next train and then goes on to make a long-winded, incomprehensible announcement that Leah cannot hear properly or decipher. Disappointment and frustration fizz up inside her. All she wants to do is get on that train, settle back and think about arriving at Aunt Mary's door unannounced. A warm glow blooms in her chest at the thought of the expression on Mary's face when she opens the door and sees Leah standing there. She just wants this damn train to get here. She doesn't want delays and muffled announcements. All she wants is to escape, to get to Mary's safely and be welcomed home. Jacob will possibly be back at his flat by now. He will have driven like the wind, discovered Chloe's body and called an ambulance and the police who will be currently crawling all over the place, an army of white-suited forensic investigators dusting for fingerprints, swabbing everything, every surface, every piece of furniture for traces of DNA.

She's not so stupid as to think they will not investigate this crime. Chloe is seriously injured. She may still die. They will want answers. And soon. They will also be searching for Chloe's phone. Leah exhales and shields her eyes from the glare of the sun. They won't find it. She threw it in the river on her way to the station. She took a diversion and headed up to a lane where it was quiet. Nobody saw her. It landed with a quiet plop and disappeared. She had hidden herself amongst the bushes as a precaution, and then walked back to the station feeling lighter. Another piece of evidence disposed of. One less thing to worry about.

She is so close to escaping this trauma. All she wants is for this bloody train to turn up and only then will she truly begin to relax. She deserves that much. Because for all she knows she has done something terrible, she is also aware that she was backed into a corner. Both Jacob and Chloe conspired to shut her out of his life. They did their utmost to curtail her visits, to make sure they could continue with their own lives undisturbed, acting as if Leah and Jacob never existed as a couple. She was robbed of her life, her relationship, everything she ever cared about. What they did was cruel – beyond cruel. All she ever did was try to defend herself. And now look where she is.

Look at what she has done. What they made her do.

More tears fill her eyes. She thinks of everything she is leaving behind. She thinks of her diaries, her innermost thoughts and feelings that are stuffed in a bag for anybody to find and read. Her private desires and emotions. The scribblings of a madwoman. She simply didn't have the time to go rummaging for them. If she is lucky, the binmen will take them away and she will be saved the humiliation of having strangers read through her thoughts, sifting through her personal effects. And if not – well if not, then they will see what she had to endure. What they put her through.

This is their fault. They drove her to it.

A collective groan forces her out of her thoughts and back to the present. A crowd of people are standing looking at the electronic timetable, muttering to one another, their faces pink with anger.

'For God's sake,' a tall man wearing a silk scarf announces loudly. 'That's all we bloody well need. It says here that most of the trains are running late due to problems with overhead wires. There's a statement on the website.' He stares at his phone then back at the board before shaking his head in disgust and marching off out of view.

Terror grips her, spiking her stomach, curdling her blood. She needs to get on that train. The longer she waits, the greater the chances are of somebody finding her. She walks to the board and squints, running her eyes over the list of times and destinations. Something inside her concertinas, her innards squirming and shifting in fear. Her train is delayed by two hours.

Two hours.

She closes her eyes, tries to blot out the image of a police raid on the station, a siege where she is publicly dragged to the floor and cuffed before being led off to a car where a team of reporters and photographers are waiting to take her picture and splash it all over the front pages of every local and national newspaper.

Sweat blinds her. She staggers away from the board, slumps down on a nearby seat, trying to slow her hammering heart, to control her breathing before she hyperventilates and draws unnecessary attention to herself. Two hours. Two long hours of watching and waiting, imagining that every dark suit, every rustle of fabric, every heavy footfall is a police presence, scouting out her whereabouts, surrounding the station before putting it in lockdown and calling out her name as they pounce on her and read out her rights.

A vice clamps itself around her head. Her back aches, her stomach roils and knots, a strong fist grasping at her insides. It's imperative she remains calm. She can't spend the next two hours like this. She will implode, her body pushed to its limits by the sheer stress of it.

Dipping her hand into the bag, she grabs at a handful of coins and makes her way over to the vending machine only to find it not working. *Jesus Christ.* Everything is conspiring against her, even inanimate objects designed to give her some sustenance are refusing to help. She will have to simply sit and wait like everybody else here. Pacing and getting angry will heighten her unease, drawing unwanted attention from other passengers. Guilt and anxiety are written all over her face, chiselled into every feature.

She sits back on the bench, trying to unwind. It's impossible. She can't concentrate on anything, can't think straight.

Out of the corner of her eye, something flickers. A quick movement. Somebody watching her. Slowly, so very slowly, her lungs refusing to inflate properly as she heaves for breath, she turns and sees a small girl standing alone on the platform. Leah's muscles contract. Her throat closes up.

The child is shivering, crying, holding out her hands, beckoning for assistance, appealing for help. Her wails grow louder. Blood runs down her face, drips over her tiny twisted body, cascading down her bare legs. Leah dips her head, turns away, covers her ears. Dear God, what is happening? Why isn't anybody helping this poor child?

The world speeds up, everything spinning around her. The floor inclines to one side under her feet. The air is too thin. She cannot bring herself to turn around, to look at the child, to see her small pained expression.

Suddenly she realises. She knows who it is, why she is here.

Sweat courses down Leah's back. Perspiration glistens on her forehead. She keeps her head low, refusing to look at what she did.

She remembers that day vividly as if it were yesterday. Lucy is gone. Dead. She isn't here. She can't be. This is a dream, a sick hallucination. Her mind is punishing her, forcing her to take responsibility for something that was a terrible accident.

But it wasn't an accident, was it? You're lying. Always lying. That's you all over. A pathetic little liar.

She lets out a yelp, covering her mouth with her hand, coughing to mask it. This has got to stop, this self-perpetuating cycle of blame and fear. Lucy is dead. Ellis is dead. Leah is here, living and breathing, they are not and there's not a damn thing she can do about it. This is insane. She has got to stop torturing herself, delving into the past, trying to change things that cannot be changed.

Slowly, summoning up every bit of courage she has, she turns her head and looks at the little girl, holding her gaze, their eyes locked together for what feels like an age. It's seconds, no more than that. Leah blinks then widens her eyes. The child has gone. Vanished. Only an open space where she should be.

There's nobody there. There never was.

33

The woman behind the desk glances up from under her lashes. Every look, every subtle movement stokes up the furnace raging in Leah's belly. The waiting around at the station for a train that obviously wasn't coming became too much to bear.

Trying to make her herself invisible amongst the crowds of angry waiting passengers, she had headed out of the station and made her way towards a nearby guest house, a tall Victorian residence nestled between other properties. An innocuous-looking house, flanked on all sides by other houses. Anonymous. Private. No reason for anybody to suspect a violent criminal was staying there.

She spent the night tossing and turning, unable to settle, listening out for sirens or the crashing of feet as the police headed towards her door before barging in unannounced. As soon as dawn broke, she got up, got showered and sat around until a reasonable hour so as not to draw any unwanted glances from staff and other guests.

'No breakfast?' The receptionist taps away at her keyboard, her attention now focused on the screen. Leah lets out a trembling breath, her jaw quivering, her skin burning. She just wants to pay and leave. So much unnecessary fuss with receipts and breakfasts and questions about parking. Staying in one of those seedy hostels would have been easier. Less conspicuous. Fewer questions. Just slap her money on the counter and leave.

'No breakfast. I'm eating at the conference. When I get there, that is.' She makes a play of staring at her watch then looking back at the female who is now watching her carefully, her eyes dark and empty, her expression inscrutable.

'Right. All done. This is your receipt. I hope you enjoyed your stay.' A sheet of A4 paper is placed in front of her, the print a blur as she snatches it off the counter and folds it up into a neat square. She wants to run, to get out of this place but is aware that her every move is being watched and scrutinised. Remaining calm is imperative. Her name is Barbara Watson and she is a businesswoman on her way to a conference in the city centre. Her new identity bounced around her head all night; the name embedded deep in her brain by the time she came down to check out. She hoped that paying by cash would make things easier, more fluid, yet here she is, still hanging around. Still waiting.

'Thank you.' She begins to walk away, then as an afterthought, places a small tip on the counter pushing it towards the receptionist. Anything to salve her conscience. A tiny plaster over a gaping wound but better than nothing at all.

The station is busy as she buys her ticket and merges into the crowd of commuters, losing herself in the bustle and noise. She hears grumbling and is dismayed to see more delays listed on the electronic arrivals board. An hour to wait until her train arrives. An hour of waiting, watching, glancing over her shoulder for somebody to step in and arrest her. This is going to be the longest hour of her life.

By the time the train arrives, Leah is a coiled spring, her

nerves frazzled, her back and head aching from the effort of trying look and act relaxed when the tension has almost broken her in half. Her spine is rigid with a steel rod running through it. Her eyes are sore from keeping watch for the police, for small dead children, for anybody who may wish her harm.

This train pulling up in the station with a skin-withering metallic screech is the nicest thing she has seen all week. She can't seem to draw her eyes away from it as it stops at the platform with a convulsive squeak, the rubbery odour filling her lungs, the noise of the surging crowds reassuring as she pulls out her ticket from her pocket, stands up, and boards.

34

She is in Will's office. She isn't in his office. Where in God's name *is* she? She can't move, can't breathe properly. Hands reach out to her, touching her, helping her, trying to free her. Trying to keep her alive. She is trapped, unable to do anything except weep. And the pain. Dear God, the eye-watering pain. It's unbearable.

She sees a face. Will's face. He is standing over her. Behind him is the picture, the hideous burst of colour that she loathes; strokes of red and orange, ferocious flames of bright yellow. It frightens her, makes her want to shrivel up in a tight little ball to escape from it. Except it isn't a picture. It's moving; pulsing and roaring close to her. She feels its heat, fears its brutality and tries to shrink away from it. The fire billows and swirls, creeping ever nearer, ready to swallow her, a big hot hungry mouth eager to take her away. She feels herself being moved. She resists, worried it's the fire, its hot claws digging and pawing at her. It isn't. She can feel them – sets of hands dragging, pulling, trying to get her away from the danger, away from the raging furnace. She wants to laugh with relief but can't do anything. It's too much effort. Too painful.

Will's face looms over her. She can't breathe. Something is stuck in her throat, lodged in her windpipe, a hard pebble stopping her from breathing. She tries to cough, feels nausea rising, blood curdling in her neck, thick and warm. A hiccup, a belch, and then it explodes out of her, a demon exiting her body. She stares up at Will, at his face. Those marks. Blood everywhere. Sticky splatters, brown and red, smeared over his visor. He doesn't budge, stays still. No attempts to wipe it away, all his efforts concentrated on her.

'Okay, Leah, do you remember me? I'm Will. I'm going to get you out of here. Just nod if you can hear me.'

She moves her head up and down, murmurs his name over and over. 'Will, Will, Will.'

'That's right. Focus on your breathing and try to stay calm. We're doing all we can to help you. As soon as we're able, we'll give you some medication to ease the pain.'

She feels his hand pressing on her wrist. She wants to tell him to keep hold, to stay by and not leave her alone. She's frightened. Terrified. She's dying. She knows it.

'We thought we'd lost you earlier.' He smiles at her, his eyes pools of darkness, his voice the sound of summer; bright, carefree, full of promise. 'Stay with me, Leah. It won't be long and we'll have you out of here.'

'Where am I?'

'You've been in an accident. Try to lie still. There are more paramedics on their way to help.'

'Am I going to die?' She feels too exhausted to cry, but a lone tear rolls out of her eye and down her face, closely followed by another, then another. An accident. The train journey. The crash.

Jacob and Chloe.

Ellis and Lucy.

Her life, her terrible ruined life. The one she shredded into small pieces.

She tries to move but it's impossible. Everywhere hurts. Agony. Beyond anything she has ever experienced.

'Let's just get you sorted, shall we?' Will's voice is soft. He is trying to sound reassuring. She doesn't feel reassured. She doesn't feel anything. Just pain and more pain.

Seconds pass, then minutes. More minutes that seem to roll into hours. Not hours. It can't be. Minutes for sure. Only a few minutes.

Somebody else is close by. She can sense them, can hear their chatter. She wants to reach out, to beg them to get her out of here but no words will come. Will is still with her. Not in his office. There is no office. They are here, trapped in hell.

She hears things: the roar of machinery, more voices. Shouting. Orders being barked out.

Her body judders, her throat closes.

She focuses on a spot of darkness. It grows, expanding and filling her vision. It's dark and yet at the same time it is light; soft and comforting. A welcoming sight in a murky pool of shadows. She wants to reach it, to climb inside that light and lose herself. She isn't frightened anymore. She is – what is it that she feels? It suddenly dawns on her what this emotion is that she is experiencing, the sensation that is ballooning deep within her barely breathing body as her life slowly ebbs away – disappointment. That's what it is. She is disappointed.

Her eyes blur, the pain lessens. She sighs, a thick gurgling sound that feels as if it is coming from elsewhere. She thinks about things. Things she wishes she hadn't taken for granted. Not only her family. Other things as well. She wants to see the sky above her, not this distending orb of black. She longs to see the silvery moon with its iconic smiling face, as familiar to her as her own skin, or the burnt orange of the sun as it hangs lazily in the sky, its welcoming citrus glow reminding her of how good it feels to be alive. But it's all too late. Her thoughts, her anxieties, her regrets... Everything is just too damn late...

But at least she knows now. She knows why she was on the train. She always knew. It was just her confused thoughts, jumping about in her brain, trying to make sense of everything. They lost their way, colliding inside her head, jumbled up like a nightmare; her worries, her memories, her many unspeakable sins, all bashing and falling about, all fighting for space, excavating and illuminating long hidden experiences she would sooner forget. She wants to say sorry, to tell Lucy and Ellis that she wronged them and to beg for their forgiveness. She wants to see her parents one last time, to hug her mum, to throw herself onto her dad's large welcoming chest, to tell them over and over that it was never their fault, that it was her. It's always been her.

She closes her eyes. Will's voice fades into the distance, a faraway sound telling her to hang on, that he is here for her and that everything is going to be okay. She knows deep down, somewhere deep within her, that it definitely isn't.

35

Darkness growing, light shrinking, becoming smaller and smaller and smaller, attenuating and disappearing.

A pinprick. Then nothing...

'We've lost her!' Will's voice barking through the wreckage.

'Shit!'

Movement close by. Somebody coming nearer, touching his shoulder. A moment of sadness, of sorrow. A wave of regret. No more than seconds then it's time to move on. More lives to save, more people to evacuate.

A swish of fabric, feet shuffling, running. Then voices, authoritative, urgent.

'Over here. I've got an elderly man. Possible hypovolaemia. Immediate assistance required.'

36

LEAH

I've often wondered what it feels like to die. I've thought about it a lot, especially since we lost Lucy then Ellis. I lie in bed sometimes and think about what goes through a person's head in those final few minutes. Do they know they're dying? Do they make their peace with the world before taking that final juddering breath? Then when I think about it too much I have to switch off. It's too frightening to consider. Did Ellis think about us, his family, before he jumped? Did he feel any pain? I hope not. I hope it was swift and if there is some sort of afterlife, I hope he's happy there.

I also think about going to see my parents. Our last conversation wasn't pleasant. It got out of hand. I suppose I was to blame for that little episode. I usually am. Being pleasant and sociable has always felt like one huge effort to me. I can do it when I need to, when it suits me, but it's not who I really am. That's something else I think about a lot – who I actually am.

What are my real mum and dad like? Are they a pair of losers or were they just going through a blip in their lives and I got caught up in the crossfire? Unless I make an effort to trace them, then I guess I'll never really know. I've considered it – going to look for them. I know how to do it. I did some research after I left home but I've never gone through with it. I think it's because I might find them and then when I see how they live, I'll realise that the grass would never have been greener on the other side of the fence. I might find them living on some scruffy housing estate in a shitty little house and then my bubble will well and truly burst. I might see the real me in them and I don't want that. At least this way, I still have an air of mystery about me.

I know their names. Karen and Mike Segrave. They sound perfectly ordinary to me and that's exactly how I want them to stay. I've conjured up an image of them both in my head. Mike is a plumber, likes a drink in the pub after work, has a bit of a beer gut but was once a handsome lad with a twinkle in his eye. He tried drugs a couple of times just for kicks and it got out of control but he's working hard on getting his life back on track. Karen works in the corner shop, spends her spare money on hair dye and fags and loves nights out at the local bingo hall with her mates. She likes to keep her house clean and tidy and her favourite programme is Coronation Street.

Meeting them might smash that image to smithereens. They may well be better than the picture I have in my head, but I know deep down that they will probably be a whole lot worse so I've never taken that step and contacted them. I don't even know where they live and that's how it's going to stay.

I wonder if they think about me? Probably not. Their drug-addled brains are probably too focused on getting their next fix. They'll be too far gone to ever give a shit about me. I'm in limbo, caught between two families. The nowhere child.

Except I'm not. I know that. I'm not stupid. Feckless – yes, thoughtless – definitely. I've got a family, a good kind family who care about me, but everything is in tatters and the problem is, it's gone on for that long now that I don't know how to get any of it back.

PART II

37

CHRISSIE

It took them a while to identify her. That's what the police officer told Chrissie and Ralph. She had somebody else's things, you see. Somebody else's handbag and purse with their driving licence and bank cards and what not, so they thought at first that they had another person. But she still had some of her own things on her – a credit card that had expired and a couple of old photographs tucked away in the back of her own small wallet.

Chrissie hadn't known whether to laugh or not when they told her this. Laughing wasn't the appropriate response, she knew that, and she definitely wasn't happy. She was devastated. Their daughter was dead; involved in a major train crash that was making national and international news, but it was just like Leah to cause a commotion. Their Leah, their daughter. Even in her final moments, their precious girl still had the propensity to send everyone into a frenzy trying to work out who she really is.

Was.

Chrissie swallows and places her fingers over her stinging eyes, pushing at them, pressing down to stem the tears that won't stop flowing. They just keep coming and coming. There's no relief from them, no respite from the hurt and the misery and the many, many regrets that whirl through her head like a tornado, smashing into her skull, giving her headaches that no painkillers can ease. Every day is a living nightmare. She rubs at her eyes and stretches her hand over the diary that was handed to her in the days after her daughter's death. Leah's diary. She hasn't summoned up the courage to read it just yet.

Every day brings new trauma, new truths they would rather not hear. The bag was stolen apparently. Stolen. Their girl was a thief. Chrissie knew Leah was many things but hoped they had instilled enough goodness in their children, enough manners and morality, to stop them from becoming involved in wrongdoings but apparently not. Even though the train had derailed and was crushed and battered, the bag was close by when they found her.

At first, Chrissie and Ralph had refused to believe it but the police were insistent, and then they had identified her body.

Unlike Ellis, she was recognisable. Her skin was like porcelain, all pale and creamy. They wouldn't move the sheet below her chin. Chrissie had wanted to hold her hand, to tell her daughter one last time just how loved she was, while stroking her beautiful face. She wanted to lean in to give her a final parting hug and one soft sweet kiss but was told it wasn't possible. She had suffered terrible chest injuries they had said so couldn't remove the white sheet that covered her body.

Chrissie had left the room at that point, unable to hear anything else. She just wanted to curl up and go to sleep for a hundred years, leave it all behind her. But that is impossible.

She has to get up every morning and relive it. Every single day is another painful blow, another reminder of what she has lost. How much she has lost. All of her children. All gone. She sometimes wonders what she did to deserve such a terrible fate but then reminds herself that lots of people suffer trauma like hers. There's a group she can attend, for people who have been through similar things. Maybe at some point she will consider it but she's not sure she's ready for such public displays of raw emotion just yet.

Ralph won't go. The garden is his sanctuary. He's out there every day, snipping at flowers, deadheading roses, mowing a lawn that doesn't need mowing, digging and tidying flowerbeds that don't need tidying. That's how he copes with it, but Chrissie needs something else. She doesn't know what that something else is but is hoping that it will present itself to her soon enough.

The police had told them that they were conducting another investigation that involved Leah but it was early stages and they weren't at liberty to divulge too many details. Recently bereaved, desperate grieving parents, and they were still questioned about when they last saw their daughter.

Had they spoken to her? Did they know she no longer lived at her flat and had been dismissed from her job? So many negative statements and probing questions.

Their daughter had just died and neither Chrissie nor Ralph could think straight, never mind give dates and remember their movements weeks before the accident had taken place. They barely knew what day it was.

In the end, the two police officers stood up to leave, giving Chrissie a sympathetic nod and Ralph a soft pat on his shoulder. They left with no more information about Leah than when they first arrived. There was nothing to tell.

Chrissie had wanted to show them photographs of the family, to let them know that the Brownes were a good family, a caring decent family, but Ralph had stopped her.

'They're short staffed, pet. They don't have time to sit and look at people's old holiday snaps,' he had said. That had stung. Those pictures were, still are, important to her. They are proof that the Brownes aren't a damaged dysfunctional family. They're a grieving one. All families have scars, it's just that some are easier to hide than others. The Brownes' wounds are visible for everyone to see. There's no shying away from them. But that doesn't make them bad people.

She sits in her chair facing the window that overlooks the back garden. Ralph is out there again. He's off work at the minute, deliberating over whether or not to go back at all. He could take early retirement but then what would he do with himself? She visualises the pair of them rattling around the house, each of them locked in their own private world of grief, their self-made protective armour plating too tight to allow anyone else in. They will both rot if they don't do something with their lives. Winter will be upon them in a few months. What will Ralph do then? With no garden to tend, he will simply hang around the house with nothing to do. There are a few odd jobs that need doing but neither of them can muster up the energy to care about the house anymore. Without their family here to fill it, it's just simply somewhere to live – four walls with furniture inside. No soul, no happiness. It's no more than an empty shell.

She knows that soon they will have to face the world, accept their lot in life and move on, but not just yet. The papers are full of the stories about the crash. She can't bring herself to read any of them or to watch the television with those overzealous, made-up happy-clappy news presenters who cock their heads to one side whilst regaling the public with the grisly details of how people died on that train, how they were trapped in the carriage while firefighters and medics fought to rescue them, fire ripping through the metal, melting it, making it even harder to reach people.

It seems that every time she turns on the telly, it's there, reminding her of how horrific her daughter's last moments were, how desperate she must have felt. Chrissie wonders if they crossed her mind, if she thought of them before...

She closes her eyes and pushes it away. She can't. She just can't think about it right now. Perhaps another time when it's not so raw, but not now. For the time being, both she and Ralph are concentrating on putting one foot in front of another and making it through the day without shouting and screaming and raging at the sky above them that life is so bloody difficult and unfair.

The police told them that once the investigation is complete, they will release Leah's belongings. There isn't much apparently, but there are some photographs and yet more diaries. Chrissie would like those for sure. She may not be able to bring herself to read them but they are a part of Leah and she will take whatever bit of solace she can. It's something tangible at least.

The shuffle of feet in the kitchen draws her away from her thoughts. Ralph is in. He will be ready for a sandwich and a cup of tea. He always works up a thirst when he's out in the garden. He's in better shape mentally than she is. Maybe she should get out there, give him a hand. She can't seem to summon up the energy. Everything feels so onerous, her limbs leaden with misery and grief.

'You put the kettle on, love, and I'll make you something to eat.' That's the least she can do for him, poor man, keeping it all hidden away, pushing his thoughts and unhappiness deep into the earth. She has watched him out there, his fingers scrabbling about in the dirt, dread and worry carved all over his face. Yet he never moans about it. Not like she does. She makes a mental note to be nicer to him, to not snap at him every time he speaks to her or tries to cuddle her. It's hard though, when your muscles are weighed down, your flesh cold with the thought of what she went through, their Leah. Their daughter.

'Salmon or tuna?' she says as she slowly heads through to the kitchen.

And this is how it is. Life goes on. People eat, drink, sleep. The world continues to spin. Nothing changes. Babies are born, people die.

'Tuna, please,' Ralph replies as he takes two cups out of the cupboard and places them down on the kitchen counter.

He fills the kettle, the gush of the water as it hits the bottom filling the silence around them. Chrissie manages a smile. Sometimes it's the everyday things, the routine and the normality of it all that makes everything that little bit easier to bear.

'You're looking a bit better, love,' he says softly. 'You know, all things considered.'

38

THE DIARY

Everything will be over if we don't get back together. I'm getting desperate now. I've let other areas of my life slide and as a result I'm unemployed and practically homeless.

Once I persuade Jacob to let me back into his life, I'm confident that everything else will just fall into place and we'll be back to how we were all those months ago. It was a mistake, us drifting apart. It's my fault, I know, and now I'm going to have to work really hard at getting him back, getting him to believe that I'm truly sorry and am willing to try harder at being a better person, at being humbler and less controlling. I guess we all have our faults, and being bossy and bad tempered is one of mine. We can't all be like Jacob, can we? All calm and cool and considered.

Maybe I should have watched him more and learnt from him instead of keeping tabs on where he was all the time and who he was with. That was my downfall. I drove him away and now I'm paying the price.

I'm willing to learn though, that's the thing. I'm willing to change and will be the person he wants me to be. I can be the one he chooses to spend his life with if only he would give me a chance to prove what a decent and caring person I can be. I've got it within me. I've just let things drift. I'm prepared to be a better person. I owe him that much. He made me so happy. Everything was perfect when I lived closer to him. Seeing him every day gave me a sense of purpose.

When I lost my job the first time and had to move to a different part of town, I felt like I'd been kicked. It wasn't the losing the job that did it, it was not being able to see Jacob every day that almost saw me off. I suppose that was when everything accelerated, the downward pull of my life and all that followed. You could say I did it to myself. Many would.

But as I said, I'm trying to improve. I don't only owe it to myself, I owe it to lots of other people too. Too many to name. Sometimes things seem to happen to me, stuff occurs and before I know it, everything has gone wrong and ends up ruined. That's how it's been for as long as I can remember. You'd think I would have had the courage to do something about it before now. Sometimes we have to be down on the ground before we realise we can't go any lower and that it's time to start looking up at the sky once again.

39

JACOB

The knock on the door wakes him, sending a deep thumping through his head as he is ripped from a much-needed slumber. He rises and staggers to his feet, clumsy and ungainly as he struggles to see through a fog of sleep. He's exhausted, fatigue gnawing at his muscles, working its way into the very core of him and settling there.

Another night at the hospital. Another night sitting at Chloe's bedside, willing her to wake up, willing her to breathe unaided. It's been two weeks since he found her, here in their bed, battered half to death. Two weeks of sitting idly by, stroking her hand, talking to her. Two long weeks of waiting for his beautiful girl to rouse herself, to sit up in bed, smile at him and help unravel this awful fucking mystery that has eaten away at him. Initially he had his suspicions. It was immediate, instinctive, to think of *her*. For so long she has bothered them, stalking them, harassing them, making their lives a complete sodding misery.

The police had descended after he found Chloe and made that call, combing his flat looking for clues, scouring every corner, every surface, every inch of the place and coming up with very little. 'It's early days,' they said. 'The DNA results are due back anytime now.' Not that they need them anymore. Not since the call from the police saying they had a solid suspect in mind.

He gave the police as much detail as he could but they initially went down the route that it was a burglary that went horribly wrong. Chloe's jewellery was missing. Pictures were stolen; and more bizarrely, his crockery. He asked them what rational explanation they could provide for such an odd list of items going missing; that the intruder goes around collecting Marks and Spencer's plates and stealing other people's photographs? It didn't add up, he had said to them.

He argued with them, his instinct telling him that only one person would do such a thing. He had given them Leah's name, told them about the harassment and as much background information on her as he knew, but they appeared to have already made up their minds, telling him that manpower was thin on the ground and that they already had a few names in mind; local drug users who routinely break into houses and steal anything that isn't nailed down. A burglary gone wrong, that was what they told him. A disturbed burglary. They had panicked, hit out at Chloe, ransacked the place and left her for dead.

'They'll take a necklace worth £200 and sell it for a tenner. Anything for a quick fix. That's all they're interested in. They're just crackheads who can't see any further than the end of their noses. They don't know the value of anything,' the policeman had said to him as they swabbed his flat and dusted for fingerprints. 'I hope they didn't have any sentimental value, those bits of jewellery. I doubt you'll get 'em back. Not unless you're prepared to trawl round all the local junk and pawn shops, and car boot sales. That's where they'll be. We see it all the time.'

Jacob had thanked the police for their time and showed them out, feeling deflated. They were compassionate, cocking their heads sympathetically and nodding and smiling in all the right places, but had their own agenda, their own ideas as to who they were looking for, taking little notice when he explained how Leah had stalked them relentlessly. Perhaps if he and Chloe had gone through with their earlier threats and called the police when she had appeared outside their door, then maybe they would have treated his claims with a greater degree of seriousness.

Even when he told them about the message that he received on the phone, they didn't appear shocked or fazed. He has since tried calling Chloe's phone but received no ringing tone.

'It's been switched off or broken apart, the SIM card ripped out and sold for pennies,' the police officer said. 'Probably dumped it somewhere once they realised it could be traced. Smackheads aren't interested in mobiles or technology. Just the high they'll get from their next fix.'

Part of him had hoped they were right, that it was a random attack – somebody looking for money which they probably got. Chloe's bag and purse were also taken. She always carried cash around. He had told her time and time again how daft and dangerous it was but she said it was a good way of keeping track of how much she spent. In her early years of teaching she had got into trouble with some debts and it had scared her so she would always keep a couple of hundred pounds with her rather than use her cards and now this attack has happened and somebody somewhere has got lucky with it.

Somebody.

Not somebody.

Leah.

Because he was right. It wasn't a random attack. He didn't know whether to be relieved or terrified when the police called back and sat him down to explain, asking him questions about Chloe, about her cards and missing purse. They had found it, they told him. They had found it with another person and asked him if he knew of her, this lady who had taken the bag and its contents. Again, he told them about Leah, about his suspicions after finding Chloe. They took notes, nodded as he spoke and said very little in return, but he knew then that it was Leah. She had done this. Madness had pushed her much further than even he had ever thought possible and now Chloe was seriously injured and, according to the police officers sitting on his sofa, Leah was dead.

They had found a body, they had said. A body. Not a person.

It was a train crash. The one just outside York that was making national news. Jacob had struggled to process it, to sort all that information in his mind and work out what had happened and why. Not that it mattered anymore. The last thing he wanted to do was climb inside Leah's head and work out her motives. She was beyond that sort of effort, as was he. He was too exhausted to think straight, too angry to care about Leah. She didn't deserve his exertions. She didn't deserve any of his time.

The knock comes again; rhythmic, insistent. He runs his fingers through his hair. He needs a shower. He can smell his own skin, the pungent meaty aroma of unwashed flesh as he makes his way to the door. He should care but doesn't. Everything is too much of an effort, his reserves of energy sorely depleted.

In the background, the muted TV displays images of the recent train crash, calling it a national tragedy. News of the local vicious attack on an innocent woman who is currently in a medically-induced coma, has already been overshadowed by a larger catastrophe. Chloe has already been forgotten about, relegated to the middle of the newspapers, cast aside for a more interesting story; more bodies, a greater impact. A wider audience. More revenue.

Jacob winces as he makes his way to the door, disgusted by

the news, disgusted by the state of the world. In the past few weeks, he has come to the conclusion that people are selfish ignorant bastards, only interested in the misfortune of others, turned on and alerted by how much money they can make out of somebody else's misery.

Eyes screwed up in concentration, he stands and stares through the peephole in the centre of the door at a middle-aged couple who look as dishevelled as he does. An uncomfortable heavy feeling presses down on him. The floor takes on a magnetic pull, dragging him down. He hangs on to the door frame for balance, his limbs suddenly weak. He is no fit state for visitors and besides, he has no idea who these people are. He also has no idea what they want from him. He hopes they're not neighbours, spurred on to do something beneficent after hearing what happened. He has neither the time nor the energy for their probing questions and faux concern, for their need for grisly details dressed up as sympathy and compassion. He is beyond being polite and isn't a fan of surprises so these people had better have a good reason for being here.

They're obviously not journalists; he knows those old hacks now, can spot them a mile away and see through their thin veneer of jocularity. How much he has learned in the past few days and wishes he hadn't. They've been waiting for him, an army of reporters, there every time he enters and leaves the hospital, even hanging about at the end of the street when he came home for a nap and a change of clothes. But now there has been a huge train crash which has taken centre stage. He isn't sure which upsets him the most – being probed and prodded about Chloe's attack or his beautiful girl being ignored and forgotten about simply because a better story has come along and nudged her out of the way.

So many times he has wished he hadn't gone to that bloody stupid conference. If only he had turned it down and stayed at home. Jacob fights back tears. He is past going over the long list of if onlys... if only he had been there to help her, if only he had driven back faster. If only, if only... Too many to count. Chloe is seriously injured, her chances of her making a full recovery still touch-and-go, and there's not a damn thing he can do about it.

Swallowing down the lump in his throat, Jacob gingerly opens the door, his fingers clasped around the frame. Experience has taught him that anything is possible. Even these two tired middle-aged folks could have a nasty trick up their sleeve. Trust nobody. That's his new mantra. Trust nobody, take nothing for granted. Especially happiness. He thought he had it all, that apart from Leah's constant unwanted presence, his life was as settled as it could ever be. How wrong he was.

'Hello?' He deliberately jams his foot in the door, stopping these jaded folks from barging their way in. Looking harmless and affable isn't always an indicator of innocence and virtue. He can't be too careful. Not after what happened.

'We're sorry to intrude,' the man says, sneaking occasional glances at the woman as if looking for affirmation of his words, 'but we were wondering if we could speak to you about our daughter?'

Jacob gazes at them, assessing them, trying to work out what their ulterior motive is. *What daughter?* Chloe's parents are separated and live on different continents – her father in America and her mother in Australia with her new husband. He has spoken to them on the phone frequently over the past few days. He knows Chloe's family and is almost certain these people are not relatives.

A sickly sensation creeps under his skin, squirming and nestling in his chest, curling and coiling itself like a viper waiting to unfurl, to strike at the very heart of him. He opens his mouth to reply, his voice low and gruff, the words hard to say out loud. 'What daughter?' he says, a tremble evident in his timbre.

But even as he is speaking, a terrible unthinkable idea begins to take shape in his head, a shadow, looming, filling the darkest corners of his mind. *It can't be. Surely not. Why would they even consider coming here?*

They don't reply, staring at him instead with doe eyes, an unspeakable sadness tattooed onto their greying skin. He can't hold them at arm's-length for any longer. They look completely stricken, as if they have been sucked dry by the woes and worries of life, chewed up and spat out as desiccated empty pods. He isn't the only one who's suffering here. These people look despairing, worse than him, if that's at all possible.

Letting out a sigh of resignation, he steps to one side, waves his hand, indicating for them to come into the hallway and closes the door behind them with a muffled click.

40

The hallway is disconcertingly silent as they stand opposite one another, clearing their throats, rummaging in pockets, trying to work out how to break this awkward moment with the right words. Words that hopefully won't bring the conversation to a close before it has even begun. Myriad images and ideas flit through Jacob's brain as the couple slouch their way past him and stand cumbersomely, their eyes flitting about, their gazes landing on everything except his face while they wait for him to speak.

'So, how can I help you?' He is beyond attempting to sound cheerful, his usual social niceties stripped away by recent events leaving a painful rawness, a gaping, bleeding lesion that he feels sure is visible to anyone who meets him. He is certain it will never ever heal. Perhaps, given time, it will, but right now, anybody saying the wrong thing to him, cursory careless words and phrases shoved his way, feel like salt tossed onto an open wound.

The older gentleman speaks first, a hint in his voice that this conversation isn't going to be an easy one. Too many pauses, too much emphasis on the sentence structure, making sure each word catches Jacob's attention. He chooses them with care, stumbling over every syllable, casting his eyes downwards, wringing his hands together inelegantly.

'There's something we would like to share with you. Is it okay if we all sit down?'

Jacob nods, feeling suddenly numb. He follows them through to his own living room thinking how strange it is that their roles have been reversed in such a short space of time. It's as if it is they who are the homeowners and he their visitor. He thought that recent events had left him desensitised to anything else life could throw at him but now their solemn expressions and grave manner are making him feel anxious, as if they are about to reveal something dreadful that he doesn't want to hear. He puffs out his cheeks and shakes his head surreptitiously. Like anything could be worse than his current predicament. It's not as if his life go could any lower, is it? He stops, checks himself, thinks about how close he came to losing Chloe on that first day. She's here, clinging on to life and for that he should be grateful. He should not think such morbid thoughts.

He notices how antiquated they look, the man in his pale blue slacks and dark sweater, and the woman in her thick tweed skirt and matching jacket. Her hair is scraped back into some sort of clip and the puffiness around her eyes suggests she hasn't been sleeping too well. They're probably only in their late fifties or early sixties but look so much older, as if life has given them a good kicking.

I'm not the only one, he thinks as he lets out a deep breath. *I'm not the only one.*

Still, Jacob doesn't want to speak, doesn't want them to speak either. He has had a gutful of bad news and can't bring himself to listen to any more of it. Whatever it is that they have to tell him, he feels sure he would be better off not hearing it. No matter how tired and distraught they look he still wishes they would take their misery and bad news elsewhere. He's having a difficult enough time dealing with his own problems at the minute.

'I'm Ralph, by the way, and this is my wife, Chrissie. We felt we had to come and see you, to speak with you and thank you for making her happy, our daughter. She wasn't the easiest of people to get along with and admittedly we hadn't seen her quite a few years.' Ralph's eyes dart towards his wife.

She is staring ahead, glassy eyed, her skin almost translucent, as thin and fragile as bone china, stretched over the sharp contours of her face. If anybody is in need of some decent sunshine, plenty of nourishment and a decent night's sleep, it is this lady.

Ralph continues, 'But we felt we had to thank you. At least the latter years of her life were happy ones. And that's all because of you, Jacob. You don't mind me calling you Jacob, do you? It's just that we've been through some of Leah's things and read some of her diaries and in them she writes about you with such fondness that we felt compelled to come and see you. Your relationship with her was a positive thing in her life.'

The room shrinks around him, the floor wobbling and teetering under his feet. His head swims. He has no idea why these people are here. What are they saying? Do they know how erroneous their words are? How far off the mark they are with what they're saying to him? It's apparent they know nothing about what has happened, about what their daughter did. Either that, or they are as deluded and deranged as she is. Overcome by a sudden need to move away from them, Jacob stands up and marches towards the door. If they refuse to leave, he will threaten them with the police. For all he knows they may want to harm him. Something tells him that isn't the case but he isn't about to take any chances. Not after what he and Chloe have been through.

Standing by the living room door, Jacob stares at Ralph, hoping he will do something. Both he and Chrissie remain seated. They sneak a glance at one another before continuing. 'We know that you and Leah had a bit of a tiff before her accident. We hadn't seen or spoken to her for a good few years ourselves, but death puts a different perspective on life, doesn't it? We decided it was time to put the past behind us and to focus on the good memories of our daughter.' Ralph looks at Chrissie, reaches across to her and grasps her hand tightly before looking back at Jacob. 'And you were one of her good memories.'

'We just wanted to meet with you to tell you how grateful we are that you were around for her, that you made her happy. We may have had our differences with Leah, but at the end of the day she was still our daughter,' Chrissie says before dipping her head and weeping quietly.

Jacob feels his stomach tighten. Leah is dead and although he feels sympathy for their loss, he wakes every morning flooded with relief at that fact. Never did he ever imagine he would celebrate the death of another human being but in this case, he will make an exception.

'She said in her diaries that her relationship with you was the best thing that ever happened to her and that she knew it was her fault you had broken up. She admitted being too controlling,' Ralph says softly as he stares at his hands. 'We just thought you should know that.'

Jacob moves back away from the door and sits, time stretching out in front of him. How in God's name is he supposed to tell these people the truth? How will he ever find the words to verbalise to them what a sick and twisted individual their daughter actually was? That she stalked him relentlessly, waiting outside his flat, staring up at his window, banging on his door in the early hours of the morning demanding to be let in and then attempting to assault him when he refused? His fingers brush over the bridge of his nose at the thought of that night, the memory of her hand connecting with his face, her furious expression. The dead look in her eyes. That's something he has tried to forget.

He should have called the police back then but it's too late now for regrets and mulling over what he should have done. Time to move on and stop punishing himself for what he didn't do.

He stares at Ralph and Chrissie, at their broken expressions, their quivering shoulders as they sit and weep silently. How is he going to do this? How will he ever tell them that he barely knew Leah and that she was just a neighbour? Somebody he passed in the street from time to time. These poor misled people have no idea that he barely knew their daughter. She was a neighbour, not even an acquaintance. They were on nodding terms, people who smile at one another as they pass in the street. He wants to tell them that he met their daughter by chance as she was moving in and that he made the mistake of helping her with a few boxes and since that time she has been an unwanted presence in his life. In their life.

It was Chloe, in the end, who bore the brunt of her madness. How can he ever begin to tell them that their daughter would turn up on his doorstep begging to be let in, that she followed him to work, waiting outside the college gates for hours at a time. All of this is the truth, but so often the truth is so much harder to relay. Why is it that falsehoods flow easier and faster than cold hard facts? He finds himself thinking that this is why people lie. It's no surprise to him that the world runs on mistruths and mendacious gossip. The truth is so often an ice-cold slap in the face and few can deliver it with the respect and reverence it deserves. Falsehoods can be moulded and shaped to suit the narrator whereas the truth simply is what it is. No frills, no dressing it up to soften the blow. The truth is a cold hard mistress and nobody is immune from her blows.

Jacob decides to take another route through this messy labyrinth so these people don't have to suffer yet another hard setback. They don't look able to withstand more bad news. Perhaps they already know the answer to the question he's about to ask but feels duty-bound to ask it anyway. He can't sit here, voiceless and helpless. Something has to be said. 'Have the police been in touch with you?' His ears buzz with anxiety, his pulse thick and solid in his neck like a drumbeat. 'About anything other than the train crash, I mean?'

He can tell by their reaction that he has hit home. Any remaining colour drains from Chrissie's face. Her eyes appear to droop and he watches as her fingers tremble in her lap like the wings of a small bird attempting to escape from a predator. Ralph clasps her hand tightly, makes an effort to catch her eye before speaking but she has already zoned out, distanced herself from what he is about to say.

'Aye, lad. They have. It's all such a mess, isn't it?' Ralph's voice is low and croaky, laced with desperation. 'That's why we're here really. Not just to thank you, but to apologise as well. The police haven't given us too much detail but we've worked out what happened. We're not the daft old codgers everybody thinks we are.'

A lump fills Jacob's throat, a resisting force as he tries to breathe properly. He didn't expect such a visceral reaction to Ralph's words. His skin is burning and his head feels too heavy for his body, his neck unable to support it. He slumps back in his seat and waits for the moment to pass.

'We had our kids late in life. When Ellis and Leah were teenagers, people used to sometimes think we were their grand-parents.' Ralph lets out a loud gravelly chuckle. 'We didn't mind it so much. We were just glad to have a family at all.'

There is a silence, the air heavy with his words, heavy with the regret and sorrow that all three of them are experiencing, laden with a thousand other emotions that are too difficult to say out loud.

'We shouldn't be here really,' Chrissie finally says, her eyes shining with more tears. 'The police said they're still conducting the investigation and that we should wait until more details are available before we say anything but...'

'We couldn't just leave it, could we, love?' Ralph says, finishing the sentence for her.

She nods and more tears spill down her face, closely followed by a muffled sob. Her hands rummage in her bag for a handkerchief. Jacob stands up and hands her a box of tissues. His own throat is constricted, his eyes bulging with tears he cannot shed. Not here in front of these people. Another time, another place perhaps. But not here.

Chrissie takes the box and thanks Jacob. She can't meet his gaze. He's thankful for that. His emotions are fragile at the minute and he has no idea how he is feeling about their knowledge of how he and Leah were acquainted. How can he ever begin to tell these distraught people that before things took a more sinister turn, they were no more than neighbours who sometimes stopped to say hello and chat about the weather and the fact the bins didn't get emptied on time.

He knew Leah had her sights set on him and that she saw Chloe as an obstruction. He's not an idiot. He presumed she was lonely and slightly unstable, but this? This idea that they were actually in a relationship is so far from the truth that it makes him sick to his stomach. Never in a million years did he imagine that this was what was going through her head when she stood outside his flat gazing up at him. He thought she had designs on him, that she imagined in some weird and warped way, she could split him and Chloe up and then perhaps muscle her way in, but to actually think she was already a part of his life, that they were actually lovers? It's insane. He has no words. He feels pity for these people but has no answers to make any of this sorry mess any better.

Sensing Jacob's growing distress, Ralph stands up, helping Chrissie to her feet with gentle guiding hands and a strong arm. 'We'll be off, then. We don't want to keep you any longer, do we, love? We just wanted to say thank you and sorry. Please tell your partner that we're so sorry as well.'

They slouch away from him into the long hallway. Jacob swallows down his fears, knowing he should say something, tell them that they've got the wrong idea and that he barely knew their daughter, but every time he opens his mouth, nothing comes out. How can he possibly do it? Isn't it bad enough they are grieving for their daughter? Is he really going to be the one who exposes them to yet more hurt and heartbreak? He knows as well as anybody, that life is tough enough.

Besides, the police will inform them of their findings soon enough. Let people who are paid to do this type of thing inform these poor people. Let them tell Chrissie and Ralph what sort of person their daughter really was. He hasn't got it in him to do it. The police are better equipped to deal with these sorts of situations without causing even more trauma and rupturing what little life these two people have left.

Jacob shows them out and leans back on the door after closing it, thinking he should have seen this coming. He should have called the police many months ago, taken control of this situation and nipped it in the bud. But he didn't. He let it escalate and now he's having to deal with the fallout.

Clutching his head, trying to alleviate the pain slicing through his skull, he returns to the living room, drops down onto the sofa and closes his eyes.

41

RACHEL

She bites at her nails nervously, tearing at a small strip of skin just beneath the nail bed and spitting it out onto the floor. A disgusting habit and one she had recently kicked, but now, here she is, at it again, tearing and spitting, tearing and spitting before shoving her hands under her armpits and holding them there tightly.

The café fills up around her, the echo of voices and the deafening clank of crockery pounding in her ears. She suddenly feels conspicuous, as if everybody knows what she's up to. As if they all know what a fraud she is, spilling the beans and making a hefty amount of cash out of a tragedy. She lived when others died. She was fortunate when others weren't. She shivers despite the dry heat of the room. Blood money – that's what it is. Blood money. She swallows and sinks down in her seat, her feet crossed at the ankles. Why didn't she request this meeting somewhere more private? Somewhere more conducive to the sensitivity of the story she is about to reveal? Stupid, so very stupid. Maybe she shouldn't have come at all. Maybe she should have gone with her gut instinct and said no.

The chatter behind her grows in volume, people drinking

and eating, laughing, feeding their children, making small talk, while she is sitting here, wondering if she has done the right thing, wondering if, rather than tell her story to the masses, she has actually sold her soul to the devil. It doesn't feel right, giving this interview, and yet here she is, waiting for him to turn up, waiting for the devil incarnate to scribble down her words and put them in print so the waiting world can gorge themselves on them, so that they can slake their thirst for stories that include blood and guts and the misfortune of others. Her stomach is in knots, her knees knocking together.

She needs the money, that's the thing. She needs the money and it was too good an offer to refuse. She has debts from her days as a student. The amount she is being paid won't wipe them all but it will get rid of a good chunk for sure. It hadn't even been her idea to do this sodding interview. It was her mum's neighbour who suggested it. She's a receptionist at the local newspaper and said she would ask around, see who was interested in Rachel's story. They came back to her within hours, ringing her, emailing her, asking when they could meet up. As it turned out, the local paper was trumped by a national newspaper who came up with money that the local paper simply couldn't offer. And she couldn't refuse. Not with her debts. So she said yes, and now here she is, sitting waiting, wondering if she is doing the right thing.

The urge to chew at her nails again is overwhelming. She keeps her hands tucked firmly under her armpits. It's the only way she can stop herself. Hopefully this reporter will arrive soon, they will talk and then she can settle herself down but right now she's as tight as a spring, ready to bounce all over this place.

She removes her arms and glances at her watch then spins around in her seat, her eyes roving all over the café, searching every dark corner for a slimy individual with devil horns and an evil twinkle in his eye. Where the hell is this man? She's been here for over ten minutes now and if she doesn't–

'Rachel? Rachel Blakeley?'

Her heart thuds in her chest at the mention of her name. She blinks repeatedly to clear the grit that seems to have settled behind her lids and fixes her eyes on the man looming over her. He's taller than she expected. And better looking too. She imagined him as a sad squat old man with a portly belly and a receding hairline yet here he is looking more like a film star, standing right in front of her, hand outstretched, teeth glinting like diamonds as he gives her his best smile.

Rachel's stomach flips. She would have worn make-up if she'd known, done her hair, put on some nail varnish or something. As it is, she has barely dragged a comb through her hair. Still, at least she brushed her teeth this morning. That's got to count for something, surely?

'Yes,' she says quietly, her throat as dry as sand. She makes to stand up, her trembling hand meeting his.

He flaps his other hand at her and smiles. 'Stay seated, please. I'm not royalty. Far from it. What I am is thirsty and in dire need of caffeine.' He flashes her another winning grin and pulls out a chair. 'What can I get you? I'm having one of those mahoosive cappuccinos and an even bigger slice of chocolate cake.'

Rachel tries to swallow down the flurry of nerves that have gripped her. The thought of eating and drinking makes her feel slightly sick but knows she can't just sit here watching him while she spills her story. 'Erm, just a small latte please.' Her voice sounds disembodied, the words disjointed.

'Oh, come on, Rachel,' he says, winking at her and patting his stomach. 'I make it a rule to never eat alone. How about one of those flapjacks? Or a slice of carrot cake? I've heard that they make the best cheesecake here too. All homemade. You can't go wrong.'

She feels her cheeks flush. Her skin prickles, a thousand sparks lighting up her face as he watches her, waiting for her reply. She isn't used to this level of attention. When they were together, Luke her ex-boyfriend, barely uttered two words to her. She became used to his sullen abrasive manner, thinking all men behaved in this way and that it was how relationships were conducted. And now this. All this attention. All these smiles and generosity. Her stomach contracts and expands and she finds herself relaxing after all despite her initial misgivings.

She returns his smile. 'Okay. I give in. I'll have a latte please and since you're obviously an expert on desserts, I'll let you choose the cake.'

She watches as he swaggers his way to the counter, confidence oozing out of every pore while she sits, wracked with nerves at what she is about to do and say.

By the time he arrives back at their table carrying a large tray stacked with enough sugary snacks to keep an entire classroom of children hyper for the rest of the day, she has decided that she will be truthful. That's all she is going to do – tell her story exactly how it happened, no lies or embellishments. What can possibly be wrong with that? She will stick to the truth, not be led into any dark corners with his questions.

'So, Rachel, I got you the special of the day – key lime pie with a splash of fresh cream. And a latte. There you go,' he says, handing over her cup of creamy frothing coffee. 'And chocolate cake for me. Can't go wrong with a bit of good old stodge, can you? Helps to kick-start the day.'

He sits and tucks into his cake with all the passion of a man who hasn't eaten for days. She is all fingers and thumbs, her dexterity abandoning her as she carefully spoons a piece of pie into her mouth, almost missing and placing it in one of her dimples. He's right. It is amazing. The citrus of the lime sizzles across her tongue, hitting the back of her throat with a punch. She takes another spoonful and another and before she knows it, her plate is empty save for a scattering of crumbs.

'That's better,' he says, leaning back and dabbing at his mouth with his napkin.

'Sorry,' Rachel says, her usual reserve settling back down in her gut. 'I've forgotten your name.' In her haste to get here, wracked with nerves, she didn't pick up her notebook or her phone that contained his details and now her mind has gone blank. She holds her cup stiffly to disguise the tremble in her fingers, and takes a sip of the steaming liquid, wincing as it catches her tongue with a scorching bite.

'Keith,' he says as he hooks his finger through his large cup and lifts it to his mouth. 'Keith Rayner.'

Rachel nods. As soon as he says it, something clicks in her mind, a sudden recognition. Why is she so useless and so bloody nervous about this whole thing? She's doing nothing wrong. People do this sort of thing all the time. They get rich on it, telling whopping great lies and having their faces splashed all over the newspapers and the internet. All she's doing is speaking the truth, enlightening those who weren't there and have no idea what happened that day. It's a story, a simple story that makes her feel lucky to be alive, and if it gives others a modicum of comfort knowing we're all here just by chance, then why not?

So why does she still feel so damn worried? Why is her stomach doing somersaults and her heart dancing about beneath her ribcage like an Olympian gymnast?

'Okay,' Keith says, his smile, his eyes, everything about him giving off an aura of poise and sureness, the likes of which she has never seen before. 'I think with stories like this, the best place to start is at the beginning.' He pulls out a phone, fiddles with buttons and places it on the table between them. 'So,

Rachel, let's start with the basics. Tell me a little bit about yourself – you know, where you're from, what your interests are, what you get up to in your spare time and then we'll get down to the nitty-gritty. The day of the accident and how you managed to survive. That's the bit people want to hear about.' He leans forward, touches his phone and sits back with a smile. 'Right. Ready when you are.'

42

'Okay. So you say that you changed seats with this woman, yeah? You were meant to be in seat 26B but due to suffering from travel sickness, you swapped with her?'

Rachel swallows, wishes she could look elsewhere. His gaze is piercing, his eyes the deepest blue, like an ocean. She nods and clears her throat. 'Yes, that's right. She very kindly changed seats with me. And then–'

Keith holds up his hand to silence her, something in his eyes switching, altering, becoming darker. 'Hang on, Rachel,' he says, softening his voice as he uses her name, 'we'll get to that bit in a minute. Softly softly, catchee monkey. One thing at a time, eh?' He gives her one of his winks, his face creasing as he settles himself back in his chair and crosses his arms over his chest.

She feels herself shrink just a tiny bit. She wants to tell him that she doesn't care for that phrase, that it has its origins in British colonialism and makes her feel uncomfortable. She visualises her Granddad John's face, how he would laugh at her political correctness if he could hear her now, telling her to lighten up and reminding her that she makes everyone too worried to talk to her for fear of offending her ideas of what constitutes fair and free speech. Maybe Granddad John was right. Maybe she is too uptight and needs to chill out and not concern herself with what is right and wrong but she can't seem to relax. The little amount of confidence and surety she had about doing this interview is slowly ebbing away.

'So,' Keith says, his usual affable manner returning. 'You swapped seats. Did you chat with her? What sort of things did you talk about before...'

'Before the crash?' Rachel says a little too loudly. That's why they're here, isn't it? She has no idea why he is being so coy about the accident. If it's for her benefit then he can stop it right now. She's the one who lived through it, not him. Something inside her bristles. She suppresses it, thinking of the money, how an injection of cash would make her life so much easier. Since breaking up with Luke things have been tricky. She has moved back in with her parents and is keen to get her own place. She's too old to be living back with her mum and dad. They have their own lives, their own rigid routine, and she has impinged on it. And then of course, there is her student debt. Always there, never decreasing or lessening.

Her recent promotion at the hospital was welcome but her salary increase has seen her monthly take-home pay rise to the point where she has to pay back her student loan. So she is worse off than she was before. The money she will receive for this interview, this small trivial interview, could be life changing for her. As well as reducing her student loan, she could use part of it as a deposit for her own place. She has been trawling estate agents' windows, imagining what it would be like to have a property of her own. Nothing too grand, just a small townhouse with a spare bedroom and maybe a nice little courtyard. It was Luke's house that they had lived in together, not hers. He had owned it for two years before she had moved in. When she discovered he was having an affair with one of their close friends, she packed up her things and left, telling him to shove his house where the sun don't shine and shouting over her shoulder that she hoped they would both be happy there. Word on the street was the pair of them split-up just two weeks after she left. Good enough for them. She's better off on her own. Nobody to moan at her for using the last of the milk, nobody clomping around in the early hours of the morning after coming in late from the pub doing God knows what with God knows who.

'We didn't chat too much,' Rachel says, snapping back to the present. To this interview. She catches the look of disappointment in Keith's expression. 'We spoke briefly about the weather.'

'As people usually do,' Keith says, his interest suddenly renewed. 'A favourite British subject, the weather. Something that binds us all together.' He has a nasally twang as he speaks. How did she not notice it before? And a slight southern inflection in his tone. The twang is starting to irritate her.

'And then I mentioned an article in the paper about a woman who had been attacked in Durham. We were pretty quiet after that,' Rachel says, averting her gaze.

The next part is the bit that haunts her, makes her realise that life really is for living. 'I just keep thinking that if I hadn't swapped my seat for hers... well, I might not be here. I saw the photos in the paper of the people who died and she was one of them. I recognised her straightaway. It's all so awful.' Rachel bites at her mouth pensively, her front teeth resting on her bottom lip. 'I can't stop thinking about it. About her. That poor woman who lost her life because she was kind to me and allowed me to take her seat. Everything could have turned out so badly for me. As it is, I'm here, alive, and she isn't.'

She averts her gaze, counting the crumbs on her plate before looking up again to Keith. He is nodding and smiling. Why is he smiling? Has she said something amusing?

'Sorry,' he says, suddenly changing his expression to one of concern. 'It was just something you said that caught my attention.'

'What?' she replies, desperately thinking over what she has just said and wondering if all of this is a scam, a phoney attempt to get her on his side, his initial pleasant demeanour and mischievous grin now slipping to reveal the real Keith underneath. The one that preys on vulnerable people. The one who uses the suffering of others to further his career.

'You mentioned that there was an article in the paper you were reading, about an attack?'

Rachel nods, wondering what is coming next. Her hands are ice cold but her face flushes hot. *What now? And how could such a thing ever be construed as funny or amusing?*

'I've been doing some investigating,' Keith says excitedly, as if what he is about to tell her will take her breath away, make her sit up and suddenly start paying attention to his words, 'and the woman in question, Leah that is, is linked to the person who was in that story, the victim of the attack. Talk about coincidences, eh? I can't disclose how she is linked as yet but I'm pretty sure it will soon be common knowledge. At least it will once I get this story out there.' Another wink. Her guts flip about like a fish on dry land.

Rachel can't manage to summon up any strength to respond to his revelation, or to match his enthusiasm with even the weakest of smiles. Despite the pie she has eaten, her stomach suddenly feels hollow as if the contents have been scooped out and her innards scraped clean. She has never been one for getting excited about somebody else's misfortune. It hits her in her solar plexus when she hears of the suffering of others.

Clearly, Keith doesn't feel the same way. His eyes are twinkling, his complexion pink with excitement. 'Obviously, I can't reveal my sources but I know a fair bit about your lady, the one you swapped seats with. I've been doing a bit of digging around and without sounding too disrespectful, she has some backstory, I can tell you, and not a pleasant one at that.'

'Her name is Leah Browne,' Rachel says sourly. That much she has remembered. She saw it in the paper, pored over it, cried and then cried some more. She, Rachel, left that train with minor grazes. Leah died. It could have been her and she will never forget that fact. Ever. Leah could have said no, could have ignored Rachel's request to change seats and turned away, but she didn't. She was kind enough to do it and that fact will never dim in Rachel's mind. She will be forever grateful to her, be forever in her debt.

'So anyway, apparently the police are investigating a link from Leah to the attack in Durham. And there's something else.' Rachel can feel Keith watching her. He's baiting her, wanting her to get all excited like he is, all wound up and frenzied like a toddler who has been promised candy if they can behave. It's not going to happen. That's not who she is. Getting fired up by gossip and malicious rumours isn't her thing at all. 'Her brother died when he was a teenager. And get this – he threw himself on the train tracks at Durham, the same station where Leah boarded the train.' His voice has gone up an octave, his skin now shimmering with beads of perspiration that glisten under the glare of the overhead lights. 'Now that,' he says, almost beside himself with exhilaration, 'is a story!'

Rachel says nothing, unwilling or perhaps unable to share his joy at this finding. The key lime pie swirls and sloshes about in her belly. She doesn't feel cut out for this – this spreading and smearing of dirt in the name of selling papers. Leah is dead. She can't defend herself. And what about her family? Where do they fit into this awful turn of events? She came here to publicly thank Leah for saving her life, to let people know that she, Rachel, is alive because of the generosity of another human being. Not this. She didn't come here for any of this.

As if he can read her thoughts, Keith pitches in, his voice now calm and measured. 'She fell out with her parents and didn't see them for many years. Do you want to know why?'

She doesn't. She really, really doesn't, but feels frozen, her body glued to the seat, her feet nailed to the floor. She can't do anything except listen to these stories. Gutter gossip about a woman who inadvertently saved her life.

'The brother, according to what I've gleaned from people who know the family, pushed a little girl over a cliff. Leah told everybody she saw it but then retracted her story to the police saying she couldn't remember what actually happened. There was nobody to corroborate her story but apparently even after her retraction, people continued believing that he was a murderer.'

'Hence his suicide,' Rachel says quietly, sorrow welling up in her chest for these people. For this poor blighted family who have lost so much.

'But what a story and what a coincidence, eh?' Keith struggles to conceal his delight. Rachel imagines that many journalists go through their entire career never coming across a story with so many bizarre events and horrible coincidences and now here he is with one and he can barely hold himself together. He is delirious at the prospect of managing such a scoop. 'I've already got the bare bones of the story written and when I found out about your link to Leah and the thing about swapping seats, I was jumping, I can tell you! Stuff like this happens so rarely. I just about bust a gut getting here today. Hence the need for cake and coffee.'

He smiles at her, that broad glinting smile that now she has seen beyond his façade, isn't sitting so easily with her. In fact if she is being perfectly honest, it repulses her. *He* repulses her with his fake smile and boyish charm and complete lack of integrity.

'I mean, she's probably travelled from that station hundreds of times since her brother died there, but for her to die further up the line is just so unbelievably freaky, isn't it? This is the sort of stuff people love to read about. It sells newspapers big time, I can tell you.'

Rachel doesn't doubt for one minute that stories involving the misfortune and distress of others, sell; that there are people out there who adore seeing folk dragged through the mud, their horribly blighted lives made public and their dirty laundry held bare for the world to gawp at and pick through. But she isn't one of them and never will be. No amount of money will turn her head. She has heard enough. She stands up. This is too much. It's all too much for her. She needs to leave.

'I've changed my mind,' she says suddenly. 'I don't want to do this story. I don't want the money and I definitely do not want my name or my conversation with Leah to appear in your paper.' Her heart hammers around her chest, her extremities tingling with both fear and anger as she glares at him from under her brow. 'If my name or anything to do with me appears in your paper, or any paper for that matter, I will sue you. You're the only person I've spoken to about this, so I'll know if anything gets out. It will lead straight back to you. I haven't signed any sort of contract and you haven't given me any money so you have no right printing anything that I've said.'

She doesn't wait for his reply, for him to shout after her that she is turning down a massive amount of money, the sort of windfall most people only ever dream about. She turns and heads to the door, leaving him sitting there, surrounded by empty coffee cups and plates and a handful of stale crumbs. A metaphor, she thinks, for the life he leads.

His voice calls after her, his southern drawl that even after her words, after her acerbic manner, still oozes charm and confidence. He isn't fazed by what she has just said. He's used to it. He is used to being turned down and insulted because of his profession. He is used to being threatened with legal action and told *no* by people who are poor enough to be tempted by the wads of cash thrown their way for the stories they have to tell. She supposes that many do fall for it; taking the financial remuneration and running as fast as they can in the opposite direction. Everyone has their price. But not her. Not this time. Being alive is her reward. Not being Leah and breathing clean air is enough for her. No amount of money will ever make her think otherwise.

'You know where I am if you change your mind, Rachel.'

She tries to stop herself from turning around to see him one last time but can't. She needs to do it, just to confirm what her gut instinct is telling her – that he is a duplicitous individual, saccharine sweet on the outside but poisonous within. And she is right. Keith is leaning back in the chair as if he hasn't got a care in the world, a nauseatingly twee smile plastered across his face. He picks up his phone, waves it in the air to remind her of how to get in touch should she change her mind, and then gives her a casual wink. That manner, those eyes with that look that almost sucked her into his revolting little world before chewing her up and spitting her out once he has had enough. She almost fell for it. Dear God, he almost had her there.

Clenching her fists until her nails dig into her palms, making her wince with the pain, she spins around, storms through the door and slams it hard behind her.

43

CHLOE

I see her everywhere – sitting in cars behind me, standing in bus stops, waiting in queues at the checkout. She's everywhere I go, a face in the crowd, a flutter in my belly, a spear in my heart. My pulse quickens, my chest constricts, I find it hard to breathe, to stay upright, and then I realise that it isn't her, that it can't be her because Leah is dead, her body buried deep in the ground. She is no longer a threat to either me or Jacob. We're safe. So why do I still feel so frightened? Perhaps it's because she stalked us for such a long time that she became an integral part of our lives, an unwanted presence we simply couldn't shake.

Leah was the reason I kept my flat. We figured that if she was outside my, more often than not, empty flat, then at least she wasn't outside Jacob's, bothering us. Had we only had the one place then her energy would have been focused on us there, day after day after day. We would have woken to see her standing there, staring in, a dead look in her eyes, her face creased with envy and malice. I used to dread looking out of the window, wondering if she would be there, watching. Waiting.

Part of me feels sorry for her, just a tiny part of my overstretched emotions that is, as I know that she had nobody and was disturbed and lonely. The remainder of me is still terrified of her. She may be dead but her face still haunts me, stopping me from sleeping at night, filtering into my thoughts and reminding me of how close I came to death. Reminding me of how precious life is. How precious our lives are – Jacob's and mine.

I should have locked the door that day. I know that now, and that is another thing that stops me from sleeping, from getting my life back on track and living it to the full. Jacob had left for the week to attend a conference just north of Edinburgh and I was busy and tired. I had had a demanding week at work and tiredness made me lackadaisical. It was an oversight and one I will have to live with for the rest of my life. I can't change my mistake any more than Leah could have changed her behaviour. We are what we are and it is now time to stop punishing myself and forge ahead with the rest of my life.

I'm seeing a counsellor, hoping it will stop the nightmares and help me to sleep again. Leah standing there in the bathroom is a vision I don't seem to be able to erase, but I'm trying. Julia is my counsellor and seeing her always fills me with a mixture of emotions, a tension of opposites that always feels like I'm putting my emotions through the shredder, forcing me to work through that event until I reach the other end, a less frightened person, ready to move on. Talking through it helps to lighten the load, but it also means I have to relive it, to remember the fear and the pain, the terror that I was going to die. I have to remember that I thought I was going to be murdered in my bed by a frenzied woman who thought of me as an imposter in her imaginary life when all the while it was she who was the intruder in mine.

It took the police some time to work out her identity after she was pulled out of the train wreckage. She had with her my handbag and my purse with my credit cards and driving licence.

They assumed I was dead and contacted Jacob while I was in hospital fighting for my life. I almost died twice in one day.

Many thoughts went through my head as I lay there unable to fight off her blows. Why was she doing it? Who would find me? How it would feel as I drew my last breath, that final gasp of oxygen before I departed this life and disappeared into an empty endless pool of blackness beyond. That moment will never leave me, of that I'm sure – the pain – which was bad enough – and the unknown future. No amount of counselling will erase it.

But I'm pleased to say that I survived and I'm still here telling the tale.

I do often wonder what went through Leah's head as she lay dying in that train carriage. Did she think of me and what she had done? Or did she simply slip away from this life into another without any regrets or reflection, hoping I was dead? People often say that your life flashes before your eyes before you die which makes me wonder about Leah and what she saw before she passed away. I like to think that she had grave misgivings about my attack and was sorry but I suppose I'll never know. She was a deeply disturbed woman, detached enough from reality to be able to distance herself from her actions.

I knew Leah was slightly off-kilter but never in a million years did I think her unbalanced enough to try and murder me. Even as she held me captive, I harboured thoughts of her setting me free, threatening me with all kinds of punishments if I dared to report her to the police. I was naïve enough to think she had a shred of empathy and compassion. Obviously, I was wrong.

I'm a psychology teacher. I like to think I should have been able to read her, make some connection or gain an insight into how she thought or what motivated her and save myself, but it wasn't to be. Terror rendered me helpless. I did fight back but my failed attempts enraged her all the more and, in the end, I was at her mercy, surviving purely by chance. I was unconscious for two weeks and by the time I came to, the police had already established what had taken place. Despite her clean-up attempts, her DNA was all over the flat. I guess I'm lucky she died otherwise I would be spending the rest of my life looking over my shoulder, always wondering if she will be coming back to finish what she started.

The police investigation didn't take too long to complete. Despite them initially thinking that it was a bungled burglary, finding the purse helped point them in the right direction. They more or less knew who had done it before I regained consciousness and could identify her as my assailant. Jacob told them about Leah and the forensic team soon confirmed what he already knew to be true.

Once the DNA results came back, everything fell into place. When I say 'fell into place', some parts of the investigation still baffle me. The police found mounds of incriminating evidence at her old flat to back up our accounts of Leah's stalking of us. Her landlady had bagged up her belongings after evicting her and fortunately they were still outside under a large shrub in the back garden. Even knowing how unbalanced she was, some of the things they told us made my skin prickle.

It was as if she had written about both of our lives in reverse. There was one account that left me reeling. DC Ingram asked me about a purported assault at Jacob's birthday party. No such incident ever took place.

What really troubled me about her words was the fact that on that night, I thought that I had spotted Leah, standing in the doorway of the pub, watching us, but when I checked again, she had gone. I put it down to the excitement of the event and the three glasses of wine I had downed in rapid succession after a stressful afternoon of organising the delivery of the cake while I decorated the back room of our local pub.

I wonder if she was so far gone in her delusions that she actually believed her version of events; or was it no more than a fantasy world she had fashioned where she could create her own desires and outcomes? I guess we'll never know.

There were so many of these fantasy episodes written in her diary that after a while I asked the police to stop talking. Thinking about it made me bone weary. I had thought Leah was just a sad lonely individual when in fact, she was so much more than that. So much more.

The papers have had a field day with the story – the suspect killed in a major train accident after leaving the victim close to death. It doesn't get much better than that, does it? The public love that sort of stuff and for a good while, Leah's face was on every front page, on every television channel, her dark-eyed stare and sullen countenance piercing my thoughts. Jacob did his best to protect me from it but I wanted to read about it, to watch it until my head hurt, to stare at her pictures if only to convince myself that she really was dead. It gave some finality to the attack and my own near-death experience.

I've been fortunate in many respects. I have recovered, not fully, but I can get out and about with Jacob's assistance and I consider myself lucky that I've got him in my life, something Leah always desired and never had. I'm hoping to get back to work once my physiotherapy sessions are over and I can walk unassisted. I suffered traumatic brain injury, or TBI as my doctor calls it. I have some disequilibrium issues and suffer bouts of dizziness but they will pass in time.

The psychological problems, however, may never leave. My mind keeps roving back to that day, forever reminding me of how my carelessness almost cost me my life. I keep telling myself that she would have found a way in regardless. That's just how she was. She would have knocked, I would have opened the door and she would have forced her way in. Her previous behaviour gave us an indication that something terrible was imminent. She was a loose cannon and it would have happened anyway. I tell myself that to stop the endless rounds of self-inflicted punishments I continually put myself through.

The mistake she made was sending that rogue text to Jacob. He knew immediately that something was wrong and drove straight home. Had it not been for him coming back early, I would have been left there to rot. She'll never know it, but her message saved my life. I would now be dead and she would have succeeded.

I have a lot to look forward to. Jacob and I are getting married later this year and I'm going out looking at dresses this week. My confidence is finally growing now my facial wounds have healed. The scars are still visible but time will play its part and I'm hoping that by the time I walk down the aisle they will be hardly noticeable.

The doctors worked miracles on my fractured skull and broken nose. Bones are solid and soon fuse back together but skin is far harder to fix. By the time Leah had done her worst, I was unrecognisable with two black eyes and an atlas of scars criss-crossing my face.

It's ironic that Leah's mad attempt to split us up actually brought Jacob and me closer together. We have survived a massive trauma and nothing can now come between us.

I've had an offer on my flat which I have accepted. We're also selling this place once I'm well enough to move. Somewhere with a garden and a spare bedroom would do us nicely. Maybe one day we'll have kids but not just yet. I need to learn how to look after myself and make sure I'm fit and healthy again before I consider looking after somebody else.

There's another thing that has changed in my life and it's not something Jacob entirely approves of. Once a week or thereabouts, I speak with Chrissie and Ralph, Leah's poor forlorn parents. After hearing about their lives, what they have endured, I capitulated and met up with them.

They had asked Jacob and the police if they could see me to apologise and try to make up for what their daughter did to me. I don't mind admitting that I was initially nervous and extremely reluctant but after giving it much thought, I relented and am so glad I did. It's not your average friendship, borne out of hate and tragedy and near murder, but it works. It's asymmetric and unorthodox but deeply cathartic for all of us, I think, like a kind of restorative justice. We sometimes meet in the park, a neutral area that holds no bitter or unwanted memories for any of us, and we just chat. Sometimes we walk.

When I say 'walk' it's more of a hobble for me. Ralph often takes my arm and helps me along. As he does it, I want to scream to the sky above, to ask Leah if she knew how fortunate she was to have these wonderful caring people in her life. Strangely enough, apart from their initial apology, we don't talk about Leah at all. I think it's too big a topic for any of us to tackle. How do you even begin to cover such a subject? Far easier to avoid it altogether. Instead, we chat about gardening, Ralph's love of roses and Chrissie's need for a new hobby. I've told her that when I'm feeling better, we should visit the local theatre. I've always loved going there and when I mentioned it, Chrissie's face lit up. She so rarely smiles that it made me jump, and also gave me something to work towards. I've made her a promise and am not about to let her down. When I'm not up to leaving the house, we speak on the phone and that works just as well for us. It's the contact that I crave, the solidity of speaking to someone who suffered at her hands, just as I did. I know that sounds strange and I can't begin to explain it. All I know is that it works for the three of us and that's what counts.

I have changed irrevocably for sure. Whether she intended it or not, Leah has done me a favour. She has altered my trajectory and changed my outlook. She has made me more appreciative of life in general. I live my life afresh every day, appreciating every little bit of sunshine, every glimpse of blue sky. Even dreary grey days make me glad to be alive. Winter is simply a colder extension of summer.

I'm just delighted to be me, to be here, breathing the same air as my love, seeing his handsome face every morning when I open my eyes.

'Right, you ready?' Jacob hands me my walking stick and stands back, pretending to look elsewhere, knowing how I hate being given assistance. It makes me feel like somebody's nan, having him place his arm under mine and haul me upright. I need to learn to do it myself. Got to get my limbs working properly. Leah will not be the ruin of me, of that I am certain.

I do my best to not groan or make any sounds as I force my weary bones into position. There are days when I feel well enough to walk independently and then others when I feel like the Tin Man deprived of oil. I'm not going to lie and say that everything is hunky-dory because it isn't, but we're getting there. I am nothing if not determined. Resilience is my middle name. It has worked its way under my skin, and is nestled deep inside me, pushing me on each and every day.

'I'm ready,' I say, my hand clutched tightly around the stick, my knuckles white with the effort.

We've come for a drive in the car to the North Yorkshire moors. The last two weeks haven't been so good. I've only managed to chat on the phone with Chrissie and Ralph rather than meet up with them, and with Jacob being out at work, I was going stir crazy sitting in the house on my own, hour after hour, day after day. I needed to see the greenery, to hear the birdsong above me, to see the cerulean sky and feel the air as it whistles around me, past me, over me. Being immersed in the elements reminds me that I'm alive, that Leah didn't get her way and kill me off. She made me stronger. Her attempts to end me have given me a new lease of life.

'Right,' I murmur determinedly as I link my free arm through Jacob's and look up at him. 'Let's see if we can make it to that small hillock, shall we?'

The landscape is magical, swathes of heather and velvety moss stretching as far as the eye can see, curling over the hill-tops and across the distant horizon. Nature at its finest, surrounding us on all sides.

'C'mon,' I laugh, leaning on my stick and grinning at him. 'Race you to the top.'

We set off at a lick, the wind gathering in strength, invisible fingers of air, guiding us, pushing at our backs as we laugh and head across the rugged terrain.

THE END

ACKNOWLEDGEMENTS

Writing a book is hard work, there's no denying it but it's a little-known fact that writing acknowledgements is almost as tricky (although a lot less time consuming and fewer bouts of uncontrollable weeping). There are so many people out there who, over the years, have supported me and helped me in my dream to become a published author that it's difficult to know where to start.

I will begin close to home and say a big thank you to my family and friends who have been there for me every step of the way, allowing me the time and space to write, regularly enquiring about my latest endeavours – 'How's it going?' 'When's the next book coming out?' 'I don't know how you do it! So many books!' – your comments are always welcome. If I shrug my shoulders and give a quick reply, it means I'm at the end of writing my latest novel and too exhausted to think straight. My dismissive response has no bearing on your questions! Give me a week away from my characters (and a glass or eight of Prosecco) and I'll be able to answer coherently and not be the bumbling wreck standing before you who can barely string a sentence together.

As always, a huge thank you to everyone at Bloodhound Books – Fred Freeman, Betsy Reavley, Heather Fitt, Tara Lyons, Alexina Golding, Clare Law, my editor, for her sage and welcome advice, and of course the publicity team who work hard to make sure my books get noticed and sell.

Since being published with Bloodhound Books I have made some good friends – Anita Waller and Patricia Dixon – thank you for being there when I repeatedly message you with my worries and questions. You guys are ace; a pair of stalwart ladies I am lucky enough to have as friends. Also, Vikki Patis – thank you for all your support. You are a star. Thank you to Stuart James (Dunne) for your many retweets. You've taught me more about Twitter in the last few months than I learnt on my own in the past few years. Keri Beevis and Valerie Keogh, you are the cogs that keep us Bloodhound authors moving with your support and publicity day shares. Diamonds, the pair of you. So many names to mention that if I've forgotten to include somebody, I apologise! We are a great team and you are all brilliant.

I am so fortunate to have a wonderful group of ARC readers, many of whom I am privileged to call friends. A big thank you Dee Groocock, Gail Shaw and Craig Gillan for not being afraid to contact me with those pesky errors that still manage to slip through after countless edits and proofreads! Your help is very much appreciated, I can tell you. I do actually believe I have the best ARC group ever so thank you all again for your support and reviews.

I can't write this without saying a huge thank you to the many book sites that help to promote my work. Mark Fearn and Susan Hunter, you have been amazing, always allowing me space on your pages, Crime Fiction Addict and Book Mark! Also, a big thank you to Philomena Callan's site, Cheekypee, Promote your Books with Me, for allowing unlimited promos. There are so many book sites that are worthy of a mention and I'm afraid that I'll miss some out but I'm also going to thank Skye's Mum & Books, Book on the Positive Side, The Paperback Writers, UK Crime Book Club, The Book Club, Book Connectors, Crime Book Club, The Fiction Café Book Club, The Psychological Suspense Authors Association and Strictly Suspense. Sorry if I've missed any. You are all fantastic, running these sites in your spare time and giving authors the chance to have their books noticed and also giving us the chance to interact with readers. Writing is a lonely business and time spent chatting with like-minded people about books and writing and, of course, giggling at the rude memes helps keep me sane.

This is the second book that I edited during the lockdown of 2020, a strange and surreal time for many and a time when I lost a good friend. Pauline, I will miss you terribly but will remember the many laughs we had together, especially your commando-style crawl across the snooker table in the local golf club, something which still makes me chuckle all these years later. I hope you're managing the odd glass of wine up there and watching over us.

Finally, thank you to you, dear reader, for buying and reading my book. I hope you enjoyed it and if ever you feel like contacting me, I can be found on Facebook or Twitter. Feel free to follow me at:

www.facebook.com/thewriterjude/

www.twitter.com/thewriterjude

Best wishes,
J.A. Baker

Printed in Great Britain
by Amazon

48991298R00183